D1798149

# Introducing
# JARROD BLACK

## An Unashamed Football Novel

# Introducing
# JARROD BLACK

## An Unashamed Football Novel

## Texi Smith

P PCORN
PRESS

First published in 2019 by Popcorn Press, a division of Fair Play Publishing

PO Box 4101, Balgowlah Heights NSW 2093 Australia

www.popcornpress.com.au

ISBN: 978-0-6484073-3-1

ISBN: 978-0-6484073-4-8(ePub)

© Texi Smith 2019

The moral rights of the author have been asserted.

All rights reserved. Except as permitted under the *Australian Copyright Act 1968* (for example, a fair dealing for the purposes of study, research, criticism or review), no part of this book may be reproduced, stored in a retrieval system, communicated or transmitted in any form or by any means without prior written permission from the Publisher.

Design and typesetting by Retta Laraway, Looksee Design.

All inquiries should be made to the Publisher via sales@fairplaypublishing.com.au

A catalogue record for this book is available from the National Library of Australia

## Disclaimer

To the maximum extent permitted by law, the authors and publisher disclaim all responsibility and liability to any person, arising directly or indirectly from any person taking or not taking action based on the information in this publication.

To my Dad.
Get some chaaalk on ya boot.

# Contents

# Chapter One:
# Repose

A heavy downpour was never the best way to start the first day of the holidays, but for Jarrod Black, the sweet smell of rain evaporating from the hot tarmac was a sensory experience that took him back to fond memories of childhood. There he sat, freshly made coffee in hand, on the balcony, a strangely calm Atlantic Ocean in the distance at the end of the street.

It was the morning after a long journey across the Channel and down through France. They had set off the previous night, a warm June night, and travelled all day, so it was a surprise to Jarrod himself to be up and moving at such an early hour.

The season was now but a distant memory. The two weeks or so that had passed since the play-off defeat had provided their fair share of restless nights; it was a blessed relief to be away from the town, the people, and the disappointment lingering in the air.

Their holiday house that could only be described as 'homely', a byword for ageing and tastefully renovated for its time, sat right next to a huge flat expanse of beach not far but far enough from the swanky Biarritz, just off the main route South to the Spanish border. A former teammate from ten years ago had the house in his family and had offered it to him a couple of years ago for a week or two. At the time there was no opportunity to take him up on the offer, this year though the timing was right. The kids were a bit older, they could afford a couple of weeks out of school, even if it was just before exam time. Marianne had more than enough annual leave, and they were going to make the most of the six weeks between the end of the football season and the start of Jarrod's next pre-season regime.

The silver octagonal pot bubbled away on the stove, filling the air with the strong aroma of fresh coffee, which he thought may have stirred his wife, but sleep was obviously more important. He was a dreamer, quite content to go along with the notion he was the king of this new castle, surveying his new domain from the safety of the balcony.

With no sign of life from any of the bedrooms, he slipped on a crumpled but not unwearable shirt, quietly unpacked some trainers and was soon off to see what was open at this early hour, perhaps a chance to sample the local patisserie and buy the local newspaper. He always liked this ritual when in a different country, even if the language barrier prevented him from understanding the bulk of the news. Sure enough, with the sun starting to peek through the clouds, the local corner café was in the process of opening.

A young lady in a white apron was putting out the A-frame advertising boards, and the adjoining tabac was already busy with locals grabbing an early edition of the newspaper, catching up on the local gossip, and sampling the first rosé of the day.

Jarrod browsed the offerings, conscious that he was conspicuous in his under-dressed state, picking up a copy of the ubiquitous daily sports journal l'Équipe and a slightly out-of-date newspaper that he had never seen before, maybe it was something local, maybe a new daily that had come into circulation since the last time on the continent. There was yesterday's Sun also, and as he had been on the road for the majority of the day yesterday, it was effectively up to date.

With papers in hand, he rustled up his best apology, 'désolé', to the shopkeeper for only having a 100 Euro note, but the gentleman behind the counter happily gave him change and wished him on his way with a cheery, 'bonne journée.'

The next stop was the patisserie counter, and again in the pidgin French he had preserved from his school days, he managed to correctly acquire a half-dozen calorie-filled croissants, one of those big baguettes that he couldn't remember the name of ('pain' as it turned out), but which the hand gestures happily explained, and two mille-feuilles, not just because he liked the name – he also knew that Marianne would eat more than half of his if he offered a bite.

Again, exchanging smiles and pleasantries with the shopkeeper, he made his way back up the street and round the corner to the house. There was no sign of life, although it was clear that someone had been up, as there was a trail of water drops from the bathroom to the kids room; a sign someone had been up and had done the right thing by washing their hands but forgone the towel in favour of flicking their hands dry.

Jarrod sat down on the balcony, pouring over l'Équipe, looking almost frantically for football news amongst the twenty or so other sports that took preference in the summer months. A mere half page was scant reward, and even that was difficult to decipher, with a few words he had never seen before making it tricky to work it out.

The Sun threw up a few interesting stories as it never fails to do; another Premiership player audited for tax evasion, and another involved in an altercation in a resort in Mexico, all standard fare for that awkward post-season pre-transfer window period, where there's not much else concrete to talk about. The short section about rumoured transfers, always rife with pure speculation, saw that a teammate was in line for a move to Liverpool, and there was alleged ill-feeling amongst the fans regarding that possibility. He rustled through the third paper.

A shuffling at the door made him turn around. Aneka was

there, squinting at the sunshine. She ran up to him and jumped on his lap, the coffee, cooling by now, extended at arms' length to avoid spillage. Aneka was a prodigious girl, a great talker, a fabulous dancer and athlete, and someone who would always be the centre of attention even if she wasn't trying.

With blonde hair, and cute set of freckles, she was definitely the apple of her Dad's eye, and even the onset of angry tantrums and issues at school could not break the bond between them.

"Was that you who went to the bathroom?" enquired Jarrod.

"Yes," replied Aneka, running both her hands through his slightly matted hair, causing his head to tilt right back as she found the knots.

"Is your brother still asleep?" he went on.

"Yes," Aneka replied, with a brisk slap of both cheeks.

The factual questions out of the way, it was time to open the questions up, in the style that the teachers had suggested to the parents in the first year of school.

"What would you like to do today?" he asked, taking a sip of his cup with the expectation of a long reply.

"I think we should all go to the beach, and then have some yummy food at a nice restaurant for lunch, and then..." her eyes danced around, before continuing, "and then we should come back to the house and all have a nice long rest."

That was essentially what Jarrod would call a great day for a holiday, and whilst he didn't commit to it, he said he'd run it past Mummy, who he knew might have different ideas.

"But first, I'm going to have an hour in the gym. I can get you some breakfast, would you like that? I've got croissants," said

Jarrod, in expectation of an excited reply.

"And orange juice, and pens. I'll colour in your newspapers," was the response.

"Done. Come grab a seat at the table and I'll bring it through for you."

With Aneka at the table, an orange juice in front of her, two croissants and some strawberry jam, part of the very kind and unexpected 'welcome pack' they had found when they arrived, and pens retrieved from the bottom of the big bag sitting by their bedroom door, Jarrod was ready for a short, sharp gym session.

That was the draw card of this place. There was a full-on gym underneath the house next to the garage, and it was done out in a modern style that belied the style of the rest of the house. There were four machines, a set of weights of all different sizes, a black mat, a punch-bag suspended from one of the beams, and a long bench with a compact kitchen, and a TV up on the wall.

On closer inspection the machines were so new there was a range of connections on each: HDMI, USB, Bluetooth, that sort of thing. There was also a connection to the TV mounted on the wall that, when Jarrod plugged in his iPad, the TV came on, and his iPad screen was displayed up on the TV. He quickly flicked to his emails and ran through the long list of unread messages to see if there was anything of interest, and then into the junk folder to see if anything had slipped in there by mistake.

One email did catch his eye, a bulk email invitation to trials for Darlington FC, one of the neighbouring teams to his own. He opened it up and had a quick look, by this time realising the short gym session was going to be delayed. The trials were in just over two weeks, and interested parties were invited to be present at the training ground with no obligation and privacy assured - presumably behind closed doors away from prying eyes of local and national newspapers.

A scraping of chairs, a loud yawn and stretch from above signalled the waking of the remainder of the family. This kicked Jarrod into gear, quickly bringing up some energetic music on the iPad, starting a fifteen-minute session of random one-minute intervals of varying difficulty. The thought of trialling for another team, and local rivals, was lingering, but soon forgotten as the machine kicked to maximum for a minute, getting the sweat going.

Half an hour later, a little sooner than planned, Jarrod appeared in the doorway at the top of the stairs to find Marianne sitting out on the balcony, pretty much going through the same routine he had done an hour before, sunglasses on to avoid the glare. Aneka sat where he had left her, with an intricately coloured front page of l'Équipe. Jarrod strolled through the dining area to the balcony, a towel over his head to keep the sweat from pouring on the floor.

"Quite a change," he said to Aneka. "Very colourful indeed."

"Hi Darling," stirred Marianne, still too tired to be up. She put an arm up to stroke his arm.

"Seb up too?" he enquired, putting his hand on hers.

"Just up now," Marianne replied. "He's been playing his DS all morning. You know what he's like. He can't sleep, even when he's exhausted."

Jarrod turned to see Seb, coming out of the kitchen with a huge bowl of cereal, sitting next to his sister.

"Hey Dad," was the casual greeting. "You look wiped."

Jarrod indeed did feel a little ragged. The two weeks since the last game had proved to be very unproductive ones. There had been a distinct lack of motivation for keeping his body in shape, something he knew would become more prevalent as he was well in to his thirties.

# Chapter Two: Beginnings

Jarrod James Black began his professional footballing career in his native Australia. Born to a migrant father from England and a local girl from the North Western Sydney suburbs, he was unsurprisingly guided towards football; "soccer" as it was more readily known to identify it from the other codes of "footie".

Being young for his age group was always a slight disadvantage going into each season in his formative years, but his skill levels made up for his lack of height and bulk, and often by the end of the season, he would definitely stand out from his peers with his knowledge and understanding of the game.

There were back-to-back championships in Under 10s and Under 11s, preceding an Under 12 season where the only wins were the first and penultimate games, a season that could have derailed his interest if it hadn't been for the fact that he was the player with the most potential.

Moving away from teams coached by Dad when he was in the Under 14s and playing in the top grade with a solid team gave him an opportunity to shine, and his performances and goal-scoring feats from midfield attracted the interest of a number of scouts, as well as the local representative team.

Instead of taking the normal route through the rankings, an opportunity presented itself with the recently formed Parramatta SC. Signing up initially for a six-week trial, he adapted very well to the change of level and Jarrod was quickly handed a start in the youth league at the tender age of 16. This provided the platform to been seen by the Australia Under 17s coaching staff, and only three months after signing a youth contract for Parramatta, he was given a squad number for a selection of Australia Under 17s matches.

That mini tournament, held only a few hours' drive up the New South Wales coast, gave him no game time, but an appetite for more, and those six days in camp were much more beneficial than he knew at the time.

Two seasons on, with school on its way to completion, and a very fruitful time in the youth team and a handful of appearances in the reserve side, Parramatta SC offered Jarrod a full-time professional contract just shy of his 18th birthday. Despite having that new contract drawn up, interest suddenly appeared from overseas after Jarrod and his teammates were featured on a TV show challenging Melbourne City players to a crossbar challenge. After a hilarious segment and a short comical interview, Jarrod was instantly on the scene and not only for his football. His profile on social media took off.

It was at this point that Dad enlisted the help of a player agent. Manny Leonard was a friend of a friend of Dad's, and although Jarrod had never met him, in the first two days he whipped up a flurry of activity. An opportunity was devised through one of Mr Leonard's seemingly endless contacts for Jarrod to visit Kashima in Japan, before continuing to Scotland to trial in Perth with St Johnstone, and then a couple dates in England.

Clubs would run the rule over him and Mr Leonard would gauge interest and give feedback. Things were moving incredibly quickly. Dad decided the whole family would make the trip. It was a good time to have a break and revisit the motherland where there was still a large contingent of his side of the family.

When Dad had eventually told Jarrod about Mr Leonard, the whole process was met with scepticism and a little bit of scorn, but when he explained what Mr Leonard was proposing, Jarrod felt sick with nervous excitement, a hundred thoughts going through his head.

The Blacks were going on tour.

Dad was always embarrassing on planes, joking with the flight attendants and asking for more of something and something extra with his meal. This was a journey like no other though, with turbulence causing some hair-raising moments and spilled drinks, especially towards the end of the flight. A smooth final approach to Narita meant the unpleasant part of the trip was soon forgotten, and the Japan experience was set to be very exciting.

They had little knowledge of the language, and even less knowledge of the fast-moving modern-day culture. The two days Jarrod and his family spent in Japan were a total blast. The Antlers' facilities were space age, the training ground was as good if not better than any of the stadiums he had ever played in, and the area it was in was like one big shopping centre.

The whole family went out to the stadium after checking in to the compact hotel, and he was even allowed to go out alone for dinner with his sister, which he absolutely loved.

The players at the club were an exotic mix of Brazilian, Croatian, and Polish players, interspersed with local talent, and in the trial training session he was the only player from Australia and the only one who spoke English as his mother tongue.

Even though he didn't feel the trial went that well, not getting as much time with the football as he expected, he loved the experience, and was absolutely thrilled with the opportunity. He made a point of phoning Mr Leonard before they left to thank him.

Scotland was a totally different experience, a thoroughly enjoyable one though. The arduous journey via Glasgow airport, and having had an hours' wait for the car hire place to open and then find their booking, left him with little time to recover before hitting the pitch in a training session with the St Johnstone first team.

Jarrod was a little daunted that he was training with players who were routinely rubbing shoulders with top players from powerhouses Celtic and Rangers, but in the training session he got 'stuck in hard' as Mr Leonard had suggested, and even managed to get the whole team laughing with a totally unnecessary mazy dribble when trying to round the goalkeeper to score his team's winning goal in the small game at the end of the session.

After the training session, Jarrod, along with his Dad, was invited to lunch at a nearby pub with the commercial manager. Mum and Anna left them to it to meet up with some of Jarrod's distant family near Edinburgh.

The late lunch, in a relaxed atmosphere on a sunny school day, gave Dad the opportunity to grill the commercial manager, Mr Noel Fawkes, about the youth academy and the opportunities that would be available to continue with higher education. Mr Fawkes' wife Stella, a glamorous cougar of a lady, chatted about life in Perth and what he could expect from the social scene. That was something he hadn't really thought about.

The general feeling after they had all exchanged farewells and good lucks was that the day had gone remarkably well and exciting times were ahead, whether it be here or elsewhere.

Mr Leonard was pleased they had spent time getting to know his old friend Noel when they spoke on the phone back at the hotel. He let them know the next leg of the journey, which was not for two days, that was just down the road and over the border in Gateshead. Dad was delighted, as he had planned to take time out to visit family in his native Newcastle.

After meeting up later with Mum and Anna, the mood suddenly

turned festive. More family members turned up, great uncles and second cousins that Jarrod had only heard of, and soon enough the single malts and sherry appeared. In his unwavering attempt to be always courteous, Jarrod slammed back a malt whisky, and his face grimaced to the extent the whole room was in hoots of laughter, and that was the end of his drinking for the night. His Mum and Dad were enjoying themselves so much, chatting to people they had not seen for twenty years or more.

Jarrod soon began to loosen up, and that was likely thanks to the single drink, as he stayed on water thereafter. The evening was a beautiful night of fun and laughter that ended with them leaving just after midnight to get back to the hotel.

A very late morning was quite obviously needed by the whole family, and a late breakfast in the hotel restaurant was taken well after one in the afternoon, everyone quite happy to make the least of what would effectively be a lost day.

St Johnstone were playing that night, and there was talk they would go along to watch, although Dad was quite keen to head South and into England to visit some more family. In the end they agreed that Dad would drive to England with Mum, leaving Jarrod and Anna to get themselves to the game and back to the hotel in one piece.

Jarrod was a little nervy about the whole idea, but Anna pleaded with him. They ended up thoroughly enjoying their evening together. St Johnstone had played fantastic football but were staring defeat in the face, trailing to an early goal against Hearts. The vocal crowd urged them on and the goal came right at the death to share the points, a moment that gave Jarrod a real thrill.

On the train to Newcastle the next day, Jarrod picked up a discarded edition of a Scottish newspaper. It was full of praise for the players, mentioning some of the players he had trained with, and that St Johnstone were a team heading for good things the following season, all food for thought.

The train pulled in to Newcastle in what seemed like only an hour, and after negotiating the concrete bridge over the platforms and the awkward barriers, they were greeted by Mum and Dad, who had driven in from Uncle Craig's place nearby.

The 3pm meet at Gateshead International Stadium was an unusual time to meet, but Gateshead had a game on that night and having played only two days before, had foregone the day's training session in favour of a rest day. They had about two hours to get there, but Dad knew the way.

Dad had always been a Newcastle fan after spending his formative years on the terraces of the old St James Park, and there was no choice in team that Jarrod would follow. Even from his earliest memory, Dad had the latest shirts for Jarrod in the most miniature sizes and was often very tired on a Sunday morning after staying up through the night to catch his team live on TV. "It's not the same if you don't watch it live," he would say, then when daylight saving moved the kick offs to 2am during the summer months, he would record the games and watch them in the morning. "It's a good way to watch it, this," as he fast-forwarded through the pauses in play.

Gateshead Football Club had gone through a remarkable change since they had been promoted to the Football League from the National League a few years back. They were a club constantly on the rise, narrowly avoiding relegation in their first season, making the play-offs the following year and then romping League Two in their third season back in the big time.

Clearly Dad was more excited than Jarrod for the visit to the International Stadium, and when they presented themselves at the reception, it was Jarrod who did the talking while Dad looked around at all of the memorabilia on the walls.

The receptionist ushered Jarrod and his family through a side door and up a long corridor to meet up with the manager, a burly local man who had obviously played the game but had not been a player for some time.

They sat down for a quick chat. The manager, Steve Bruker, was a man who had won trophies in Europe and in England as player, who had been in charge of some of the top players in the world as a manager, and here was Jarrod Black sitting in front of him for a chat.

Dad was slightly unnerved, and wasn't his usual chirpy self, and later it would turn out he had an innate distrust of the man due to his past connections with rivals Sunderland, even though Dad didn't really dislike anyone.

Mr Bruker was a warm, eloquent man, who explained everything Jarrod would need to know, making Jarrod feel right at home. After exchanging greetings and getting changed with two other triallists in the otherwise deserted dressing room, it was time to join the rest of the squad out on the field. He would go through a very light session and then split up with some of the reserve players for some extra training while the first team continued their preparations for that evening's game.

The training was the easy bit. Jarrod gelling with the other trialling players and dominating the training session, to the extent that when the three of them were in a group of four doing a pass and chase exercise, the fourth member, a sleek looking winger, couldn't get anywhere near the ball for a good five minutes. It was smiles all round, and Jarrod was invited back the next day to an actual training session and offered the chance to stay and take in that evening's game with his family.

After showering in the very impressive dressing room and being ushered out by a tutting cleaner just before the away team bus turned up, they all went off to a local pub in quite a desolate-looking housing estate for a quick bite to eat.

This was a big game. Gateshead found themselves in the lower half of the table and scrapping to stay away from danger. The visiting Rotherham, who brought a hefty contingent of orange-clad fans, were looking themselves to get out of the bottom three.

In reality, it was a fairly drab game, no goals and not many chances, but Jarrod knew straight away that this could be an interesting place.

After getting back to Uncle Craig's house well after ten thirty and saying 'hi' to everyone, they were out for the count an hour later. The next training session was at 10am the next day.

Mr Leonard was on the phone almost as soon as Jarrod got up, the man obviously never sleeps, and told him that the remaining trial had been cancelled in Luton, and they were to make their way back to Glasgow for the flight in two days. He also mentioned there were a couple of A-League clubs showing great interest in him now, given the news he was trialling in Europe had been craftily spread.

Buoyed by this, and a quick toast and obligatory cup of tea, they were off to Gateshead's new training ground, making a point of driving via the Tyne Bridge, "to see if it was still better than the Harbour Bridge."

Mr Bruker was not there, nor were the players from the previous night's game, presumably given a break after their efforts, but the reserve team was starting to file in, and the two trial players from yesterday were also there again.

They were met by a lovely lady at the reception. She formally introduced all the triallists to each other, the first being Tommy Moody, a local player and a midfield workhorse who had a tattoo of the Newcastle United crest emblazoned on his upper arm, and the other being Regis Westmann, a lanky Southern sounding guy, who looked as though he would win every header in attack or defence, and who had also brought along his exotic cousin Marianne, quite a looker.

The training session this time was more physical. The three of them found the going tough as the coach barked orders for more sprints and more sit-ups. The rain started teeming down as they were on their backs doing a simple leg raising exercise, shirts and shorts getting totally sodden, but this was part of the romance of the place for Jarrod, and he was loving every minute.

There was time for a short sharp game at the end, eight on eight, and Jarrod was immediately in the thick of the action, shouting instructions and trying to dictate the play.

The coach came up to him afterwards and had a chat, asking Jarrod whether he had any leadership experience, and giving him praise about the positive attitude he had. Signs were good then. The coach shook his hand and hoped he would see him again in the near future. Jarrod popped in to the office on the way out to fill out a contact form, and the formal part of the journey was officially over.

That afternoon Jarrod made the pilgrimage to the shrine known as St James Park, where he walked right around the stadium, past the newly relocated Sir Bobby Robson statue, peering through the gates in the carpark under the Leazes End to get a glimpse of the field, and then spending a good hour in the club shop browsing through the thousands of items he never knew existed.

That was where Dad caught up with him, and after making a few purchases of branded pencils and last season's shirts for friends and family back home, they headed down the hill to take a photo with Shearer's bronze statue and then on to the Newcastle Arms for a beer and bite to eat.

Jarrod had never really been into beer and was not much of a drinker since he disgraced himself at a 16th birthday party - chugging away on the sickly sweet Breezers until he eventually vomited on the dancefloor while slow-dancing with a young lady - while Dad seemed to enjoy his ale without ever seeming to go past two or three drinks.

That afternoon though was different. Without the car in tow, without the girls, without any more football, and with holiday mode kicking in, the afternoon turned into evening with ease, and there wasn't a care in the world as they met up with the girls and Uncle Craig's family in a homely Greek restaurant near the Civic Centre. It was another fabulous night of laughter and happiness, with all the usual stories, and some new ones coming out. Dad and Uncle Craig were so glad to be together again.

Next day, they were back on the road to Glasgow for the afternoon flight out to Sydney. Jarrod absolutely loved flying, and despite a lengthy delay at Glasgow airport, they were on their way via Abu Dhabi.

They called Mr Leonard during the short stop-over to update him of their travels and to organise to meet up, and some twenty-five hours after setting off from Glasgow, they arrived back to a surprisingly damp Sydney.

And so ended the trip of a lifetime.

# Chapter Three:
# Break

It was not until two days later that things began to happen. After a warm winter training run with some mates from his old Rovers team, the first contact was made via a text from Mr Leonard. It was from Japan.

The Kashima club had come back with an offer of what was effectively an apprenticeship, with a view to signing professionally after two years, to which the immediate reaction was pride and delight.

Jarrod quickly started to ponder, and it began to sound like a second-best option to him. He reserved judgement though until he and his Dad had spoken to Mr Leonard.

"This is how it works," said Mr Leonard as they all huddled around the phone. Dad had leapt to the phone to get the call and was now on speaker. "They will sign you for two years as a junior player, which means they will pay you a nominal salary, house you, feed you, and look after your education needs, while you play in the junior team, with the possibility of moving up to play professionally if you impress. After two years they are not obligated to do anything."

The boys all looked at each other, unsure whether to smile or frown.

"So, if Jarrod gets injured, you know, long term, what then?" asked Dad.

"They will look after you, of course, but it would set you back and you might struggle to get back to the right level before the two years are up. If that's the case then that's it, you're out"

"Sounds harsh," muttered Dad.

"It is harsh, and that's the reality of football over there. They give you a chance, but if there is any bad luck, your chance may be taken away."

Jarrod was silent, hoping for any sign, good or bad, from Dad.

"Anyway, we have Parramatta keen to re-sign you, and there is also a bit of interest from the Super League, so nothing ventured, nothing gained. Don't feel like the trip was a total waste of time," stated Mr Leonard.

Jarrod was at a bit of a low ebb by this point. The impatience of his generation had come to the fore, and that sinking feeling stayed with him all day and well into the next week. Training was due to start the following week for Parramatta and they were keen to meet up with Jarrod as they hadn't seen or heard from him for three weeks. Mr Leonard had called again to tell him he had been in contact with Parramatta and he had let them know he would be Jarrod's representative from now on.

Checking his emails on the new MacBook set up in the study later that day, Jarrod saw one from RWMan, a name he didn't recognise, and suspecting a SPAM mail, opened it gingerly. It was a personal mail from Regis Westmann, or Reggie as he signed it, from the Gateshead trial, updating him with his news. Turned out Reggie had been invited back to Gateshead and had another trial, and he was surprised not to see Jarrod there. There was also a photo attached of Reggie, Jarrod, Tommy, Dad, Reggie's cousin Marianne and Tommy's Dad. Seeing Marianne caused Jarrod's heart to jump.

In a moment of timing that could not have been scripted any better, the phone rang in the kitchen and Dad answered it. Mr Leonard was on the phone, and Dad sounded like he was calm, but talking loudly, a sure sign he was either flustered or excited, or both.

"So, they've done all background checks, all references, all t's crossed and i's dotted? They want him there?" said Dad. "I'll phone you back in half an hour Mr Leonard...yes, definitely."

Dad slammed down the phone as if it was a plastic toy, turned to where Jarrod had now crept up near him, and gave him as big a hug as he had ever given anyone in his life, lifting his son off the ground.

"Jarrod James, professional footballer, welcome to the Football League," he said, knowing Jarrod had cottoned on straight away to what had just been said on the phone.

Once Dad had filled in a startled Jarrod about Gateshead's offer of a two-year professional contract, about a solid wage, not far off the wage Dad himself pulled, and that they wanted him to be with them in ten days, he phoned Mr Leonard to confirm.

Some minutes later, they were quickly changed and in the car to drive the half hour over to Mr Leonard's office in the Northern Beaches. Jarrod was surprised when he met Mr Leonard for the first time. Not quite what he had envisaged on the phone, as Jarrod hadn't even asked his Dad what he looked like, assuming he was a tall, overbearing man with a sharp suit.

On the contrary, Manny Leonard was a stocky, short man, obviously very fit having once been a professional football player himself, and his booming voice seemed less so when faced with the man himself. He was hot and glowing with sweat.

"Excuse the demeanour," he said. "Just back from lunch time futsal, and with this mild weather, it gets hot in there."

Jarrod was delighted he was being represented by a real football man, and a man who clearly was not giving up his passion for playing despite his advancing years.

"Come into the office," beckoned Mr Leonard. "I've printed

out the contracts. We need to sign them all. I'll give you a copy, I'll keep a copy for my records then I'll scan and send back to Gateshead, and send the hard copy afterwards in the post."

Dad was already reading the contract papers, not as many as he expected, only four pages, while Jarrod was looking around the office at some of the photos on the walls. Mr Leonard either had a passion for memorabilia, or he went to a lot of events with silent auctions. There were signed photos of rugby league teams, a signed bat by the Australian cricket team, and a lot of signed photos of players that he didn't know from the Sydney Swans.

"There's not much to it, is there?" exclaimed Dad, looking at the back of the papers expecting to find more to it, puzzled by the lack of fine-print and clauses.

"It's a standard document," explained Mr Leonard. "There are no clauses, no complicated bonus system to explain, and I can explain it all in three sentences." Which he did. "This is a two-year contract as a full-time professional player, earning £600 a week. That's just over a grand a week, with a win bonus for first team players of £200. Relocation costs, including airfare and the first six weeks accommodation, will be covered by the club. Most importantly, there is a club constitution that must be adhered to. This details the expected code of conduct of a Gateshead player - I have heard that any breaches of this code are dealt with very strictly. Jarrod, are you prepared to be a saint for the next two years?"

Jarrod was surprised to be addressed with such an outright question as he wasn't really concentrating, his eyes focused on a fabulous photograph of Parramatta Stadium at capacity, and his mind already elsewhere as he contemplated the days to come.

"Of course," he said without looking. "Great opportunity and all that, blah blah…"

A moment of silence was shattered as Dad slammed the desk he was sitting at with the palms of both hands and shot up as if he had been challenged to a fist-fight.

Mr Leonard was already standing, shocked at the answer he had received from Jarrod.

"If that's the way you're going to answer a simple question like that, you're not signing ANY contract," yelled Dad. "That just proves to me you've got NO respect and you're NOT ready to go and live overseas."

"Jarrod. Don't EVER speak like that to anyone who is in control of your career," continued Mr Leonard, instantly in a much calmer tone. "Just don't."

He turned to Dad, who was gurning at his son and breathing heavily through his nose and beckoned for him to take a seat. Dad was livid but didn't say anything else as Jarrod was stunned silent and virtually sitting on the desk behind him.

The realisation he was going to be on his own was very stark at that point. This was the moment he had to become an adult, and the shock it gave him was enough of a lesson.

Mr Leonard walked over slowly and put his arm around Jarrod's shoulder in the manner of a Sicilian mafia type,

"Son, it's time to grow up," he said, clicking the top of his silver pen as if he was going to ram it into Jarrod's jugular. He then placed the pen in Jarrod's hand and walked him over to his desk to sign the contract.

Which he did, and with a bruised ego and thirty minutes of awkward silence in the car home with Dad, Jarrod Black had become a professional footballer.

Mum, Dad, and Anna were all at Sydney's Kingsford Smith

airport to see him off, and he was in tears by the time he made his way through the gate into immigration and it became real. He was excited enough, but also daunted by the fact that he was venturing out of his comfort zone and into a new chapter of his life.

His resolve was to keep a level head, and that teenage moment of flippant cheek in Mr Leonard's office two weeks earlier was weighing heavily on his mind as he made his way onto the plane. With Uncle Craig set to meet him at the other end, he had a good 24 hour journey time ahead of him.

After collecting some duty free, remembering Dad's instruction to get a bottle of Irish whiskey for Uncle Craig and spending some time sorting out a playlist on his iPhone, it was time to board. Within the hour, the plane took off and Jarrod settled back for a rest.

It was going to be an adventure from here on in.

# Chapter Four:
## Tempted

Jarrod's mind had wandered all over the place in the first three days of the holidays. Two weeks already eaten into with thoughts of how the season had ended and how the next season would go.

By now, he had been at Gateshead for 13 years, and had seen the club go through some big challenges, with two relegations back down to League One, but two joyful promotion seasons, and another two seasons reaching the play-offs to get in the Premier League, culminating in making that play-off final last month where some wretched luck left them short a goal in a scintillating 4-3 defeat.

A photo had appeared on the front page of the local paper, the Journal, the next day. Jarrod standing forlornly on the Wembley turf, shin pads in hand, head bowed, and red-eyed, as the City players celebrated with their fans in the background. Oh, how different it could have been.

The thought of being overlooked in favour of more youthful but less experienced players was bittersweet. He could understand if the younger player could do more physically, but he was just beginning to think of himself as an experienced player - that extra sense where he could see the play happening before it unfolded, intercept passes by anticipation rather than speed - that was giving him an extra sense of enjoyment from the game.

But to have that wasted by sitting on the bench or in the reserves was not an option; fair play if he wasn't playing very well, but there were no half measures with Jarrod, and he had his sleeves metaphorically rolled up every time he entered the field.

While he thought of himself as a Peter Beardsley, Lionel Messi type player, he was perceived more as a Steven Gerrard or David Batty, blood and sweat sprinkled with class and the occasional magic. Jarrod was definitely a player who gave his all for the fans, always staying to applaud the away support, last off the pitch, never too rushed to sign autographs - his signature had morphed from a Keegan-esque masterpiece into a symbol written in less than a second.

Having been at the club for as long as he had, and with only a short loan spell at the beginning of his career, those thirteen rollercoaster years had seen him cemented into the folklore of the Gateshead club.

Players had come and gone in that time, and he had played with some of the best. Didier Foy, the current Belgium captain, was the name he used when asked who was the best player he had ever played with.

Managers had also come and gone, but the merry-go-round had ceased when the stadium and the club was bought by a local businessman, and they installed Nigel Shackleton. He was not a fancied name at the time but was a well-respected player in his era, and they had stuck with him since that move almost seven years ago. That included an FA Cup semi-final appearance that saw them go so close to making the final, eventually undone in extra time at Old Trafford against Spurs.

The club was also heavy in to giving time to local causes, charities, schools and colleges. Jarrod had taken on an ambassadorial role after his many years living in the Newcastle area; charity dinners, visiting people in hospital, taking the disabled out for excursions, always left a warm glow and allowed him to make friends in totally different circles.

His relationship with Nigel and the rest of the behind-the-scenes team was exemplary, so why on earth was he having the urge to see what the grass was like on the other side? Nigel had ushered him into his office last season to discuss a new contract, without any agents or directors present, and gave the indication he wanted him to stay for the rest of his career.

Jarrod had held the belief he would remain loyal to the cause until his body gave out, but with many players moving to the Indian Premier League and to China for one last go at the big time, and with club loyalty a strangely foreign idea these days, there was always a thought in the back of the mind.

Jarrod was club captain, feeling responsible for keeping his fellow players in check as they visited and partied in some fabulous places.

So the seed was there in his mind, but the reality of the situation was he had lived in Tyneside since he was 18, his kids were born and schooled there, he had two more years on his contract which would take him up to well after his 33rd birthday.

He continued to be in a good place, with no financial worries for the future, coming into the twilight of his career.

# Chapter Five:
## Return

There were now eight days left of the holiday, and Jarrod had clicked right into holiday mode. His two-hour fitness regime early every morning left him feeling refreshed and awake, and ready to welcome his family when they arose from their slumber. He knew that, despite it being a tough gig to get up after some late nights and the odd glass of wine, he would benefit immensely from keeping up the training.

The week had seen them do a bit of travelling. A trip to Lourdes one day was requested by Marianne, as Sebastian had done a project on it at school, and Aneka was likely to have to do the same project next year. There had been gawdy trinkets for sale and lots of desperate, ill people with carers, not something he had been looking for on a holiday, but in the end they'd had a lovely time, and the kids, Sebastian especially, had been delighted to be seeing something they had learned about in school.

Travelling had slowed the last five days of the holiday. They were bathed in sunshine, and the beach seemed like the right place to be. Aneka, who had befriended a younger Dutch girl staying two doors up, was distraught when they had to leave. Jarrod had been upset seeing his daughter and her friend in tears. They swapped contact details with the girl's parents so they could share photos.

The holiday was officially over then, and the long car journey saw them head straight up the motorway, around the outskirts of Paris and back to England via the tunnel.

They arrived home in Tyneside, tired and grumpy, but with great holiday memories and effectively totally relaxed.

# Chapter Six:
# Test

Jarrod had bought a calendar. It was something he had never used in the past but he had bought it and had it hanging next to the blackboard in the kitchen. Having missed a couple of catch-ups with friends, and having numerous clashes with Marianne and school events, he had decided it was time to use a calendar to plan the coming events more transparently, and for all to see.

He had gone through an old address book to mark birthdays of friends, then family, and the two kids' class lists with kids he knew. When Marianne came in from the food shop later in the day, she failed to acknowledge, or even notice, his creativity, much to Jarrod's disdain.

Along with the numerous events he was signed up for through the club, and dates of pre-season, and the beginning of the season, there was an entry on the calendar marked DFC for the coming Thursday. No explanation, just the three letters, marked to disguise that Jarrod was still contemplating the trials at Darlington he had read whilst on holiday.

There was no clash. Jarrod just had to drop the kids at school that morning and had the rest of the day to himself. He decided to check again via the internet about the trials and then decided he should make a discrete phone call to the advertised number. After hesitating a couple times, he dialled. A receptionist answered. He explained he was interested in coming to the trials on Thursday. She explained what was happening, where to go, and who to ask for. With the instructions written down, he had what he needed. Now he just needed convincing it was a good idea. Nothing ventured, nothing gained as his Granddad used to say.

Wednesday came and Jarrod met up with his friend and teammate Nikolai for lunch, a ritual he absolutely loved. They had the same taste in food venues, and always had plenty to talk about. This time they tried out a Yum Cha restaurant that had opened up in Old Eldon Square in the centre of Newcastle. The restaurant turned out to be a bit fancier than they had both expected. They were seated immediately. There was no hint of them being recognised as professional footballers.

After a short catch up on the holidays and news, exchanging various shots they had taken on their mobile phones, Jarrod turned the conversation to his "quandary."

"Oz, you have to be kidding me!" was the response from Nikolai, referring to Jarrod by his nickname from way back. "Why would you do that?"

Jarrod hesitated and then replied, "You're making my mind up if you say things like that, you know how bloody-minded I can be." That was quite a revelation from Jarrod, and a hard thing to admit.

"You're in a good team looking for promotion to the Premier League, and now you want to drop down two divisions and play a Sunday league style of football. Why don't you wait until you're 40 for that? You've got at least four good years left in you." Nikolai went on. "Remember all those players who drop down divisions or retire early and try to get back, it never works! Sol Campbell! Remember him? Notts County…"

"I know it doesn't look right," interjected Jarrod. "It's a timing thing. Moussa's in a good place right now, breaking into the Morocco team, and he'll get my spot. He's a good bloke. I just feel as though I'll never know what it's like to play somewhere else if I don't do it now."

"Think of Michael Owen then - sign a week-to-week contract

- but keep yourself in the highest division possible. You'll regret it," promised Nikolai.

Nikolai had the look of disgust as he always did when the slightest thing didn't go his way.

Jarrod added. "Look, Niko, we go back a long way, you're the first person I've told about this, and I'm really happy with the way you've reacted to it. It's good to know that I can get some realistic advice from you."

"I'll be very disappointed with you," Nikolai said, by way of ending the subject, and pulling his stern face which led to them both bursting out laughing. Jarrod knew Nikolai would be a mate whatever happened, and that made him realise he was surrounded by good people and had a good life. So what on earth was making him think this way?

They left the restaurant just before one; the place was at its peak. The ladies going around with the dessert trolleys had obviously clicked to who they were and offered dessert five times. They both eventually caved in and chose the mango pancakes. The memory of that taste stayed with Jarrod as he mulled over the conversation in his mind. He knew that once he made his mind up about something, it was difficult to change.

That night, with the kids fed their staple of pasta and Bolognese sauce, homework done, bath, a little TV, and Marianne not due back until late, Jarrod had time to do a ring around.

First was Dad. He caught the old man at a good time, just out of the shower and ready for a chat. The time difference meant it was close to six in the morning back in Sydney.

"Jarrod, so good to hear from you," said Dad in a slightly sarcastic tone, knowing it was before their holiday in France they had last spoken.

"Yes, yes, I know. Sorry about that. It is about time we spoke."

"Very early to be calling here, something up? Everyone's well?"

"All good, holiday was good, got to San Sebastian - took your advice."

The small talk out of the way, Jarrod turned to footballing matters:

"Look Dad, I have been doing a bit of thinking about my future here at Gateshead, and I've been invited to a trial with Darlington tomorrow."

"I was wondering when you would start thinking like that," was the surprising reply from Dad. "Darlington though...I would have picked Belgium or Switzerland or even Dubai. There can't be much money in a move to Darlington."

"You're right, I've just got a feeling about this. A club on the move, having risen from the ashes you know, doing a Wimbledon, going up through the leagues and in a few years might be hosting Newcastle, Gateshead, Sunderland, Boro, in some pretty big games"

"Yeah, but you'll be 36 or 37 by then. Do you think you can play 46 games a season when you're well into your thirties?"

The rest of the conversation was basically Dad pouring all his thoughts down the phone. He wanted the best for his son and was a little surprised such a minor name in football had caught his attention. Having checked on the welfare of the rest of the family, his sister and her crew, Jarrod ended with the line, "Don't worry I won't do anything without running it past you."

# Chapter Seven:
# Dabble

It was Thursday morning and Jarrod had just dropped the kids off at school with a wave and watched them go in before driving back home to collect his gear.

It dawned on him that almost all of the football kit he had was branded Gateshead. It took a bit of a rummage around to find a playing shirt and shorts with no branding or team colours. He was pacing around the kitchen, almost erratically. A mild sense of panic had overcome him, he checked his bag twice to see if he had everything; a snack, an extra drink bottle, and three types of boots for all surfaces.

With the clock trickling towards 10am, this would be a good chance to test the drive time from home to Darlington, to be there for the advertised 11:30 start. Traffic was non-existent at this time of day, and the journey took just under forty-five minutes, with an extra few minutes to locate the stadium and find a good spot to park. It was a much longer journey than his current three-mile drive.

Jarrod turned off the engine and clicked one more time to stop the radio and the silence left him sitting there for a moment. Why was he doing this? Was he making a mistake? Was this a massive backward step? It was time for a sharp intake of breath and he stepped out in to the warm glare, like taking the first step into a new era of life.

It was a two-minute walk to the stadium gates of the newly reconfigured Feethams. No sign of cameras mind you, which was an instant relief, but there was definitely a good turnout for the trials. Jarrod wasn't even in the first wave to arrive. After getting through security at the narrow gate, he was welcomed by a young man in a tracksuit, who was evidently part of a welcoming party for the day and escorted him the short distance to the club office.

One of four in corporate attire, the receptionist was taking details of the players as they entered. Jarrod was given a blue bib and invited to use the changing rooms if needed, drop his bag in a designated area, and meet with the other triallists, through an open turnstile onto the field.

A few handshakes and surprised looks later, the mood was buoyant, and a potentially entertaining day was underway. Darlington had achieved promotion back into the Football League only last month, after finishing fifth and coming from 2-0 down at half time to win 3-2 in the play-off final at Wembley. Making the play-offs was surprise enough after a six-match winning run saw them belie their average season to scrape in on goal difference, but to take the play-offs by storm was even more of a surprise, 1-0 wins in both legs of the semi-final against second placed Tranmere giving them their ultimately successful shot at the big time.

Pre-season training was due to start in one week and this was the first major trial session being undertaken to try to attract some talent to the club. The majority of the players had been sourced via a network of scouts who had invited a selection of players from the National League and League Two, as well as some well-known local non-league talent. After chatting to a young ginger-haired player up for the day from Macclesfield, Jarrod could sense that places at the trial were not being taken lightly by the players at this level.

The day would consist of two half-field games of eight-a-side in a round-robin fashion, with players being moved between teams accordingly. After the briefest of warm-ups, the whole group did some light jogging and turning. Jarrod joined up with his blue bib teammates and shook some hands, a couple of familiar faces, but no names springing to mind. Any nerves or doubts were forgotten as the assigned coach sorted the team into positions and the whistle sounded to get the trials underway.

Jarrod, despite being assigned as a central midfield role, tucked in behind as a central defender so he could see everything going on in front of him. The quality of the football was high, the intensity higher than he had anticipated, and he found himself enjoying a tussle with a nugget of a forward who kept tight hold of Jarrod's shirt whenever in close attendance.

Word had obviously been passed on that Jarrod was at the trials, and at the break the first team coach Des Davis took him aside for a quick chat, expressing his thanks for him turning out, while also questioning why he was there. There was heavy investment expected in the playing squad and some big financial backing imminent, so Jarrod fit the bill perfectly and was singled out as a good example to form the backbone of the new squad.

The final game against team red was an even affair as everyone started to wilt a little in the sunshine, and Jarrod took off the shackles, ditching his defensive spot and embarking on a storming run that led to a neat through ball for the striker who dinked an even neater finish for the only goal. Applause all round for a good team goal, and it was clear the fitness regime maintained in pre-season had set him a step ahead of everyone else.

Jarrod was half expecting to be given some preferential treatment but to his delight he was treated the same as everyone else and told the club would be in touch. A quick signature was needed on the sheet that had already been filled out for him when he arrived. After quick handshakes all round, it was back to the car and the drive back to Gateshead.

Jarrod had plenty of time to get back home and sort his gear out, put on a load of washing including his sweaty kit and get the sandwich press out to toast a ham and cheese roll.

The school pick-up was impending. Jarrod was always happy to mingle with the Mums and Dads at school pick-up. After turning off the sandwich press and wrapping his steaming roll in a paper towel, he grabbed his keys and headed out to catch the kids at afternoon assembly.

Sebastian came out in the first wave, chatting with his mates, totally oblivious to his Dad's presence, then a good four or five minutes later Aneka straggled out with her young classmates, spying him instantly and giving a big smile and wave.

Jake Stakis' mum rushed in looking flustered as she often did and stood next to Jarrod.

"You back training yet Jarrod?" she asked quietly.

"Hey Serena, training starts back in a couple days. Why? Do you think I've put on weight?" retorted Jarrod in a jokey manner.

"Word is there's a big signing in the next couple days. But I guess you'd be more up to date than me," Mrs Stakis continued. "Biggest signing in history, I'm led to believe."

"Keep your eye on the papers, Serena," said Jarrod with a fake twinkle in his eye, not having any idea what she was talking about.

His smile was interrupted by Aneka, who had run and jumped at him with pace. Jarrod was now cornered by three seven-year-old girls peppering him with questions and observations. Jake Stakis had joined his mum with his big brother and they were about to head off.

"Jake, have you got football practice tonight?" asked Jarrod as they started to leave. Jake had made it to the Newcastle United Academy and was in the area team for school. The Stakis family was a family who would know a lot about football, and would obviously, to Jarrod, have local football knowledge ahead of everyone else. Jake turned, about to speak, but his mum cut in.

"Night off tonight, first one in three weeks." she said rather wearily, and they turned away and continued out of the school gate as Jarrod was again distracted by Aneka and her entourage.

Despite being glad that his life was nowhere near as busy as the Stakis family's non-stop juggernaut, he did have a twinge of sadness that Sebastian wasn't into football as he would have hoped. By all accounts, Seb could hold his own in a game, but the spark of interest just wasn't there, and he seemed more interested in scoring a new high score on whatever game was flavour of the day on his iPad than getting out there with the lads.

Still, he had only just turned ten years old, and was being totally immersed in football culture thanks to his Dad's job. Hopefully something would rub off. Although he didn't realise it, Jarrod had been very similar when he was younger, up until he was at least the same age. But memories of being ten can be selective when berating a young son for wasting his days playing video games.

Jarrod was lost in thought as he drove the kids home. How could Serena Stakis know something about his own club he didn't know? The club captain? Jarrod kept a poker face going through different scenarios in his head, unable to shake the feeling he was out of the loop.

That feeling was forgotten as the afternoon got underway, and the blender was untangled from its hidey hole to whip up a quick milkshake for afternoon tea. Aneka was adamant she wanted a strawberry milkshake, despite having pleaded for chocolate milkshake mix at the supermarket.

The kids loved this special time with Dad, even if it was also homework time. Jarrod had time to give them as they spread their books, pens, and pencils across the kitchen bench to signify the beginning of 'serious' time. Sebastian was straight into his maths homework while hunched over his milkshake, straw in mouth, eyes sharp right to see over the top of the tall metal cup. Aneka was on her iPad, trying to find her homework sheet. Jarrod was impressed with how quickly she found it and printed it out.

Jarrod's mobile phone buzzed, it was a text from Massa, his teammate:

JUST MET FERRAZZO. HE'S GONNA SIGN. WOW.

A rush of cold air seemed to envelope Jarrod, as though the footballing Gods were at play - Emilio Ferrazzo was a long-time target of neighbours Sunderland, a central midfield workhorse from Inter Milan, about three years younger than Jarrod, and had been spotted in the area on more than one occasion.

The papers had put out stories about house-hunting and looking at schools, when in fact his managing agent was simply whoring him out to every club in the top two divisions. Everyone in the footballing world knew it, and the story was so old that nothing had happened in four weeks.

Sunderland had stalled on the transfer fee, and that appeared to be that. For Gateshead to be mentioned in the same sentence as Ferrazzo was very surprising, and Jarrod had to know more. He excused himself from the kitchen bench, leaving his untouched chocolate milkshake that Aneka immediately made a play for, and he moved to the lounge room to ponder the text.

Surprisingly, his first call was not to Massa, but was straight to Nikolai, who he had been at Yum Cha with the other day. Straight to voice mail, fair enough, and Jarrod chose not to leave a message. He sat there staring into space for a moment before his phone rang in his hand and he answered it straight away.

"Hey, that was quick," chuckled Nikolai, unsure of the subject matter of the conversation ahead, so keeping it light. "Missed your call."

"Did you get the text from Massa?" Jarrod asked.

"No mate. What's it say?" came the puzzled reply.

"We've got Ferrazzo - signing as we speak," said Jarrod in a less than enthusiastic tone.

"Really? He was off to that lot down the road, wasn't he? What happened?" Nikolai asked.

"Don't know Nico, don't know. I'll let you get back to it anyway, off to find out more," Jarrod continued. "Big news for the club. Later." He hung up before Nikolai had a chance to continue the conversation.

It just dawned on Jarrod then that he had received the text from Massa who was on the spot and in-the-know. Pre-season training was due to start on Monday after the fitness day on Sunday, and it was still just Thursday now, so why was Massa at the club?

A feeling of utter paranoia was shrouding his thoughts, and he was making up the plot of this scene in his head, arriving at the conclusion that Massa had been invited to meet up with the new signing to greet him, and was therefore considered as the club captain and Jarrod was not. Things were going to change for him very soon.

This was more than a hunch. It was as though Jarrod was drifting away, especially after Serena Stakis had given him the news in a roundabout way - how much further removed could he be?

Aneka broke the thought process with the usual "Daaaad!" call from the kitchen, and Jarrod turned off his phone and pushed it in the front pocket of his jeans. Aneka had retrieved her homework sheet from the printer and had been busy preparing to do her homework, creating a document on her iPad, copying the questions across from the online homework sheet, and setting it all out in a very neat way - all preparation and no substance, her trademark homework style.

"Can you help me?" came the question once Jarrod appeared in the doorway. The question was non-specific and simply portrayed the desire to have her Dad in the same room.

"Of course," came the reply, and with that, any thoughts of Emilio Ferrazzo and the whole situation were instantly forgotten.

The kids having showered and now in their pyjamas and the rice cooker steaming away on the bench, the beginning of the evening was marked by the arrival home of Marianne, the sun catching the windscreen of her little sports car. He was fortunate to have Marianne in his life. She was very social and always had things going on away from football. Her golf pro duties did take up a lot of her time and she led a clean-living lifestyle.

Jarrod had proposed in a hotel room in the chic St Germain in Paris during a winter break in fixtures caused by an early FA Cup exit. A simple country wedding then followed a few months later in the post-season in the Pyrenees foothills, which had been an absolute blast. Jarrod's family all came over. They made the most of the festivities that went on for days post-wedding in the fabulous June sunshine.

Jarrod and Marianne had been very young, and that was a cause of much concern from Jarrod's Mum and Dad, but when the announcement of baby number one came soon after, any doubts about the longevity of the relationship were dispelled. The new family found their ideal home in Gateshead not long after Sebastian was born.

At that point the mantle of hot couple that had been bestowed upon them moved seamlessly on to one of the Newcastle players and his new fashionista wife, and Jarrod could now get out in the garden and don his tracksuit bottoms when he went down to the corner shop for milk.

Marianne bustled through the door, carrying two grocery bags and two golf clubs while perching her mobile phone between her ear and neck, talking loudly about the following day's golf. Once the phone call had ended, she rushed over to the kids and gave them a big hug each, almost tipping over the remnants of Sebastian's milkshake before moving over to see what was cooking in the kitchen.

With a sniff and a nod of approval at the stir-fried vegetables that had just come off the cooktop, Marianne whisked past Jarrod, with a gentle pat of the bottom and a cheeky smile, to their bedroom to get out of the restrictive golfing clothes into something more relaxed.

Jarrod thought about talking football and new signings but chose to keep quiet. Marianne was clearly in a good mood and Jarrod didn't really want to be grilled about the new signing. Yes, a quiet evening, he hoped. The phone interrupted him as he went to finish preparing the dinner, it was a number he didn't recognise, but in his jumpy state of mind, he had to answer.

It was Des Davis, first team coach at Darlington.

"Hello Jarrod. Caught you at a bad time, have I?" asked Des, clearly knowledgeable about when is a good time to call a family man. Jarrod replied with a laugh that no time was a bad time.

Des had been itching to talk to him since they had met that afternoon, and things had obviously been happening behind the scenes after the trials had finished. He was very upbeat and very keen to talk, even more so than earlier in the day.

Des continued after some niceties. "Look. We've been in deep conversation with the owners since this morning, and we want you here. They are not convinced you really need or want the move, but as it was you that turned up at trials and not us that pursued you, they're keen. We are keen, I should say."

"Keep talking," said Jarrod. "Give me an idea of what's on offer."

Des then proceeded to give Jarrod the lowdown about what the club was preparing to offer, as if he was reading from a prepared statement, and to be fair he probably was reading from notes he had taken from a meeting that afternoon.

The club was after a star to head up their new season. A big-name player, and they were keen to get someone in place to make a statement of intent and attract more quality players to what would be a massive first season back in the professional football league.

The money on offer was surprisingly good, though not in the same league as his current wage, but more than he would have imagined any club in the fourth tier of English football being able to afford. They had huge sponsorship deals bubbling away. The owner, a local businessman who had brought the club up from the depths after their inception following the demise of the original club, was an established multi-millionaire with very deep pockets and an open cheque book. It all sounded too good to be true.

The speed of Des' words led Jarrod to believe he was very excited about what was happening, and it was a surprise when he realised he had been on the phone for five minutes already. Marianne was hovering in the kitchen ready to pan fry the strips of sirloin he had sliced.

He slowly edged away giving Marianne a wink and a smile, suggesting there was nothing going on, listening to the stream of information pouring at him through the phone. After a while, Jarrod decided to cool the conversation.

"Des, look, I'm a bit pressed for time right now, I'll need to get back to you," he said. "Can you send me something via email with what you think should happen next. I'll have a chat with my agent and we'll see what happens."

Des replied, "You're on. I can tell you're serious, we're serious, and we're ready for action. Check your emails in about an hour or so, I'll send you something in writing to make it a bit easier to follow."

"Good on you, Des. Speak soon." Jarrod clicked off his phone and headed to the kitchen where the stir-fry and sizzling steak were being served by Marianne. She was keen to tell him all about her day rather than pursue the content of the phone call.

She had given some of the guys from Sunderland a private lesson today, and talk was rife about some transfer news about to hit. Marianne quizzed Jarrod about what it could be.

"I'm a little in the dark myself," he said. "Maybe we'll flick on the TV for the news. It should be coming up to sport time about now."

Marianne was not one for TV dinners, so took the remote out of Jarrod's hand. She asked Sebastian how his Science presentation had gone and who Aneka had played with at lunchtime. As they discussed their day, Jarrod tucked into his stir-fry, which was a burst of flavour in his mouth - he must have been hungry after the day's efforts down at Darlington.

He took a moment to reflect on life; a ten second thought pattern that makes you feel warm and glowing, where you stand back and take into account how good things are, how good the simple things in life are. It also made him get off his stool and go searching for a decent bottle of red wine in the pantry.

Would this all change? Would it all be a little different if he shook things up and made a big move? Would he spoil it all on a whim?

Jarrod cleaned away the few dishes and moved his iPad closer to check his emails. Sure enough there was one from Darlington FC, authored by owner Gerry Lincoln, with a few words alluding to an attached document. He opened it. The iPad took a few seconds to decide how to open it, and up popped a very professionally laid out letter of offer.

In between carefully stacking glasses in the dishwasher, he read a few lines at a time, taking them in and giving them a lot of thought over the next items to stack. The offer was as club captain, well over half of his very generous current wage for four years, which would effectively take him up to the standard use by date of thirty-five, with an option to sign for two more depending on appearances in the third season.

Performance-related bonuses for promotions and cup success were detailed. Jarrod did have to "speak to his agent" aka his Dad, and the thought of speaking with him was something he wasn't looking forward to. He didn't have an agent these days, after the mercurial Manny Leonard had retired, and he had no reason to need one either. His Dad provided just enough stubborn advice to allow him to negotiate his own contract renewals at Gateshead and end up on a very good wicket indeed.

The stacking of the dishwasher took longer than normal, and Marianne found Jarrod with his elbows on the bench, hunched over the iPad, when she had taken a break from the phone.

"The kids are ready for bed, hon," she said. Sebastian and Aneka having done the tooth-brushing routine in efficient time to afford themselves a good twenty minutes of relaxing on the beanbags in the lounge with electronica in their hands.

"Oh," blustered Jarrod, having been startled out of deep thought. "Yeah. I was just reading a few emails."

"Something interesting obviously," Marianne pried.

"Nothing of note," side-stepped Jarrod, grabbing his wife around the waist in a tender moment and reaching in for a welcome kiss. "Nothing of note."

# Chapter Eight:
## Arrival

The descent into Newcastle airport was a rocky one. The plane seeming oversized for the scene of rolling hills and small villages. The familiar coded announcements came from the pilot, seeing all the stewards head to their fold-down seats and buckle up ready to get the flight on the ground.

Jarrod was about to embark on the rest of his life, and in a sense, he knew it - he had control over everything up until he walked out to the arrivals hall. It was freestyling after that.

There were only two other people filling out their forms when he got to the immigration check. The busy EU Passports line was going quickly through. Jarrod was instructed to fill out a small form, before heading through to get his passport stamped. The immigration officer flicked past the stamp for Japan, the last one from the return to Sydney after the trials, pondered for a moment at the visa on the last used page as if to give dramatic effect, and stamped the empty page next to it.

Jarrod hadn't even considered he might need international clearance to play for an English team, after all Dad was born in England. It turned out there was no need to get a clearance from FIFA due to his English family member, but the five hours spent in the passport office in Canberra before he left were an eye-opener to the work that goes on behind the scenes when club A signs player B.

That theatrical pause by the immigration officer brought immediate doubts in his head and a rush of relief when the stamp hit the page. Jarrod collected his passport and moved on through to the baggage collection area, the bags still nowhere to be seen.

It didn't take long though for the whoop of the siren and the flashing light beamed on for a moment. The carousel was off and running, the bags appearing from the hatch as if on a supermarket conveyor belt. His bag was soon through the hatch, and he spied it immediately.

A sharp intake of breath, a moment to put on his small backpack before flicking up the handle on his suitcase, and Jarrod was off, striding confidently through the "Nothing to Declare" gate and through the automatic door into the arrivals hall, where he was hoping Uncle Craig would be waiting in plain view.

Jarrod did a double-take - there stood a casually dressed man, not much older, but much taller than himself, who was in a branded Gateshead polo and was smiling ear to ear. It was Regis. It took a second to recognise him, but as soon as he saw Regis, he smiled and offered his hand and they pulled in for a rapper-style embrace.

"Ha ha, surprise," cheered Regis. "Thought it would be a nice touch. How're you doing?"

"Awestruck, mate, totally awestruck. Tell me I'm not dreaming," came the reply. Jarrod was scarcely able to grasp what was happening and wondered what had happened to Uncle Craig.

"Is that all you've got?" asked Regis. "One little suitcase?"

"New beginnings, mate," retorted Jarrod. "No need to bring everything."

They walked through the arrivals hall and out through the first available door, the fresh summer air hitting him, then through the carpark to Regis' car, an old blue Ford that was looking a little worse for wear. Regis pushed Jarrod's suitcase in the back seat and Jarrod placed his backpack alongside. They both hopped in the front.

Training had already been on that day, so there was nothing official for the boys to do. That gave Jarrod time to get acquainted with his room at the guest house, unpack a few bits and pieces, and get settled. Regis was keen to show his new friend the sights and sounds of Tyneside. They drove about ten minutes against traffic heading the other way, Regis finding a spot in front of a shopping centre.

"Come on, let's have a look around," he said, keen to bring his new accomplice on a scouting mission of the local youth hangouts.

"Hey, this looks good," said Jarrod. Regis glanced quizzically as if he disapproved of what looked like an upmarket child-minding facility. "Let's have a drink."

Jarrod's enthusiasm won and in they went, grabbing two stools at the counter, like in a scene from a Wild West cowboy movie. A young girl sidled up behind the counter and passed them an over-sized menu and gave them a cheery smile. Jarrod nudged Regis.

They were mere teenagers and had only met for a matter of hours, but they were clearly way ahead in their relationship and already had some unspoken communication. After a while the waitress returned to their spot.

"What can I get you fellas?" Her manner was relaxed, her eyes already fixed on Regis, and she certainly was pretty. Jarrod and Regis ordered a drink each.

"Hey, you've been here before," exclaimed Jarrod, once the waitress had left them. "And you've got the hots for that girl."

Turned out that she was just about to finish, and whilst she had to be at her next job at the local working men's club, she came across to them after removing her apron, and sat next to Regis. Jarrod was in awe of Regis by this stage. If this was how it was going to be, living life in Gateshead, he could get used to this. The waitress, Charlotte was her name, or Charlie for short, made her exit, declining the offer of a lift. The boys followed soon after.

"Hey, before I forget," said Jarrod. "My Uncle Craig was meant to pick me up from the airport."

"Oh, shit!" exclaimed Regis. "He'll still be there waiting."

Regis started running for a metre or two, causing Jarrod to panic and start running too, before Regis turned his head and smiled as he slowed to a walk.

"Aaaaah, gotcha!" he smirked.

"Bastard," said Jarrod, and they laughed. Turned out Uncle Craig was on holiday and couldn't be there. Regis had offered when it had come up in conversation on his first day.

Regis was conscious that the next day Jarrod was due to meet up with his teammates for his first day on the job. After a quick shower and being formally introduced to Doris, the friendly but stern-looking lady who ran the guest house, they were down for dinner in the dining room.

While this was not exactly the high life, he felt a sense of adventure being away from home and having to fend for himself and make his own decisions. There was no-one to remind him to take off his boots, there was no-one to make him eat his green beans, it was all down to him now.

A quick check to see if he had everything for the next day and he was straight into bed.

# Chapter Nine:
# Eager

Jarrod had been given instructions before he had set off from Sydney that he was to meet at the stadium at 10am, and Regis had been given the same instructions. They set off from the guest house at 9am. The drive was a very quick one.

Jarrod grabbed his bag from the back seat and carefully pulled it out of the car. They confidently strode in through the main entrance of the stadium, Jarrod recognising the lady behind the desk from his last visit a few weeks ago.

"Jarrod Black," she said extending her hand. "My name is Wendy. We have been expecting you. Welcome to Gateshead. I trust Regis has helped you settle in with Doris?"

Jarrod was a little taken aback that someone knew his name, before the realisation set in that of course they knew his bloody name.

"Pleased to meet you, Wendy," came Jarrod's response, remembering his mum's advice that repeating someone's name when you meet them increases the chances of remembering their name next time. "It's great to be here."

"I'll take you through to meet Mr Bruker. Just a second…" she paused as she walked around the corner to see if Mr Bruker was in his office before beckoning with her hand. "In you go."

Wendy smiled at Jarrod as he peered around the corner and then he bounded towards the office once he was comfortable. Regis followed, remaining in the background.

"Mr Bruker," started Jarrod. "Great to see you again"

"Jarrod," came the reply. "Welcome to Gateshead. Glad to see you made it in one piece, especially being driven by Regis in that thing."

Regis coughed comically to re-iterate the fact he was in fact in the office with them.

"It was good to see Regis at the airport, nice touch," replied Jarrod.

"We have training at 10am sharp out on the training field out back," continued Mr Bruker. "Regis here will show you around, get a locker sorted out, and introduce you to the kitman, Rodge. Training will be over by 1pm, when you can take a shower, and you are expected back here at 1:30pm in your club tracksuit where Wendy will run you through your contract and our code of conduct. Regis will be waiting for you after that to take you back."

Regis was startled at hearing his name, and it was clear he had not been paying attention, and was lucky to have caught that last sentence, to which he nodded authoritatively at Jarrod.

"Any questions?" asked Mr Bruker, clearly in a jovial mood.

"None so far," replied Jarrod.

"See you on the field then," concluded Mr Bruker before standing and ushering the boys out.

Jarrod and Regis blustered back through reception and out the back door that took them to the changing rooms. Rodge was where he was expected. He stood up to greet the boys, extending a big hand to Jarrod. Rodge had his tape measure out within seconds and instructed Jarrod to stand, feet apart, much in the way a tailor would have you stand to get a suit fitted.

He took Jarrod's measurements, including almost strangling

him to get his neck measurement, before tutting to himself that he may be out of a certain size. He already had a pile of clothes all wrapped in plastic on the table next to him, and then went to select a few more pieces of equipment as well as a big sports bag which he started to fill.

The final thing Rodge located was a key, and he gave that to Regis, with instructions to try the locker first before giving the key to Jarrod, because some of the locks were "a bit special," and Regis might have a better chance of getting it if it was just like his.

Jarrod was laden with all the gear and wished Rodge a good day, and the boys headed to where the lockers were located, in a small room just inside the changing rooms. Regis was trying the lock when Jarrod managed to catch up, the big bag having got stuck in a doorway en route. Regis opened the locker and handed the key to Jarrod, before snatching it back and putting it back in the lock where it should have been while it was open.

Jarrod gave him a sideways glance and placed his new bag of gear on the floor and began pulling things out, Regis saying "Yeah" or "Nah" to every item of clothing, so Jarrod would know what he needed for training today.

A few players were in the changing room by now, rifling through their lockers, and giving each other handshakes or slaps on the back. There was a good vibe, and Jarrod tentatively introduced himself to the first player he met, and it turned out to be one he recognised, Richie Bernard. He was one of the older heads on the team who was making a long-awaited return from injury, and he introduced Jarrod to the rest of the boys. This was starting to feel real now, and Jarrod immediately felt part of the family.

Out on the field, there were 26 players. This was a mix of

youth and experience, it was the youth team and the reserve team squad, with another handful of players missing who were either undergoing treatment or rehabilitation or were excused as they had first team duty the next day for a pre-season friendly in Scotland.

The squad was split into two, one made up completely of young players, the other an array of players of differing age, from the grey hairs of Richie Bernard to the pimply faces of some players that looked younger than Jarrod himself.

Mr Bruker strode out onto the field just as the coaches were counting the players in each group, and stood between the two groups and gave a speech:

"Gentlemen, we now have sixteen days until the beginning of the new reserve and youth league seasons, and nineteen days until the start of our Football League season. Today we welcome our newest recruit Jarrod Black. Please everyone, make him feel at home."

All eyes turned to Jarrod, who gave a slightly nervous smile before Mr Bruker continued. "Today we will work hard and at the end some of you will be asked to join our squad for the game in Perth tomorrow. We're looking for commitment, accuracy and energy. I'll leave you now with your coaches."

Jarrod heard the name Perth and his senses heightened, maybe due to it being a reference to Australia, before realising that Perth was where he had been only a few weeks back as St Johnstone rallied to a 1-1 draw in a great tussle at the end of the previous season.

Jarrod was surprised just how much he wanted to go there, even if only to see someone he had seen then and let them know that he had been signed up. It was maybe a reflection of his character that he let that thought dictate his performance in the training session, and he was absolutely buzzing, concentration levels at an absolute maximum. He most certainly made an impression on the coaches, and on his new teammates, with some quick thinking and shrewd positional play, way ahead of his years.

Jarrod also managed to pick up a first nickname of his career after calling out "Far out!" in frustration at a misplaced through ball in an attacking drill, which could not have been any more Australian. Hence the nickname Oz was coined by the coach the next time he referred to Jarrod, no doubt in reference to a character in an old TV series re-running at the time about a bunch of Geordie bricklayers. And so the nickname was born, with some of the players now only knowing him by his nickname rather than his real name.

The end of the session was a full game, reserves against youth team, with a few of the youth players having gone with Mr Bruker for a meeting leaving ten on eleven, one of the coaches joining the youth side to give a bit of grit to the midfield.

Jarrod played a very reserved game for the first twenty minutes, making tackles and offloading, without attempting anything out of the ordinary, but was obviously saving himself for the final few minutes. He picked up a loose ball on half way after a tackle spilled the ball his way and scurried off as if he had literally stolen the ball. He dummied his way past one defender before advancing to the edge of the area at an acute angle. A quick glance up and he delicately curled the ball to the far post where a waiting striker was on hand to slam the ball home with his head, a goal worthy of winning any game.

Jarrod was on fire, and when the opposing team broke through when the coach had called, 'last goal,' he sprinted at full speed to slide in and make a last gasp tackle, trapping the ball in the process and getting back to his feet in one movement before booming the ball out of play.

The younger of the two coaches, Senthil Dharam, made his way towards Jarrod when the final goal had triggered the end and a slow warm down was in progress.

"Great start, my friend," he said cheerily, giving Jarrod a pat on the back. "We hope to see more of that tomorrow. Training at 10am, okay?"

With that, any chance of Jarrod making the bus to Scotland the next morning was out the window, and the deflated feeling was almost masked by the encouraging words of the coach. He had to take things slowly, one step at a time - after all he was a rookie, first day on the job, it wasn't all going to happen immediately. There was still a twinge of disappointment.

# Chapter Ten:
# Change

The first week was a blur.

Jarrod was also suffering from jetlag although he didn't acknowledge it, crashing early one night on the couch just after dinner down in the dining room. His body was adjusting to the daily training sessions, and the afternoons were spent at the pool doing laps, something he had never done before. He had been advised it would be a good way to condition his body to the rigours of pre-season.

The Thursday after he had arrived, he was called in for a chat pre-training with Wendy, and she explained there might be an opportunity to gain some experience at a lower league club, Carlisle United, on loan, not too far away, and that Mr Bruker was offering the opportunity to go for a trial the following day.

Jarrod was a little confused, as he had his eye firmly fixed on Gateshead, and voiced his concerns to Wendy, who was quickly taking on the mother hen role. She was more than happy to give him words of wisdom but didn't push the loan deal and that made any decision more difficult to make.

As it turned out he had to make the decision that day, as Mr Bruker had committed to sending a couple of players for trial at Carlisle and was expecting at least two of the three players he had asked to make the commitment.

Taking advantage of Mr Bruker being out of his office, Wendy ushered Jarrod to use the phone and make a call, and he hovered over the phone for a while, knowing what time it was back in Australia, probably after midnight if his calculations were right, and decided to give Manny Leonard a call. He had, after all, told him previously that he could give him a call any time day or night, and perhaps this was the time to put that offer to the test.

"Yes…" came the response from the other end of the line after five or so rings. Mr Leonard had clearly been asleep.

"Mr Leonard, it's Jarrod Black here," said Jarrod, after all Mr Leonard might have five different Jarrod's on his books, all overseas. "Just hoping for a quick chat."

"Well, well, Jarrod, what can I do for you?" asked Mr Leonard, obviously sitting up with a strain in his voice.

"I have an opportunity to go to Carlisle for a trial tomorrow," said Jarrod. "With a view to going there for a loan spell. Not sure how long for and if they would want me, but it's an opportunity. What do I do?"

Mr Leonard was surprised at the news. It was a little early in his Gateshead career to be farmed out to a lower league club, but as he knew that Jarrod was quite a robust player, capable of handling himself, he came back with his immediate thoughts.

"Okay. So, Steve Bruker wants you to get some real life experience of the football league, that's a good thing. Carlisle have a paper-thin squad," he continued, not seeming entirely convincing. "The chance of playing first team football is higher. You're obviously not the finished product," he went on, thinking of good and bad points as he went. "Perhaps you haven't made that quick an impression…"

Jarrod wasn't liking what he heard.

"But, knowing Steve, Mr Bruker," he corrected himself. "He will be doing an old mate a favour, and from memory Carlisle's coach played with him at Man United. This could be a good move. A good move."

56

Jarrod excused himself for having woken Mr Leonard, and the call was over soon after. The parting words gave him some hope. "You're young and you need experience."

Wendy came in when she had noticed the talking had stopped, and Jarrod was deep in thought, staring at the door and pushed right back in the comfortable seat.

"Making yourself at home there?" called Wendy. "Mr Bruker will back any time."

Jarrod leapt to his feet, rearranged the papers he had been nervously toying with as he spoke, and bolted out the door, straight for the changing rooms to grab his kit and get changed, ready to put it all out there on the training field.

The training session was high intensity, and Jarrod was wearing his heart on his sleeve throughout, going in a little too hard at times and not making any friends with his over-eager manner. He realised this towards the end, and thought that it was time to chill out, so manufactured a situation where he cleared the ball during a defensive drill so far that it bounced over a hedge and down an embankment. He was egged on by the coaches to go and get it.

That gave him a couple minutes of down time, by which time he had calmed down and was beginning to think rationally. By the time they started to play a high-paced four-on-four game, the smile had returned, and he remembered how lucky he was to be doing what he loved.

He enjoyed the praise towards the end, and even got a playful hug from one of the first team players when he had slipped the ball through Jarrod's legs and left him for dead.

No time for showers. Jarrod went straight to the office area after training, after being told to check his feet for mud by Rodge who was passing in the opposite direction. He asked Wendy if Mr Bruker was available. Again, she went around the corner to check and guided Jarrod in, and this time he didn't hesitate, breezing in and shaking Mr Bruker's hand.

"Jarrod, Wendy has explained the situation," he said almost as a question. "Can I count on you to make the journey over to Carlisle tomorrow with Rodge and spend the day with my old friend Gary?"

"Sure thing, Mr Bruker," was the reply. "Happy to help out where needed."

"That's the way, my friend," smiled Mr Bruker. "Be here at eight and Rodge will drive you over. He'll hang around and drive you back afterwards. You should be back by four."

# Chapter Eleven:
# Unknown

It was a struggle to get out of bed the next day and be ready by quarter to eight. Regis was kind enough to be up and ready to drop Jarrod to the stadium in time.

The expectation was that there would be no-one at the stadium and the gates would be locked up, but the place was already alive, some workmen tending to one of the big metal gates at the entrance.

Rodge wasn't anywhere to be seen, but he arrived a minute later, Jarrod jumping out of the car. Rodge had an old Rover, the type that Regis would be looking forward to upgrading to if his car ever died, and it was in immaculate condition and shining in the morning sun.

"In you get, Jarrod," said Rodge, beckoning him towards the car. "Colm's already called shotgun." Colm Baker was in the front seat, looking like a real 18-year-old punk with his fake Burberry hat, one eyebrow sporting a gap, and chewing away. He did have the full Gateshead uniform, and he gave the air of a professional sportsman, at least from the neck downwards.

Rodge roared on the accelerator and they passed the front gates out onto the open road. Road trip! He was full of anticipation over his latest in a growing line of adventures coming his way.

As it turned out Colm was a bit of a character, the sort of guy who had a story for every occasion and was not short of a word or two on any subject. Rodge had suggested to the manager that Colm would be a good fit and could benefit from a bit of time away from his teammates, who might have been growing a little tired of his constant chit-chat.

The drive took over an hour, going along some windy roads, then some dead straight roads where the Rover got up to terrific speeds. Rodge slammed on the brakes when he got a ting from his mobile phone, presumably the speed camera app telling him to slow down to the limit.

They were a little early for the training session. More cars pulled up by the side of the field and players in twos and threes got out, all in blue Carlisle United training shirts. Colm and Jarrod took this as their cue to get out of the car and walk over to where the players were dumping their bags and getting their boots on.

Rodge introduced Jarrod to the Carlisle reserve team coach, Ian McFarlane, who it turned out was an old teammate of Rodge's from when they played together in non-league.

The training session burst into action with an energetic warm-up routine of short, sharp sprints of varying speed until a massive sprint the width of the field and then the players formed a circle to do some stretching. Jarrod thought this was a little unusual, having always stretched first before even contemplating a sprint, but it was clear this was the drill, and everyone knew what to do.

Jarrod was probably at the peak of his fitness, fitter than he had been in his school days when he was playing and training for Parramatta. He was really enjoying being able to run and run when most of those around him were spent. Colm was also as keen, and the two of them looked a step ahead of their peers in both energy and poise. After a break of about five minutes when the players took on water and some of the players lay on their backs to recuperate, and with Rodge having set up a field with cones, Coach Ian barked for the players to get up and get ready to go.

Following an unscientific team selection of every second player getting a yellow bib, apart from the two goalkeepers present, they were ready to play an eight on eight game. Jarrod and Colm found themselves on opposite teams, both playing in the middle of midfield and once the game got underway, they found themselves in direct combat.

Coach Ian rectified this after five minutes by instructing Jarrod to drop to a defensive role, as he obviously wanted to see both players play without cancelling each other out.

Jarrod looked assured when he had the ball, but wasn't interested in dazzling, preferring to play the simple ball left or right whenever he made an interception. That was until he nipped ahead of his man to break up and attack and found a huge hole opening up in front of him. He took a quick look around before galloping forward, drawing the defender in and slipping a tidy ball through for the centre forward to tuck away under the keeper.

That felt good for Jarrod, but he chose to stay composed for the rest of the game, even when it came down to the "last five," as Coach Ian barked, and then, "last goal."

The keepers both played blinders, perhaps because the goals that Rodge had set up were a little small, and the score ended 1-0 to Jarrod's team. The players all shook hands after the game before setting off on a slow lap of the field as a warm down.

Coach Ian was clearly impressed by what he had seen and didn't hesitate to let Jarrod and Colm know. With no showers in sight, Jarrod could feel he was soaked in sweat when he chatted with some of the players as they changed back into their trainers and packed up their kit.

Jarrod had a string of questions, talking as though he knew he was going to be offered a loan, and felt he only had ten minutes to find out about the town, the facilities, the prospects for the season, and basically everything he needed to make an informed decision.

Rodge beeped his horn to get his boys back to the car, Jarrod shaking a few hands as he made his way over. Rodge told them they were heading to Brunton Park, the stadium, to meet up with Mr Bruker's friend Gary. After ten minutes in the car screeching around corners and tailgating buses, they arrived at the stadium car park brimming with cars. Rodge parked, and they headed to the reception. Two men were having an argument, which ended as soon as they saw Rodge and the boys.

"Leave him alone, Gary," said Rodge, with a smile.

"Constructive debate," said Gary, the manager of Carlisle United. "All positive." His sparring partner in the argument smiled and shook hands with the boys.

"You saved me there, fellas." He walked out the back door into what was the office area. Gary Hollister was a tall, stocky man and former teammate of Mr Bruker.

Jarrod had never heard the name before, but if he had played with Mr Bruker, he must have been good. He spoke with a thick accent similar to some of Jarrod's local teammates and gave the impression of a laid back man who you would never expect to have an argument.

"Colm and Jarrod," Rodge said by way of introduction, turning his body towards Gary. "Boys. This is Gary," he stated. "Gary, these two boys have been training with Ian this morning and he asked me to pass by before heading back to Newcastle."

"Pleased to meet you guys," said Gary, who, unlike Mr Bruker, was never addressed formally. "Gary Hollister. Ian has filled me in and we would like to have you both here for a spell to help out our reserve side. Is that something that would interest you?"

"Sure thing," said Colm, answering on behalf of them both, before Jarrod could offer a reply. "We should have a good time here."

Jarrod wasn't really sure what he meant by that, but it was well received by Gary.

"Glad to hear it. Come look around." He pushed open the office door and they went up a big flight of stairs that came out in the stadium. Gary seemed quite proud of the stadium.

"You'll get to play here quite a bit. We haven't got another field at the moment for reserve fixtures, so we use our stadium," said Gary. "I'm sure you would enjoy it."

Colm and Jarrod agreed. When it appeared Rodge was ready to go, Jarrod jumped into question mode.

"So, where would we live?" Jarrod asked.

"We have a house nearby for our temporary players. It's a lovely spot. Home away from home." Gary was enjoying being questioned and having all the answers.

"What happens if we get injured?" came the next question.

"You will get treated here like everyone else. If it is something major, you will go back to Gateshead."

"How long do we stay?"

"We'll be in touch later today or tomorrow morning about that."

By now they had edged towards the door and Rodge was holding it open. This was the cue to leave, and after a very firm handshake, they got back in the car and started the trip back over to the East Coast. They were back at 2:30pm, and Rodge dropped Jarrod and Colm off at the door of the International Stadium. They were greeted by Wendy, who handed a document to Colm and as he started to read it, she handed another document to Jarrod.

"That was quick," said Jarrod, now realising this was the offer from Carlisle. Wendy had buzzed Mr Bruker and he walked in as Jarrod was getting to the part about the duration.

"Well done, Colm, well done, Jarrod," said Mr Bruker as he shook their hands. "Gary wants you both and wants you quickly."

"It's only for a month though," said Colm, a little agitated that it wasn't a longer stint. "Is it worth it? That'll only be a couple of games max by the time the season gets underway."

"It's a month to begin with," said Wendy. "They will request another if it's going well, and they can keep extending if you guys and our group are in agreement."

"Sounds great to me," said Jarrod. "Any opportunity to get game time."

"That's the way," said Mr Bruker. "Now, go make a few calls, speak to your folks, sleep on it and we'll see you back here tomorrow morning at 9am. I'm sure we can find someone to take you over there, or you can go on the train. We'll work that out in the morning. Get packing."

Jarrod was excited, but realised he was marooned at the stadium. His usual chauffeur Regis had finished training and had headed off.

"Anyone heading over to Doris' place?" he asked Wendy.

"I'll drop you," Wendy replied. "I'll be heading off in fifteen minutes. Go and have a shower and get changed and I should be ready."

"Thanks, Wendy," said Jarrod. "I owe you one."

Jarrod showered, and Wendy clearly wasn't ready to go, so he asked if he could make a call. The time difference meant this was going to be in the middle of the night back home, at least Dad might be up. Sure enough, Dad was up.

"Hello?" said Dad.

"Dad, it's Jarrod. Hope I've not got you out of bed?"

"No, no. I've just put Anna back to bed. She's been up sick - a bug going around."

"Ah, that's no good," replied Jarrod.

"Are you going to Carlisle?" asked Dad. Obviously he had been talking to Mr Leonard.

"I was there today," continued Jarrod. "And yes, I'm going again tomorrow for a month."

"Well done, son," said Dad. "You'll get some real experience in the lower leagues. Mr Leonard seemed keen when I spoke with him yesterday."

"I'll let you get back to bed, Dad. Just wanted you to know," said Jarrod, wrapping up the call.

"Yep, look after yourself Jarrod."

"Look after Anna. And Mum."

Decision made then, Wendy was now ready and dropped Jarrod to the guest house. Jarrod went straight up to start getting his stuff together. He was surprised to find Regis doing the same thing. The room was looking a lot neater.

"What's up, where are you off to?" enquired Jarrod.

"I'm moving two rooms up. Doris needs the room for a couple. I'm going to a single room."

Jarrod was impressed by the efficiency of everything at Gateshead. It had only been an hour or so since he had been told he was wanted by Carlisle.

There had obviously been no doubt whatsoever that Jarrod would be going.

# Chapter Twelve:
# Jolly

A week of high tempo training led to the opening friendly game of the season for Carlisle United reserves. This was an away fixture at nearby Workington Town on a warm, sunny but blustery Thursday evening. Jarrod had been named in the team to play in the centre of defence alongside an older player who would play more of a sweeper role, and Colm was centre midfield in a 4-3-3 formation.

The whole build up to the game was so exciting to Jarrod, the meet at Carlisle at 4pm, the briefing from Gary, the coach journey, the away dressing room, the team talk, all things he had done before, but this was in England and this was something totally different.

Stepping out on to the field in front of about 40 spectators was such a thrill, and lining up waiting for the whistle to sound was one of those moments when everything stops and you are afforded a few seconds to take it all in. The shrill burst on the whistle saw the stadium spring to life, and Jarrod was straight into the action, sprinting hard to make an interception as Workington started the game on the front foot. Colm was making a nuisance of himself in midfield and was playing with a smile on his face and giving lots of commentary to his team mates, to the opposition, and to the referee.

Ten minutes in, Workington broke up the left and Jarrod got pulled out of position to cover his right back, and that left the central midfielder to ghost in behind him and drill the ball across the face of the goal where the right midfielder had raced in to slide the ball into the net for 1-0. Jarrod knew that he had been caught out, but the positive talk from the sidelines and from his teammates allowed him to shake off the immediate disappointment and keep the defence tight for the rest of the half.

One down at the break and Workington had shown that they were not going to lie down for their league opponents. Coach Ian was upbeat and his relaxed demeanour and concise instructions gave Carlisle extra focus as the second half got underway. Colm went in for a strong challenge five minutes into the second half and the referee immediately brandished his yellow card, as if he had been waiting for an opportunity to silence the motor-mouth. That tackle was the catalyst for Carlisle to get stuck in and start to boss their non-league opponents. Colm absolutely clattered into his man on the hour and the referee was straight on the scene but thankfully there was no second yellow card.

From the next passage of play, the Carlisle left winger jinked past his man and swung in a looping cross where the bulky centre forward nodded the ball back down and Colm arrived like a steam train to lash the ball into the net from the edge of the six yard box. Colm celebrated as though he had won the FA Cup final, Jarrod choosing not to join in with the exuberant hugs, but gave him a thumbs-up as they lined back up to restart from the kick off, Colm still beaming.

The game was there for the taking and two minutes later Jarrod found himself in midfield as Carlisle cleared a corner and romped forward en masse. After evading a tactical foul, he chipped the ball over the last man to the centre forward who got the ball down on the ground with a lovely bit of control and steered a curling shot past the dive of the keeper and into the top right hand corner of the goal.

Jarrod was definitely in for a celebration for this one and joined his teammates in a mass huddle of roaring and somewhat high-pitched cheering and whooping. Carlisle added a third after a raft of substitutions had killed the tempo of the game, a dreadful mistake by the central defender who trod on the ball when trying to roll it backwards to change direction, the Carlisle striker nicking the ball away from the desperate lunge to steer the ball under the keeper for 3-1.

Carlisle Reserves had won, beating a team of experienced semi-professionals, and Jarrod had his hand in the victory. It all felt right and it all felt good.

Jarrod was called on to help out the youth team for one of the fixtures, simply to make up the bench as a couple of the players had missed the bus and Jarrod was on the spot at training and asked to pack up quickly and join the youth team on the waiting bus.

The opening day of the reserve league season came around and Carlisle travelled to Blackpool on the Friday night, while the first team entertained their counterparts from the seaside town on the Saturday.

The day of the game went smoothly. There was eager anticipation amongst Jarrod's teammates as they travelled down the M6 on the gleaming team bus, and there was a great deal of banter about what they were going to get up to after the game.

The game itself was played at an amazing pace. The first game of any season was often a frenetic affair, and Blackpool were dominant, scoring twice and hitting the frame of the goal on multiple occasions in a crazy half that ended 2-0 to the hosts.

With coach Ian in no mood to mess about, he hauled off both of the fullbacks without any criticism or negativity and switched from a dull uninspiring 4-4-2 formation to a 3-5-2.

Jarrod was entrusted with the task of leading the midfield that was slightly overcrowded, but which allowed him to sit deeper in a position that made him feel in control.

A thirty-yard special from left winger Stephen Colby, still rising as it hit the net at a terrific speed, halved the deficit soon after the break, and Carlisle sensed a comeback and threw everything forward. Colm lifted a corner over from the right hand side with eight minutes left on the clock and the ball looped to Jarrod, who had escaped his marker and was totally free, but he seemed to have too much time and the header glanced well wide.

Carlisle now poured forward, and it was a massive relief when they were awarded a penalty for a ridiculous handball, the defender clearly going for the kick, only to be undone by the most wicked top spin off the glistening surface, the ball smacking his outstretched hand. Jarrod was called to take the penalty and prepared his usual technique to attempt to fool the keeper, which was not received with any interest by the green-clad Blackpool goalkeeper. His shuffle to the left to make out that he was opening up to shoot right, the quick run up, and the ball was drilled to the left, but almost straight at the despairing dive of the goalkeeper who was very unlucky not to get a hand to it.

Jarrod had seen enough attacking, and was playing almost at the back, barking at the back three to get out when the offside opportunity arose. A two-all draw was the result in the end, and while the Blackpool players trudged off the field looking dejected having let a two goal lead slip away, it was contrasting emotions in the Carlisle camp.

Coach Ian applauded each player into the dressing room and closed the door behind him after he was sure everyone was in.

"Wonderful, lads," was all he could say. All the players stood to applaud their coach and his miraculous half-time tactical masterstroke.

Jarrod was loving this. The result was positive. The players overcame a difficult start to turn on the style in the second half, and they had a night out to come.

The players all rushed to get ready, to the surprise of the coach driver who was still in the cafeteria of the neighbouring sports complex. It was about a quarter past eight when they set off. It was only a half hour journey to Blackpool itself, and by nine they burst into a packed Scruffy Murphy's pub.

Coach Ian slipped up to the bar and ordered a round of bottled beers for everyone – the under 18s included. They were passed back to cheers from the throng.

Jarrod took it all in. The beer gave his head a dull haze, making it feel like a dream. With their corner of the pub now emptying, Coach Ian stood up on the rung of a bar stool.

"Lads," he barked, arms out wide with palms down to shush everyone. "You know where the bus is, you have ninety minutes to get yourselves back there. Now, go enjoy the sights and sounds, and make sure we don't leave without you."

The majority of the players downed their beers and headed for the exits in threes and fours. Jarrod joined Colm and two girls, who were happy to tag along.

Coach Ian had turned back to the bar, ordering a whisky. Quite the example to set.

Stepping out into the warm night, the fresh air left Jarrod a little disoriented, but with the taller of the two girls grabbing him by the arm, it seemed right to go with the flow and head on down the Promenade, which was very busy.

Jarrod seized the opportunity once inside one of the bustling pubs to pull his lady in for a kiss which was reciprocated with gusto. Jarrod felt like he had hit the big time. He was playing professional football. He was out on the town with a pretty girl and buzzing with excitement.

Jarrod was conscious of the time, and with his phone reading 11:50, he tugged on Colm's shoulder and pointed at his wrist to remind him of the time. Colm was looking a little worse for wear, his eyes not quite following Jarrod's as he spoke, and for a moment Jarrod thought he was going to be fobbed off and told to "get lost," but Colm simply pointed his thumb to the door, bent down to give his girl a peck on the cheek and they made for the exit, speeding up as they finally battled through the crowd.

They sprinted the two hundred metres down the main drag and up the side road past Scruffy Murphy's, arriving at the bus with two minutes to spare, everyone already there. Coach Ian was in deep conversation with a local and didn't even acknowledge their heroics to get back on time.

The next morning, there was not a lot of movement at the house they shared with two other loan players. Jarrod the first up and teeth cleaned at about ten thirty, and he made his way quietly out after grabbing an apple and checking whether everyone else was still asleep.

After meeting up with some of the first team players, shaking hands and absorbing the mood, Jarrod slipped into the line for lunch in the rather makeshift cafeteria.

Jarrod felt like a pro footballer, and despite not being in the squad, was walking the walk and talking the talk, sitting at a table with the Carlisle United back four, albeit on the end of the table and not able to readily join the lively conversation.

After lunch and a catch up on the previous night's escapades, they assembled in a part of the West Stand behind the directors' seats that was otherwise empty. The club had chosen to fill the front of the stand and leave the back seats empty to try and give the impression of a big crowd.

Much to everyone's surprise though, there was a big crowd, Blackpool bringing a huge following, and Carlisle's supporters obviously sensing a good game with relatively local rivals, and just shy of twelve thousand would be one of the biggest opening day attendances around the country.

Jarrod watched the game as though he was playing. At one point he was out of his seat to head the ball in when a cross just evaded the striker, his team mates giving him some stick, but he was loving it. The half time deficit of 1-0 was justified, Blackpool having the lion's share of the game, and Carlisle unable to get any rhythm going. The half-time break though saw a change akin to the previous evening's game.

Carlisle grabbed their equaliser. Jarrod was up cheering. His teammates now warmed to the idea they were allowed to act excited and not pretend to be cool. They were all off their seats ten minutes later. Carlisle had scored a vital second.

Jarrod was keen to talk to the players afterwards, although there was no way of getting to the dressing room, so he waited in the lounge with Colm. They did the rounds of the players, giving pats on the back and handshakes to the victorious first team stars.

# Chapter Thirteen: Selection

The first team season was now in full swing.

Carlisle United had started off the campaign with two wins, a draw, and two defeats, leaving them just in the top half of what would be a very tight division.

After overcoming Blackpool again in the League Cup in an edgy 1-0 win at Bloomfield Road, the nerves started jangling as Carlisle were read out for a home tie, and they were paired with Bury, not the glamour tie they were hoping for, but a winnable game against a team already struggling this season. It was another relatively local game that would surely draw in a good crowd.

Having been beaten in their next three games after the Blackpool cup victory and having lost three influential players to injuries, the mood at Carlisle was starting to turn a little sour.

Manager Gary asked Jarrod to meet him in his office after training on the Monday morning, and Jarrod had thought it was something to do with his loan agreement. The second month had come to an end and both parties were negotiating to keep him in Carlisle for another month.

As it turned out, the manager asked Jarrod if he thought he was ready for first team action - the midfield had been decimated by the injury situation, and what's more, captain Jon Miller was suspended for the next game, the following day's visit of Bury in the cup.

At the first mention of this, Jarrod switched into ultra-positive mode, letting Gary know in no uncertain terms that he was ready, and Gary let him know that he would probably have to start the game, and they would take it from there.

Gary knew the risks, Jarrod chose not to take in the risks when Gary went through them - the main one being that Jarrod could be scarred by a heavy defeat and it could be a black mark against his name so early in his career - but Jarrod was 100% in for this one, his first team debut.

Dad was thrilled when he heard the news, Jarrod calling home after midday from the chairman's office and catching him just as he was getting ready for an early night. Anna even got a quick word in, wishing her brother good luck and making sure he knew to collect every bit of memorabilia from the game.

Back at the house, and Colm and the boys had got wind of the news and were straight up to him with handshakes and pats on the back when he came through the door, a really nice touch as they were all in the same situation and all striving for the chance that had just fallen his way.

They talked for a couple hours, all four of them, filling in the gaps about their past history and their path that led them to Carlisle, and the collective joy they were all feeling for their housemate was clear. This was a true show of mateship and Jarrod really enjoyed it.

The boys were all due at early evening training, a four thirty start, and it took Colm a moment to process the fact that his watch said four o'clock. He burst out laughing.

"Look at the time, we're going to be late..." he said, before they all scarpered to their rooms to get what they needed and assembled at the front door to make their way back over to Brunton Park.

The receptionist at the office let Jarrod know that Gary

wanted a word first, while the other three continued through to the changing rooms to pick up their kit and get changed. Gary was quietly typing an email when Jarrod showed up at his door.

"Jarrod," said Gary, offering a smile.

"Mr Hollister, er, Gary should I say," said Jarrod. "You wanted to see me"

"Yes, my friend. Just wanted to know if you know where and when you need to be here tomorrow evening for the game? I remember my first game, and no-one told me anything, so I wanted to make sure."

Jarrod was immediately at ease and delighted to be asked the question.

"So, we have to be here by 5pm at the latest," said Jarrod. "Er, that's all I have!"

"That's a good start. Let's have a look now," said Gary, reaching down for a piece of paper that had found itself on the ground. It had the word Runsheet at the top.

"The stadium is open all day as the TV cameras will be setting up. You need to be here by 5pm, at the latest," Gary continued as he looked up approvingly at Jarrod. "I would suggest you get here at 4.30pm for a bite to eat before the game. Bury team bus arrives around a quarter to six, interviews are at 6.10pm, warm-up at 6.30pm...that pretty much covers it."

Jarrod thought for a second before interjecting.

"So, interviews, what does that mean?"

"Ah, yes," pondered Gary for a moment. "The local papers, the local TV news, radio, and the like, they do pre-match interviews as well as post-match interviews. We try to have these preplanned, but they can request to interview players at any stage. Do you have any interview experience?"

"Nothing substantial," came the reply. Jarrod had no interview experience, outside of a few interviews he'd done in the media room for the school TV channel.

"That's okay," said Gary. "You'll not be expected to make your interview debut tomorrow. Plenty of time for that. Right, off you go Jarrod. Put in a good training session tonight and get to bed early. Big day for you coming up."

Jarrod turned to leave.

"Oh, yes," concluded Gary. "And don't forget to dress smartly."

Jarrod nodded and left.

He had a lot of energy, despite not having eaten anything during the afternoon, other than a couple of ginger snaps with his cup of tea, and perhaps this was due to the excitement and the adrenaline coursing through his body.

Jarrod was called out of his training session after only ten minutes to go and join the first team squad who had just arrived on the main field. Coach Ian gave him some encouraging words as he left with the first team coach Stuart Lough.

The players were undergoing their warm-up routine which involved some really slow run-throughs from the side-line towards the centre of the field, each run-through with a twist, using different muscle groups, but gentle and methodical.

Vincent Kennedy was the first to offer his hand by way of congratulations to Jarrod. He would most likely be named as captain for the next night's game, and regular captain Jon Miller was stretching to the other side of Jarrod and came up to him and stood with his arm around his shoulder and began a speech in a deep Liverpudlian accent, the rain dripping from his nose.

"Lads, you all know Jarrod. He's been here for a couple months now and been part of the success of the youth and reserve teams this season. Tomorrow, he will be playing in midfield for the first team, making his first appearance at the top level, and we need to do our best to make it an enjoyable experience for him. We're not expected to get a result out of the game, but if there's any result worth having, it is getting Jarrod through his debut with a smile on his face."

The rest of the players gave a cheer to Jon's words, which were very well spoken, and with a tightening of Jon's arm, Jarrod knew his teammates would be there for him.

Jarrod got home way after his teammates, and Colm was heading to bed as he walked in and gave him an unexpected man hug.

"Good luck to you, mate," he offered. "We'll be rooting for you."

"Wow, thanks, Colm," replied Jarrod, conscious that Colm would be getting soaked. "You don't realise what that means."

# Chapter Fourteen: Nerves

Jarrod expected to toss and turn all night, but instead he found himself waking late after an epic sleep with dreams blowing around his head. The rain continued to lash against the window.

A quick glance at his mobile phone which he had forgotten to plug in the night before led him to quickly spring out of bed and find his charger, then he flicked on his bedside radio where CFM were running through the evening's fixtures, obviously having already talked about Carlisle - he would have to wait another thirty minutes to hear all about it.

A sudden clearing of the clouds and a brief glimpse of sunshine was enough to rouse him from the covers, the birds starting to chirp loudly and the sound of the postman walking up the front path making him sit up and contemplate the day ahead.

There was about six hours he had to kill before making his way to the game, and after a quick shower and cleaning his teeth, he decided a walk into town would be a good way to get his mind off the game.

He grabbed a backpack, donned his raincoat and set off for town. The walk being about half a mile at most, and with the sun starting to peep through, he ended up with his coat tucked roughly into his backpack after about a minute. Jarrod stopped in at a news agency to pick up the local paper and the Sun, then wandered two doors up to a café, in the thick of the central shopping area. He ordered a mug of coffee, some scrambled eggs on toast, and sat down at a table, diagonally opposite an old lady.

She had pin badges all the way up one lapel of her jacket. They were all football badges; a number of them Carlisle United, and the distinctive red fox on a blue background making it quite obvious where her allegiance lay. Jarrod had spread out his local newspaper and caught himself staring at the badges. The lady piped up, "You follow the football, son?"

"I do," replied Jarrod immediately, his senses already heightened by what was going to happen later that day, and he felt ready for anything. "Are you going to the game tonight?"

"No, love, I don't go to the games now, it's a little difficult to get around these days," came the reply. "It takes something pretty big to get me to the Park. Say, you don't sound like you're from Carlisle."

"Sydney," said Jarrod. "I'm from Sydney in Australia."

"Oh, really," the old lady replied, stopping in her tracks as the scrambled eggs and the mug of coffee were placed in front of Jarrod. "I spent a few good weeks in Sydney when I was about your age," she stated with a devilish look in her eyes. "Seven Hills we stayed, with some cousin or other, it was the middle of winter and it was red hot every day. Loved it!"

"You must have been lucky, it's not often like that," replied Jarrod, remembering all those times when football would be cancelled during the winter due to the heavy rain.

"Well, welcome to Carlisle, I'll leave you to your scrambled eggs," said the lady. She packed up her belongings.

Jarrod took a bite of his breakfast.

"Take care," said the lady as she shuffled past his table.

"You too," said Jarrod.

The lady was almost gone when she turned and said with a wave of her knitted blue and white scarf. "And good luck tonight."

It took about ten seconds for it to sink in. She had known who he was all along. He was disappointed not to have talked further with her. It was a lovely moment.

He started scanning his newspaper from the front page for a change, acknowledging that he knew very little about the town that had played host to him for almost eight weeks. But his mind was elsewhere, and the words danced around the page in front of him.

It took until the inside back page of the local paper to hook him in, and it was the team news for the game tonight, and whilst his name wasn't mentioned, there was talk that the manager would need to dig deep into his squad to cover the players who were missing.

After contemplating browsing the shops, he decided that in his current frame of mind, there was nowhere else for him to go other than the stadium. He set off back towards Brunton Park, realising half way he should take a detour via the house to pick up his bits and pieces and to make himself look 'smart.'

A quick text exchange with captain Jon Miller revealed he didn't need to wear a suit - only the first team players had official club suits - but he would need to either wear branded club casual wear or look smart.

Jarrod had a few items of branded casual wear, but struggled for smart pants, his usual choice of jeans or tracksuit not really fitting for the occasion. He clattered through the front door, the house standing empty, dropped his backpack and made for his room where he found what he was looking for - a smart jacket emblazoned with the club badge, and smart casual shoes.

He would have to make a stop at the club shop to work out something for the bottom half. Still wearing his shorts, he bundled everything together into his backpack, removing the raincoat that was taking up the majority of the space, the rain having stopped.

After negotiating the usual route through the terraced houses and across the front of the rugby club, he arrived at the stadium. The old clock had just ticked past one o'clock. The club shop was his ultimate destination, but he decided to get the opinion of the receptionist, a pretty lady called Siobhan, as to what he should be buying from the club shop to complement his jacket and shoes.

She had a chuckle at his expense, which he was totally expecting, and decided the jacket would be perfect and the shoes would do if he could find something suitable in the club shop.

She scribbled on the board behind her desk. "In club shop 1:05pm."

They headed out together across the courtyard to the shop, which was a flurry of activity.

"Hi Jerry," said Siobhan. "Have you got a moment?"

The rustling stopped, and a grey-haired man popped his head out.

"Siobhan," said Jerry. "For you, I always have a moment."

"Great," replied Siobhan. "I have Jarrod here making his debut tonight and he needs to look smart for the occasion. Can you weave your magic?"

It was clear this was not the first time she had been in this situation, and Jerry scampered over to take a look up and down at Jarrod in his shorts and sweatshirt.

"Good looking man. Shouldn't need much," he stated, without even bothering to say hello, before turning, checking a rack, and turning back to look Jarrod up and down.

The club shop wasn't exactly brimming with fashionable gear, but Jerry brought out a jacket and a pair of very straight tracksuit bottoms, which Jarrod looked at quizzically.

"Oh, he has a jacket and some shoes, don't you," said Siobhan beckoning Jarrod to get them out of his backpack. "It may be just a pair of pants that he needs."

Jerry looked at the shoes with a wince, but turned again to find something on a shelf, and this time it was a pair of black jeans, with the letters CUFC across the backside in a bold silver font. They were surprisingly stylish, and when he went to try them on, he found the leg length was just that little bit long for his liking, but they sat well on the shoes that he had.

"Great," said Siobhan. "Put that on the club account, please, Jerry."

"Of course," Jerry said, and smiled at Jarrod and opened the door for them both.

Jarrod quickly nipped back to the changing room to retrieve his shorts that were still hanging on the peg and rushed out the door with a curt smile to Jerry to catch up with Siobhan, striding towards the office door.

"So, how do I pay for these then?" asked Jarrod.

"Oh, no, you don't need to. It's on me," Siobhan said, making out that it was coming out of her pocket, which Jarrod absolutely believed.

"Wow, thanks, Siobhan. That's, er, very kind," he said.

Siobhan waited for Jarrod to open the door for her, which Jarrod remembered to do, and they went their separate ways. Siobhan went straight to the reception desk to see to a delivery man, and Jarrod through the open door to the training fields. He walked up briskly and stood beside Coach Ian.

"There's a photographer waiting for you inside. Did you see him?" asked Coach Ian.

"Er, no, I wasn't aware," said Jarrod.

"Off you go then. He's been there for a bit," said Coach Ian.

Which he did, breaking into a jog as he headed back to the office from where he had just come. As he arrived at the door, the photographer was coming out and they surprised each other.

"Great. Jarrod," said the photographer. "Just the man. Come this way. We'll get you set up with some greenery behind you. Put this shirt on."

The photographer handed Jarrod a Carlisle shirt still in its packet and he ripped it open, cast off his jacket and t-shirt and put it on, tucking it in to his new pants.

"No need to tuck anything in," said the photographer. "Top half only."

Siobhan came running out and over to Jarrod, where she did some last minute preening on him, producing a comb from her pocket to tidy up his hair, and straightening his shirt. Just when Jarrod thought he had to be ready, she came again, licking her finger and wiping away some toast crumbs from the corner of his mouth, then telling him to scratch the corner of his left eye to get some sleep out of it.

It was like a whirlwind, and after going through four or five different poses with varying levels of smile, the photographer gave the thumbs up and turned back to the office.

"Nice one, Jarrod," said Siobhan with a smile and rushed back after the photographer.

Jarrod pulled his t-shirt back on over the top of the playing shirt and his jacket over that. Another freebie!

Siobhan turned and snapped her fingers at Jarrod.

"Jarrod. Tickets for tonight's game. Do you need any for any family or anyone?" she said. "I know you have some family over in Newcastle."

"Er, I, er, I don't know," came the reply. "Do I need to let you know right now?"

"I'll give you four tickets. If you don't need them by six tonight, bring them back."

"Right," said Jarrod with confusion and doubt in his tone. "Thanks."

Jarrod's mobile phone had been buzzing furiously in his pocket and he hadn't even noticed. He had six messages and a missed call. Regis had messaged:

'HEARD THE NEWS, GOOD LUCK.'

His Mum and Dad had messaged separately to wish him all the best. There was a missed call from Uncle Craig, who had then followed up with a message asking Jarrod to call him.

How had he not noticed all these messages and calls?

# Chapter Fifteen:
# Game day

It was by now 2:30pm and his teammates had finished their training session and were getting changed, rolling out through the office and into the car park in twos and threes. Jarrod exchanged handshakes with them as they filed by Siobhan's front desk.

Sitting there in reception replying to messages gave Jarrod some appreciation of just what goes in to running a football club, and he was taken aback by two things: first, just how much Siobhan did on match day, and second, how much was actually going on behind the scenes. A van dropped off some bread rolls, the programme sellers came to collect their programmes, two TV crews were in and out of the office carrying equipment while their huge trucks were unloaded with the heavy stuff and taken on their 'dollies' through the car park and through the stadium gate to the pitch side.

A couple of tourists cruised in and asked if they could see the stadium. Siobhan was very polite and apologetic when she declared the stadium not available for touring today, offering them two tickets to the game, which they took gladly.

Time was absolutely flying. Siobhan reminded him he was due to meet his teammates in the dressing room at 5pm at the latest, and he should get himself tidied up and ready and grab a bite to eat in the adjoining room that was the makeshift canteen.

Siobhan eventually had to remind Jarrod to head to the changing room and get ready. Jarrod went along with it and went to drop off his backpack, get changed, and do his hair in the mirror. Loughy walked in just after Jarrod.

"Have you just arrived, or have you already done the walk?" he asked.

"I'm just going out to come back in again." said Jarrod, a little puzzled by what had just come out of his mouth.

He headed out to the car park via the office, going the long route to get final approval from Siobhan with what he was wearing. Back inside the stadium via the staff door, he bumped into Vincent and it all became a little more relevant once they arrived at the half way line. There was a group of fifteen or so kids with mobile phones, marker pens, and fresh t-shirts waiting for the team. Turned out this was a special event laid on by the club for local children, and the kids were having an absolute blast.

Jarrod was straight into the mix, signing a couple of shirts, albeit a little shakily as he battled the fabric with the thick pen, before taking out his own mobile and taking a few selfies with his teammates and some of the kids. His signature was quite a long affair and he started to change it slightly with every attempt, finally settling on a simpler one that saved him a few seconds.

As Jarrod and Vincent left the throng, Jarrod realised the photographer he had seen earlier was snapping away at the group, and he secretly hoped he had taken some good photos of him.

After heading down the tunnel and shaking a few hands with some of the stewards and club officials, he entered the dressing room. Jarrod's shirt was there, number 33 with his surname printed above it along with the rest of his gear, only missing were his boots and shin pads he would have to get out of the locker in the small room between the training dressing room and stadium dressing room. There was a relaxed atmosphere.

Loughy started to do the rounds with club physio Nico

Costas to check on the players one by one; asking a standard set of questions about their general mood, how they felt for fitness, and whether or not they had any concerns ahead of the game.

They went by first name, so Jarrod was early in the list.

"Hello, Jarrod. How are you feeling?" asked Loughy.

"I'm nervous but excited," replied Jarrod.

"Great," replied Loughy. "Any injury concerns, illness, anything that feels not quite right?"

"All good," was the reply. "Nothing to report."

"Good luck, son." said Loughy.

The dressing room emptied out as the players made their way onto the field for the warm-up, some greeted by cheers, others walking out unnoticed. Jarrod was one of the last out after struggling with his shin pad strap that was hanging by a thread. He had taped it around his leg, adjusting the tightness a couple times, and the sock over the top hid any evidence.

Coach Ian called in all the players for the initial warm-up, which was some simple jogging on the spot with five-second bursts of sprinting on the spot, all the players having formed into a circle without any prompting.

Everyone looked so professional dressed in identical training kit, and there were some very sleek-looking players. The opposition trotted out looking just that slight bit fitter and sharper than Jarrod's teammates.

After warm-up, Loughy came over and tapped Jarrod on the arm, beckoning him to follow him to where Gary was mulling over a clipboard.

"We have a specific job for you tonight Jarrod," stated Gary.

"Bury are playing a midfielder who was meant to be injured, and we know we have to stop him from playing. I want you to man mark him, do you know what that means?"

"Yes," said Jarrod, realising immediately he was going to be in for a very tough baptism. "I have to follow him around the field and stop him from getting the ball."

"That's it, Jarrod," said Gary. "But he will get the ball, and you just have to make sure he does nothing with it and you make sure he hates your guts by the end of the game."

"It's the guy that just came out before, isn't it?" asked Jarrod, already knowing it would be him but looking for confirmation.

"That's him. Number 8, Holker," said Loughy. "His teammates call him Freddie. He's the focal point of their midfield and we want you to be everywhere he is. Can we count on you?"

"I'll give it my best shot, Loughy," said Jarrod, straightening his back.

"Good lad," said Gary, and ushered him to the changing room. The rest of the players, coach Ian, and Nico followed as soon as they had seen Gary walk off.

There was much purpose in Gary Hollister's team talk before the game. The re-shuffle to accommodate the man-marking role would not affect the formation but would hopefully allow Carlisle to nullify the greatest threat.

It had been three seasons since Carlisle made the second round of the League Cup, and the manager was not going to waste the opportunity to get a positive result.

They were ready to go. Once the customary knock at the door from the fourth referee had been sounded, the players started to stand up to move out of the changing room into the narrow passage that led to the tunnel.

The protocol of the Cup competition meant the teams would go out together, captain first, goalkeeper second, and number order thereafter, which caused a bit of confusion as the players found their correct spot.

The players came out, and Jarrod eyed them all up. Jarrod was not the tallest kid around, but he was up there pushing six foot. The sleek and fit adversaries looked just a slight bit taller than his teammates, and Jarrod found himself smiling at himself; thinking this must be his mind playing tricks and his nerves making him think too much.

After a quick yelp from the front of the tunnel, the players began to move out of the covered area, over the concrete that fronted the main stand and on to the field. The nerves had gone, replaced by a huge adrenaline rush, and Jarrod could feel himself focusing on the task ahead.

He scanned for his target, Holker hanging deep next to his central defenders as they lined up, Jarrod on the edge of the centre circle looking to pounce early as the away team kicked off. A big noise from all sides preceded the kick off, and Jarrod quickly raced after the ball before diverting to his man and standing five metres away from him, the attempted long ball from the kick off by Bury having looped out of play.

Jarrod was a little lost and unable to make himself available for any attacks as that would mean leaving his man, but he contented himself with taking breathers in between passages of play when Holker was not involved.

Jarrod, who was tracking his man and not really paying full attention to the ball suddenly realised the right back was wrong-footed by an over hit pass and he might be able to get there, and leapt into action, sprinting after the ball that was spinning just outside the edge of the away team's penalty area. Within two seconds he was there, just ahead of the other central defender who gave him a nudge as Jarrod nicked the ball away.

He maintained his footing and glanced up to see striker Olivier Nguyen lurking at the far post, but the goalkeeper was only just getting back to his goal and Jarrod decided to take his chance and placed a right foot shot across the goal, sending the keeper the wrong way, the ball bouncing once off the wet surface and heading for the bottom corner of the net. Jarrod wasn't sure if it was going wide or going in and gave a little leap as the swerve on the ball took it onto the post and into the net.

It was like slow motion for Jarrod as he didn't break stride, running away to his right and into the corner with his arms stretched out wide, the fans already jumping for joy, and his teammates raced to congratulate him. With the hairs on his neck bristling, Jarrod turned and was clattered into by Olivier and they both fell to the ground in an embrace before the rest of his teammates joined in, making it very uncomfortable under the heavy mass of bodies.

Jarrod though was made of steel at this point, and after getting back up, he punched the air as the applause rang around the ground, Olivier jokingly letting him know that he should have crossed. United were one up.

Jarrod was starting to feel comfortable, easily keeping up with his man wherever he went. With the half entering its final ten minutes, Jarrod nipped in front of Holker and took the ball away, the Bury man deciding to lash out, bringing him to the floor, earning a lecture from the referee. He was obviously rattled, which gave Jarrod even more cause for optimism

Two blasts on the whistle signalled the end of the first half, and the players slowly walked over to the tunnel, grabbing refreshment on the way in from the substitutes and the coaching staff who were very upbeat.

"Wow, Jarrod," said Gary as he entered the dressing room. "A goal on your debut. Well done mate, and well done on Holker. Keep him quiet and we're in with a chance."

Gary didn't stop talking for the whole of the half time break. Jarrod was feeling good, his half hadn't been as taxing as it could have been, and he was ready to go out there and do the same job again. He guzzled down some Gatorade and washed it down with some water.

Into the second half and Jarrod was being teased by Holker, and the superior fitness of the Bury team and their ability to maintain possession was making Carlisle use up every ounce of energy in pursuit of the ball. Jarrod slid in clumsily the next time Holker received a pass, and felt a twinge in his hamstring as he got up, nothing to slow him down, and the field was beginning to cut up.

Holker dashed away with the ball and drew the defence towards him, slipping a lovely ball to his left where a low cross just evaded the toe of the striker and Carlisle had again escaped, the ball skidding out to the other side of the field.

Jarrod kept the ball in, totally unopposed by his own corner flag, and moved forward with quite a bit of real estate in front of him. There was finally some movement ahead of him, Olivier darting to the left up front, but more importantly Jarrod spied newly introduced substitute Hamad Absalom racing out of defence on the right. Jarrod knew he had to stall time for a second or two, so took a little touch and then looked back up before sending a raking ball over the Bury left back's head and towards the opposite corner flag.

Hamad was definitely quick, but could he get there, and could he cross it if he did? His incredible pace saw him not only get to the ball, but it allowed him to slow down and change direction, cutting in towards goal, the ball just holding up enough to allow him to turn without slipping on the damp turf. Olivier was steaming in at the far post and Hamad feigned to shoot before taking an extra touch onto his right and clipping the ball over to the left hand post where that man Olivier Nguyen dived in full length to head the ball home from two yards out. An absolutely amazing counter attack. Carlisle were up two nil and the crowd was bouncing! Jarrod didn't have the lungs to make it up to Olivier and Hamad who had jumped into the crowd.

The noise was amazing, the atmosphere lifted everyone for a second time and it really started to feel like a fairy tale. The board went up to signal a substitution, and Bury were surprisingly bringing off Holker. Jarrod could not have been happier at that moment, he blew hard and puffed out his cheeks, realising just how tired he had become.

Midway through the second half with Jarrod free of his man-marking duties, he reached for a stray ball and felt a big slap on the back of his left leg. He took one more step and when it came to put his weight back on his left leg, it totally gave way and he ended up crumpled in a heap on the floor, holding the back of his thigh.

There was a groan from the crowd, most of those in attendance knowing exactly what had happened. Jarrod though wasn't sure and got straight up, the ball still not having run out of play. One step and he knew he couldn't carry on and stood with his fingers pinched to the bridge of his nose and his head bowed, his left hand clutching the back of his left thigh, the referee beckoning on the physio.

Nico came racing over from the far side. Nico caught up with him before he had left the field and told him to stop and then go down to the ground, the opportunity to waste a few moments too great to miss.

"Hamstring injury," said Nico immediately. "We need to get this iced. You need to get your leg up and then we need to get you some compression. You okay to walk on your own?"

"Yes," said Jarrod, and he went to get up from the ground.

"Not yet," said Nico. "Take your time."

"Okay. Get up and walk the other way, towards the bench," said Nico, slowly reaching into his bag. "Don't stop if the referee says anything."

Jarrod got up and the fourth official held up the board to signal the substitution. Nico began to walk towards the bench on the far side. The Bury fans started to shout, the referee ran over to Jarrod, and when he saw that he was almost in tears, he decided not to hurry him up, instead holding his arm in the air with the other hand clasped to his watch as if to tell the Bury fans that he was stopping the watch to take into account this mini-charade.

Coach Ian helped Jarrod on to the treatment table, and the club's resident medic Dr Paul Davis appeared once he was settled.

"Off you go boys, back to the game," said the Doc. "Hi, I'm Paul. So, we have a hamstring problem. Nothing to see just yet. Let's just test where it is."

"Hello Doc," said Jarrod, as he watched Coach Ian and Nico race back out to their posts.

Dr Davis smiled and got Jarrod's ankle in a grip and shook it slightly, then lifted it and pushed on his knee to push the whole leg up in a bent position. Jarrod couldn't take the pain and let out a yelp. He gave Jarrod an ice pack, a very flat one, straight from the ice box and asked him to press it on where it hurt. He then got some bandage and, while Jarrod held the ice pack in place, wrapped it very neatly and securely around his leg.

They both walked up the tunnel and Jarrod slipped around the corner and into the dugout, the doctor following him and grabbing an empty plastic chair which he put in front of Jarrod.

"Just put your leg on here," said Dr Davis, placing a couple of stray training tops on the chair to make it higher than the bench. Jarrod placed his left leg on the pile of clothes.

"We'll have a look in the morning," continued the doctor. "Try to keep it iced and elevated when you're not standing on it. That should keep any swelling away."

"Thanks, Doc," said Jarrod, as midfielder Dean Hardacre appeared at his side, and without a word, sat down and gave him a reassuring pat on the back.

The game was still going on, Bury had obviously scored, and the crowd was sounding a little frustrated. Jarrod heard his name shouted from behind him. It was Senthil, the Gateshead coach. He gave the thumbs up, thumbs down gesture with a querying look on his face to which Jarrod waved then gave the throat-slit gesture, he was crocked. Uncle Craig was by his side and gave a big grin with both fists in the air and Jarrod mouthed, "See you after," to which he gave a thumbs up.

The victory was in sight, and after a penalty appeal by Carlisle was waved away by the referee and some expert time-wasting over by the far corner flag, they reached the end of the 90-minutes, the fourth official holding aloft his board to indicate 2 minutes.

Bury had one last chance to save themselves. A sweet ball

was played up the left to their tricky winger, who crossed low and hard, the ball flashing across the face of the goal with two Bury players unable to reach it. The ball rolled out of play. The whistle sounded. Arms went up in the air, and the whole of the bench, Jarrod included, got up to join in the celebration.

Jarrod had a mix of emotions. He was frustrated at having picked up an injury, and was unsure what was to come, but was also proud and delighted to have been part of such a good team performance and to have helped the team through to the next round of the cup.

After the post-match team-talk, showering in the buoyant dressing room and getting changed, Jarrod picked up all the ice packs and bandages he might need for his night's sleep, Coach Ian making sure he knew what to do. He popped his head out of the main entrance to see Senthil, Uncle Craig and the family all waiting patiently and beckoned them in - they could come in and celebrate with him.

"Jarrod," exclaimed Senthil. "Bloody great game my friend."

"Thanks, Senthil," said Jarrod. "Shame it was cut short."

"Yes, on that. We'll let Carlisle assess you in the morning and then we'll be in touch. You might have to come back over to Gateshead to get some treatment. We'll let you know in the morning. You go and enjoy yourself though, well done."

A journalist rushed past them and into the media room which was a-buzz with activity. Jarrod and his family peered through the open door where Gary had just appeared at the front to give a post-match interview. Gary gave a short summary of the game, telling the reporters of his surprise and delight about the way his team played tonight, then the reporters began to ask questions, although it was a little difficult to hear the questions as Gary was the only one with a microphone. The answers were fairly sterile and non-specific until it came to the injury situation, when Jarrod caught his eye standing at the doorway.

"It's thanks to guys like Jarrod Black," said Gary. "Who we can call on in our time of need, that we're in the next round of the cup." He pointed to the door and everyone turned around to stare. It felt a little confronting, but Jarrod felt ten feet tall.

All of a sudden a big roar came from the lounge, followed by another from outside where some fans were still milling around. A cheery Coach Ian came waltzing out of the lounge door and announced, "Everton away!"

That set the media room off in murmurs and led to the question being asked immediately of Gary as to his reaction of the draw.

"I think the reaction is obvious," he said. "Look at Ian McFarlane." And with that, Gary got up and left the room via the door where Jarrod was still standing. He put his arm around Jarrod and led him to the lounge, where he put his other arm around Coach Ian and they entered to a raucous welcome, Jarrod's family following in total amazement.

# Chapter Sixteen:
# Out

The next morning Jarrod woke to the sound of his mobile phone ringing - he had been given a couple of sparkling wines by Siobhan the night before as they celebrated, and whilst he didn't mind the taste then, his head was telling him otherwise this morning.

It was Dad. It wasn't exactly early, but it was probably getting quite late over in Sydney. Jarrod let it ring out knowing it would be ringing again in an instant. That was Dad's way of making sure he hadn't just missed the call.

"Hi Dad," said Jarrod in a croaky voice. "How're you doin?"

"Jarrod!" exclaimed Dad. "Your uncle Craig has filled me in on everything - I couldn't shut him up on the phone earlier on. Your Auntie Cass had to drive home as he'd had a few too many and the kids were buzzing in the background. Tell me, how are you feeling?"

Jarrod was by now sitting up and taking in the new day.

"Ah, it was great," he said. "You should have seen us. They were all over us and we just went and broke away twice and scored. They couldn't believe it."

"What about the injury?" said Dad. "What's up?"

"Hamstring," said Jarrod. "Don't know the extent yet, but I'll find out this morning. But sore as all hell." Jarrod put one foot out of the bed and felt the strain on the injury. It felt as if he had a heavy weight on his left leg which pulled downwards when he moved.

"Dad, I'm due at the doctor's in an hour, I'd better get moving. I'm not walking that freely either so everything's going to be a little bit slow today."

"All right, Jarrod," said Dad, not wanting to end the call. "Let us know how you go - just text us, anything, but let us know."

Jarrod said goodbye and walked as fast as he could to the bathroom to brush his teeth, trying to break into a jog to see how it was, and was surprised to find that he could, but it was painful.

As he was getting his shoes on, his mobile sounded. It was a text message from Siobhan - she was going to swing by and pick him up as Dr Davis had decided he shouldn't walk too far.

Jarrod flicked back a thanks and flopped on the old couch in the living room and got on to the BBC website on his phone to catch up with the football news, and to see if there were any write-ups of the game. There was a short summary of the match, which mentioned his name twice; once, obviously, for scoring, and then once describing an "inch-perfect cross-field missile," referring to the pass for the second goal.

A quick flick over to Soccernet and there was much the same thing, a short write up that could have been done by the same reporter, and then onto the Carlisle United website where there was a much longer version, and Jarrod was glued to it, reliving every moment until he got injured, reliving the rest of the game as he saw it from the subs' bench.

Jarrod's mind was racing by now, and this new found fame, coupled with the fact he was getting a lift instead of having to walk to the stadium, gave him a huge sense of pride.

Siobhan didn't take Jarrod to the stadium, instead dropping him at a nearby clinic where he had been fast-tracked to see a specialist, and after checking in and browsing through the extensive collection of ladies magazines in the waiting room, he was called in by the receptionist and a door opened.

A young doctor came out and showed him in. This was definitely not a new experience – Jarrod had been through a couple of minor of injuries in the past; the most painful being a totally bruised right ankle he sustained when he was still at school.

The doctor welcomed him in and asked a number of general questions about his health, which he scribbled down on a blank scrap of paper. Jarrod had shorts on and the doctor told him to lie down on the bench and let him take a look, asking when he had found the sweet spot when moving his foot up and down a few times.

A quick scan was next, using an ultrasound machine that Jarrod thought was only for pregnant women, and the results were displayed on the screen by his head. Whilst Jarrod couldn't see anything, the doctor had obviously homed in on something and was pressing very hard where it hurt. He took some screenshots and measurements using the tracker ball and some buttons on the console, but Jarrod couldn't make anything of it.

The doctor had him stand up and stand on his toes with his right foot only, then his left, and Jarrod couldn't support his weight on that leg which made it very difficult to keep his balance.

The doctor remained poker-faced throughout, even chatting about the game as he had obviously been there the night before, but not giving away anything.

Jarrod did ask him as they wrapped up the consultation whether he could diagnose the problem, but the doctor simply said he was not qualified to give an opinion and he would have to talk with Dr Davis. Turned out this guy probably wasn't even a doctor.

After taking a seat in the waiting room again, it wasn't even thirty seconds before Dr Davis appeared. He offered a hand to Jarrod and gave a firm shake before leading him through to his room, giving a cheery good morning that broke the solemn atmosphere, which also signalled the other doctor, if he was indeed a doctor, to come out with printed scans and join them in the room.

"Congratulations on your debut, Jarrod." said Dr Davis. "You must be delighted by the way it went."

"Yes, it went well, then this," said Jarrod, pointing at his leg. "What does this mean?"

"Let's see then," said the doctor, and held the printed scans at arm's length while tilting back his head. He had three prints and looked at the second two closely, exchanging jargon with his colleague who had taken the scan.

"Looks like we have a slight tear to the hamstring, nothing too dramatic. We usually see these injuries more in older players, but you've definitely given your muscle an episode."

"I don't see any other problems. Do you feel okay otherwise?" asked the doctor.

"Yep," said Jarrod, adding, "apart from a little achy after the game, you know, standard muscle soreness. It was quite a busy game."

"It certainly was," concurred Dr Davis. "Your marking job was very successful, that Holker guy didn't get a sniff." Jarrod was surprised to hear the doctor was also an expert tactician and had picked up on the job he had been given.

"So, I'll let Ian know," continued the doctor, referring to Coach Ian. "He will contact your club and organize the next step. You go off to training as normal - you do have training today, don't you? Ian will see you there. You can walk on it, but don't try any running. Try and ice it once today, then again tonight for fifteen minutes."

"Thanks for your help, Dr Davis," said Jarrod, and he left the room. He walked over to reception, where he asked whether or not he had to sign anything or pay anything but was told there was nothing else to do and they wished him a good day.

Jarrod stepped out into the daylight. The day was turning out to be quite a nice one, with the sun peeking around the big clouds. There was training today, a 12 noon meet for all players, junior, reserve, and first team.

He had half an hour to get there, but with his impaired walking, he knew the fifteen minute walk would take much longer. By the time he got there, Coach Ian had already talked with Gateshead and they had decided to get Jarrod back over to the East Coast for some rehab, as Gary would not be able to play him for at least three weeks.

Jarrod got the news via Siobhan, who was relaxing with a cup of tea, reading the paper. She was in a cheery mood, and that cheery mood didn't falter as she gave the news to Jarrod.

"Jarrod, Gary will see you," she started. "You'll be heading back to Gateshead today to get some treatment on your hamstring, I'm just waiting to hear back from one of my contacts who is heading over to Newcastle tonight, and he should be able to drop you off. Come and see me after you've seen Gary and I should have everything sorted."

Jarrod walked over to Gary's office, where the manager was in his tracksuit ready to go out and join the training session but was looking up something on some sort of database on his computer and staring intently at it.

"Gary," said Jarrod, conscious of not startling him. "You wanted to see me."

"Yes, Jarrod, good to see you," replied Gary, shifting himself in his seat and offering the other chair to him. "Listen, well done for last night. It was truly a memorable game and you did a great job."

"Thanks," replied Jarrod, knowing there would be more to the sentence.

"...and, well done on your time here at Carlisle," continued Gary. "You've been a pleasure to work with, you really have, and I would hope that you would consider coming back later in the season when you're back on track."

Jarrod had a mixed sense of pride and disappointment and didn't know what to think. He knew though that he was welling up and could feel his cheeks drooping as if he wanted to sniff and pull back the tears. He put his head down slightly and Gary sensed that he was struggling.

"Think of your time here as the first episode of your football career." Gary started. "When you're in your late thirties and you've played at the very top level, when you've achieved everything that you're going to achieve in your footballing life, when you're writing your memoirs, just remember your time here and write something complimentary."

Jarrod smiled. He had heard a similar line on a TV show once, and had an inkling that Gary was quoting it, but fair play, he was saying all the right things. It was all just so sudden - from the moment that second goal went in last night to now, there were only a few hours, but the whole landscape of his life had changed.

He had gained such immeasurable experience here at Carlisle and it was now cut short and he felt like he was back where he started.

"Thanks, Gary," said Jarrod. "I've had a blast." And with that, he sprung out of his chair and offered his hand to Gary, who beamed and shook it, clasping it with his left hand as he did.

Jarrod had two hours to get back to the house, pack all his gear up, strip his bed, pack the Carlisle kit he needed to return, and generally make sure he had everything, before his designated lift called to pick him up.

The middle-aged business man, with his suit jacket hanging on the hook by the back left window of his Ford Mondeo that screamed salesman to the world, was a really nice guy who had loads of stories to tell, and the run over to Gateshead went very fast.

He was dropped back at the guest house. It was coming up to dinner time, and he felt as though he was home, despite having spent more time in the Carlisle share-house than he had here. He still only had the one bag of belongings, although it was getting heavier, and he heaved it out of the boot and waved off his driver before striding in through the front door.

Doris came out of the kitchen and grabbed his arm and told him how she had read about the game the previous evening. She was so eager to talk to him, and Jarrod felt a little overwhelmed. Regis had heard from the lounge room and walked in, grabbing him in a hug.

"Welcome home, superstar!" he exclaimed. "How does it feel to be the darling of the Cup?"

"Ha ha. Hello, Reggie," replied Jarrod. "Wounded soldier coming through."

Regis picked up Jarrod's bag and led the way upstairs. They both had separate rooms now, and Regis told him they had a week to find a place to live, and he had been thinking they should find a place to share in the middle of Newcastle, where all the action is.

Regis had obviously been looking forward to having his mate back, although he had still been enjoying his time at Gateshead. He had trained with the reserve team a couple times, so had been recognised as someone having potential, and he was loving it.

They had kept up to date via social media and text message, and only a couple of brief calls over the seven weeks, but they were fast becoming like brothers, and Jarrod really liked it.

They bounded downstairs, Jarrod stopping halfway when he realised he shouldn't be bounding anywhere at the moment and sat down to the hearty dinner Doris had made, mince and dumplings with potatoes, truly a delicacy in the region.

Life was going to be back to normal now.

# Chapter Seventeen:
# Grind

The normality of life, for a few weeks at least though, was intensive physiotherapy and clinic visits, and Jarrod spent the majority of his day in the gym, working on the upper half of his body in a bid to stay strong in the absence of fitness training. He was already starting to bulk up.

Senthil had encouraged him to do at least two hours a day in the gym, in order to "fill out" and to get some strength that would be useful in direct combat with the opposition.

He was back to light running after two weeks, under the supervision of the club Doctor, Dr Muura, a svelte looking, stern woman of South American descent. She was very strict on what he could and couldn't do, and even scolded him on one occasion when she saw him run down the stairs after an afternoon visit.

By week three, with some strapping, Jarrod was told to go on a long run to test out the hamstring. The long black bruise that had appeared a few days after the injury had now gone, and Jarrod could only feel a slight pulling sensation when he lifted his leg.

Dr Muura told him that this was normal, and he would now need to make sure the sensation had gone completely before entering into any gameplay, where stop-start actions would be likely to cause further damage.

Jarrod was welcomed back to training four weeks to the day since the injury by his youth team teammates with a round of applause. Jarrod felt low on energy, carrying an extra three kilos due to the gym sessions, and it took two weeks for him to return to something like his original fitness, two weeks in which the youth team played three games and lost all three, mirroring the fortunes of both the reserves and the Gateshead first team. Jarrod sat on the bench in the third of those games

The next game was a Friday night trip to Middlesborough and with two of his teammates out with 'flu, Jarrod was given the nod to make his first appearance. It felt like his first game at Under 10s academy all over again.

It took until the fifteen-minute mark for Jarrod to get some space on the ball, and when he side-footed a pinpoint pass in between the central defender and left back for Regis to run on to, the smattering of applause gave him hope.

Jarrod found himself with plenty of opportunity to make crunching tackles in the middle of the park, coming out on top in each tackle that he carefully chose to make. By half time, Jarrod had drawn blood on both knees, but it was only when he took his seat in the dressing room that he noticed.

Senthil asked if he was okay, and Jarrod nodded as he took in almost a full litre of water from one of the many drink bottles that were dotted around. The left leg was feeling tight, but he figured it was because he was making his first competitive run out and putting in that extra 10%. There was no way he was coming off anyway, no chance.

There were ten minutes remaining when Jarrod was finally replaced, and he was red in the face and had started to slow down dramatically - no complaints from him as the board went up signalling his replacement. The high fives on the bench were welcome, as was the jacket handed to him and the energy drink. He settled down to take in the last action of the game.

Jarrod was disappointed with the result, especially after having put in so much work to get them into a good position, but he took a strange kind of solace that his team had lost when he was off the field.

Jarrod had returned to fitness, he had made his first appearance for the Gateshead youth team, and life was starting to feel whole again after the uncertainty of injury and the long wait to play.

Dad was quick to remind him that his senior stats read: Played 1 Goals 1 Assists 1, and that he had a 100% strike rate. Jarrod couldn't help but enjoy that.

# Chapter Eighteen: Plans

The mobile phone, charging on the floor next to his side of the bed, gave a ting to suggest there was something new to look at.

Marianne had gone for a 7am tee-off, and the day was just starting to get underway.

It was a text message from an unknown number telling him to check his emails, signed DFC.

Jarrod sat up and took a breath before negotiating the phone menu to his emails. Sure enough, there was a new message amongst the usual junk email. From: "Reception: Darlington FC." Subject heading: "Session 4th July—New Feethams—09:30 meet."

This was a mass email, although Jarrod was obviously on the bcc list as there were no other recipients. Jarrod read through the email, very exact and concise to keep to the very basic of information in case the email got into the wrong hands. He was invited to meet at 9:30am for a 10:00am start, with a meeting afterwards at noon.

This was only two days away. He might have some juggling to do with his timetable, but the timing was good - Marianne was on a run of early starts, so he could get the kids to school just after the school gates opened, test the rush hour traffic and be there hopefully bang on time.

He figured he had half an hour grace as it was officially a 10:00 start. There was no need to reply, no RSVP. Jarrod was just expected, along with other players invited back, to be there.

The roar of the garbage truck chewing through the rubbish

and clashing the rubbish bins back onto the ground snapped him out of his thought pattern. Aneka appeared like a mirage at the doorway with the stealth of a puma, before bounding over to the bed and throwing herself on it and launching into her usual non-stop barrage of questions and observations.

Jarrod loved this part of the day. The five minutes between waking up and getting up, and when Sebastian lolloped in and sat on the end of the bed, he knew that getting up time was coming.

"I'll be down in a minute," Jarrod said, interrupting Aneka's flow and suggesting he needed to make a phone call. "I just have to talk to Granddad."

"Can I speak to Granddad?" asked Aneka, hopefully.

"After I have," said Jarrod, signalling the kids to walk down the stairs and get on with their breakfast, knowing fine and well that Aneka would not be speaking with Granddad. The kids raced for the stairs, Aneka almost tripping down them and Jarrod could hear scuffling and shouting as he found Dad's number in his phone and rang it.

It rang for quite some time before Anna answered.

"Hello?" said Anna, wondering who this could be on the now obsolete home phone, and half expecting it to be a sales call from some faraway place purporting to be a survey.

"Surprise!" said Jarrod. "What are you doing over?"

Anna had moved out three years ago, leaving the family home at the tender age of twenty-six. She was enjoying her own success in the Australian W-League, rubbing shoulders with the elite and pushing for that elusive Matildas spot, living in Melbourne, playing for City.

"Game tomorrow at Parramatta. Came up a day early to pop in and see Mum and Dad," replied Anna. "You all right?"

"Yeah, things are good," replied Jarrod in a blasé manner. "When are you coming over to see us again?"

"Won't be for a while," continued Anna. "Game after game at the moment."

"Listen," said Jarrod, cutting his sister short. "I've got to be quick, got to get the kids ready for school. Is Dad there?"

"Sure," said Anna, thoroughly comfortable with playing second fiddle to her father for Jarrod's attention. "Give those kids a kiss from me. Ring me next week, things are getting exciting."

Anna left it at that. She gave the impression she was purposely teeing Jarrod up, so he would be keen to know her news and would ring her. Dad came on the phone.

"Hello, son, be early in the morning over your way?" said Dad.

"Yep, sure is, but time is ticking so I'll be quick," said Jarrod.

"O-kayyyy," said Dad, slowly and suspiciously.

"So, Darlington have invited me for a second trial," Jarrod said. "They've put an offer on the table already, but I'm figuring that it's open to negotiation."

"Right..." replied Dad, unsure as to what the question was or was going to be.

"I just need to know if I'm being stupid. Can we enlist Mr Leonard to help negotiate a deal?" Jarrod asked with hope in his voice.

"I'll have to see," said Dad. "It's been a while since I spoke to him, maybe six months, and he's enjoying his travel at the moment. Last time he was off to Hong Kong to play in a six-a-side tournament."

"Okay," said Jarrod. "Do you mind ringing him to ask if he can help? I'm a little bit out of my comfort zone here."

"I'll ring him tomorrow," said Dad firmly. "He wouldn't have his agent licence these days, so he'd only be offering advice. It's probably a good idea though."

"Great. Let me know," said Jarrod. "You don't think I'm being stupid, do you?"

"Trying to secure your future is no stupid thing," replied Dad. "But, I think you could be aiming a bit higher, or further afield."

"Belgium, Switzerland, Dubai you mean?" said Jarrod, referring to an earlier conversation burned in his memory.

"Exactly," said Dad.

"I'm keeping that in mind," said Jarrod with no conviction whatsoever. "Listen, thanks for doing this. Let me know how you go. Ring me anytime on the mobile."

"Will do. Keep smiling, son, and make sure you talk to your family about this. There's no use keeping secrets."

Jarrod flicked his phone off and leapt out of bed, thundering down the stairs to join the action downstairs, and made his way to his adopted position behind the kitchen counter where he would direct the morning rush hour while making lunches, emptying the dishwasher, overseeing spelling practice, and maintaining order.

With the kids moving back upstairs brushing their teeth and getting dressed, and Jarrod having completed the morning routine with a wipe of the counter top, he felt it was time to have a word with Marianne.

He picked up the home phone and dialled her number. She answered after two rings.

"Hey Jarrod," she said cheerily. "Kids ready to go?"

"Yep, nearly," replied Jarrod. "Listen, can we meet this morning after the school drop. You're not playing now, are you?"

"No. Sure," said Marianne. "Nothing wrong, is there?"

"No. Just need to run something past you," said Jarrod truthfully.

"Oh, exciting," replied Marianne, accentuating her exotic tone.

"Right," continued Jarrod. "I'll see you at the golf club café at 9:30. Your shout."

It was at that moment he realised Aneka had picked up the phone upstairs and was listening.

"Okay, bye," said Marianne.

"Byyyyyeeeee," said Aneka, giggling to herself.

"Bye, Aneka," said Jarrod and hung up before sprinting upstairs, Aneka fleeing in mock panic to her room to pretend she hadn't been listening in.

Marianne was already in the café when Jarrod arrived, looking relaxed and tanned, and Jarrod realised he rarely saw his wife in daylight hours these days as they led very separate lives.

Still, he knew what she would be drinking, a peppermint tea, and she already had a macchiato on order for him. Marianne was looking svelte in her golfing attire, and she smiled at Jarrod as he walked over and kissed her fully on the lips before taking a seat.

"Looking relaxed, honey." said Jarrod, conscious not to sound as though he was being cynical of her tough and gruelling job. "Thanks for taking a bit of time."

"No problem, babe," said Marianne, reaching in for another kiss. "What's happening?"

"What's happening? Not sure how to answer that one, but I'll try," said Jarrod. "What's happening is that I'm in an interesting place at the moment, a crossroads if you like, and we need to talk this one through."

"Oh," said Marianne, sitting upright and moving her cup closer.

"I'm being pursued by another club, Marianne, another club in the area," said Jarrod.

"Who is it, not Sunderland, no?" she asked, pretending to be horrified.

"No, it's not them," said Jarrod. "But you would be surprised to know who it was..."

Marianne gave him an incredulous glance as if to say, 'Well, who is it?'

"It's Darlington," said Jarrod, unsure about the reaction he was going to get. "Darlington FC, new team in the football league..." His voice trailed off, sure that Marianne had no interest in the make-up of the football pyramid.

"That's not too far, is it?" asked Marianne. "I was playing yesterday morning with the wife of one of their players, Suzanne Rhodes, lovely lady, seems to be very happy." And with that, Jarrod sat up and realised this was not going to be such a drama at all.

"Rhodes, yes, Jason Rhodes, plays left back," said Jarrod. "I think I've met him recently. Darlington are on the up. They've just come back into the football league and looking to hit the ground running. They would want me as their captain and marquee player."

"You're a wanted man," said Marianne. "That must make you happy."

Jarrod was again taken aback by the lack of resistance and he felt like he was falling in love with his wife all over again.

"Well, it does," admitted Jarrod. "It makes me very happy that someone with a grand plan is including me in it, and the timing, I think, is absolutely spot on."

"But you're still young, Jarrod," said Marianne. "Why the rush to move down the leagues?"

"Yep, that's what my Dad said, in a roundabout way," said Jarrod, confusing his Dad's words and Nikolai's sentiments a little. "In fact, he was keen for me to head over to Dubai."

"Does this mean we have to move?" asked Marianne, changing the subject somewhat abruptly. "I mean, I love it...we love it here, the whole family."

"I don't think we do," said Jarrod. "I think I can cope with 45 minutes each way in the car. I know I've been spoilt being so close in my time here. But, if you want to move."

"So, who knows about this?" probed Marianne, partly so she could toe the family line, but mainly so she could identify her spot in the pecking order in Jarrod's confidence.

"My Dad sort of knows," said Jarrod, sounding less than convincing. "I've chatted with Nikolai briefly. He thought I was joking."

"But you're not...are you?" asked Marianne, leading Jarrod to have a horrible thought that Marianne actually thought this was a joke. Luckily she didn't.

"No," said Jarrod, softly. "This is going to be a big decision for me to make, and I need to know if I've got you and the kids on board."

"Who can I talk about this with?" asked Marianne. "I mean, if it's all hush hush."

"We'll need to keep this under wraps," said Jarrod. "I've got a meeting this Friday and things could happen very quickly after that. If you need to speak with anyone, ring my Dad, or talk with your friend Suzanne. Hopefully she can be discreet."

Marianne nodded. "Okay. What are you doing now?" asked Marianne.

"Oh, I'm meeting with a guy who runs the Gateshead fans website at noon, no rush though," said Jarrod. "What are you up to?"

"I'm teeing off in a team match just before twelve, with a couple of your teammates. They should be in soon, Massa and Raz."

Marianne had a devilish twinkle in her eye. Jarrod knew he could trust her to keep quiet, but she would play with his head in the process.

"Well," said Jarrod, getting up. "Say hi from me. I'll see them on Sunday. First day back."

"Already?" exclaimed Marianne. "We just got back from holiday and you're going back to work?"

"That's right, my love," said Jarrod, reaching out and playfully grabbing her chin and moving in closer, planting a big kiss on her lips. Jarrod let go and made for the exit as Marianne turned to make her way back to her base at the club shop.

He smirked as he walked away from his wife. That went pretty well.

# Chapter Nineteen:
# Talk

Jarrod was aware he had let a couple of calls ring out on his mobile. There was also an email that had come through. He clicked through to emails. One caught his eye with an abbreviated subject heading: 'Gateshead welcomes you to the new season.' It was the first generic email of the season.

The email had been forwarded by the manager Nigel Shackleton who gave a cheery welcome, before the key dates were spelled out and the agenda for Sunday was detailed.

Jarrod already had an idea of what would be the agenda on Sunday: weigh in, health check, fitness test, and a long run. The only difference from previous years was the start time dramatically earlier, 7am on Sunday. Yes, 7am!

He was about ten minutes early for his meeting with Mark White, primarily because he wanted to avoid seeing Massa and Haz at the golf club. He made his way to the front entrance and was met by the Maître D, who showed him to a table in a quiet corner of the restaurant.

Jarrod was ordering a bottle of sparkling water when Mark turned up. They exchanged handshakes and pleasantries before Mark got his mobile phone out and got it ready to record the conversation. Mark ordered himself a drink and got straight down to questioning. The waiter showed up, handing them a menu each. It was clear that Mark had done this many times before, and despite not being a 'real' journalist, he knew the drill.

"Jarrod Black," started Mark. "A pleasure to be here to discuss all things Gateshead."

Jarrod nodded and added, "It's been a couple of years, Mark. It's about time."

"Pre-season is due to start this weekend," said Mark. "How have you relaxed this summer, and are you raring to go?"

"The body is never exactly raring to go at this stage of the season, but the mind is always ready. Ask me again in a month." said Jarrod in his media voice. "I've been down in the South of France for a couple weeks with the family and we had a ball."

"Is the play-off defeat at the forefront of your mind?" asked Mark.

"It was a horrible end to a great occasion," admitted Jarrod, trying to give the impression he was giving some good news to the reporter sitting opposite. "We were looking so good early in the game and then it all unravelled. The fourth goal was the nail in the coffin, but after that we played with total abandon, and we nearly nicked it."

Jarrod's voice began to rise in volume as he remembered the day.

"Martin Shovey almost did it single-handedly," said Mark. "Was his presence the reason you came back so strongly at the end?"

"Look," said Jarrod. "Martin is hardly a prolific goal scorer, but he knows how to finish, and when his second went in and three of us raced to the back of the net to get the ball, we honestly thought we could rescue it in the final five minutes."

"Your face at the end told a story," continued Mark.

"I bet it did," said Jarrod, smiling. "I have to remain stoic and I have to be strong for my teammates when they need me. But the realisation that I would never reach the Premier League was pretty hard to take, and I was welling up, I'll admit."

Mark looked quizzically and then continued calmly, "So, you don't think you'll ever reach the Premier League?"

"Ah," said Jarrod, knowing his last sentence sounded a little wrong. "I mean I would miss out again. Gateshead will make the Premier League, we have to. We've been to Wembley twice now, and we need to put it right."

Mark seemed to dwell on the subject.

"You're still in your prime, would you say? Has there been any interest from the Premier League teams to acquire your services?"

"I'll be honest and say that I don't know," said Jarrod. "I've not heard anything from any Premier League team in the last few months, but you never know what goes on behind the scenes and who is talking to who. I think I could cut it at that level, but I'd hope to do it with Gateshead."

The waiter arrived with their drinks and Mark stopped recording. They both had a cursory glance at the menu and ordered something simple, Jarrod opting for a healthy Caesar salad to go with his healthy sparkling water, playing the professional sportsman role to perfection. Jarrod took his chance to turn the conversation around while the conversation was off line.

"So, Mark," he started, rubbing his hand over his mouth in contemplation. "What do you think needs to change at Gateshead to get us up?"

"Quality players," said Mark instantly. "More quality players. It's about quality and quantity in this division. There's a lot of games and there's always plenty of injuries during the season.

Has Nigel been given the green light to sign any more since Ferrazzo?"

"To be honest," replied Jarrod truthfully. "I haven't been involved at all. I'll be meeting Emilio for the first time on Sunday and I'm looking forward to it. I'd expect that signing to get other players from other clubs excited and we might see a few more come through the door."

"He's a bit of a mercenary though," said Mark, alluding that he was being touted to pretty much every club in the top divisions in England.

"You can't deny his work rate and skill though," retorted Jarrod, going on the defensive despite not knowing the man. "As a Gateshead fan, I'm excited too."

Mark restarted the recorder, showing Jarrod he was doing so.

"Jarrod, what are your thoughts on Nigel Shackleton as a manager?" he asked.

"Nigel is a good friend," said Jarrod. "He has been with us for quite a long time now, and his playing style is wonderful." Jarrod didn't want to give any indication of a 'but.'

"Is it time for a change, with two failed promotion attempts?" asked Mark.

"I don't think so," said Jarrod, again on the back foot. "We've played some fantastic football over the last two years, and we've been very unlucky with injuries at key stages of each of the last two seasons. Not much Nigel can do about that."

"True," continued Mark. "But a fresh approach, someone to attract more players, would that be a good move by the club?"

"No," said Jarrod unequivocally. "The recipe is right, just

needs a little more prep time."

Jarrod was happy with that bit of wording, and Mark knew the line of questioning needed to change, and he went for the more light-hearted.

"Who do you consider as your best mate at the club?" he asked.

"Pffff..." Jarrod stalled. "That's not a fair question, as I do see a lot of my teammates on a social basis. I tell you what," he replied, offering some substance. "Me and Nikolai are secret foodies at heart. We love nothing more than trying out new restaurants. So, let's go with that."

"And who is the biggest joker on the team?" asked Mark.

"That's an easy one," said Jarrod. "Raz Hamdon. When he got doused in wee at the game in the Europa league, everyone who had been victim of his practical jokes cheered. In fact, it's rumoured one of his ex-teammates threw it from the crowd."

"I remember that," said Mark. "One hell of a day out."

That seemed to make Mark relax a little and the conversation became an opportunity for the two to reminisce about those days in Europe and other random escapades in pre-season. Their lunch came out and the recording was paused while they ate, the conversation continuing along the lines of 'what about the time...' Jarrod had, after all, a lot of history with Gateshead.

Jarrod finished his crispy salad and Mark almost at the end of his club sandwich.

"Jarrod," said Mark, by way of signalling the start of the next chapter. "You've been at the club for 13 years now. When do we see you lining up in a testimonial game?"

That was an interesting question. Now that he was being wooed by another club, he paused while he gathered his thoughts.

"It was always my thought," said Jarrod. "A testimonial would be appropriate at the end of your career. The fact that you've played ten years at a club should not be an automatic right to a testimonial, especially when you've still got many years ahead of you." Jarrod was being careful here, trying not to introduce any doubt as to his future.

"That's very gallant Jarrod," said Mark. "Who would your testimonial be against anyway? You've got no history at any other club."

"Well," stated Jarrod, with his finger in the air. "There's always Carlisle, where I made my first start. Or, there's VV Venlo, where my 'brother from another mother' Reggie now plays. Or, one of my old teams in Australia who would love me to make the journey over for a game. Don't worry, there's plenty of teams."

"Going back to your first seasons at Gateshead," said Mark, seizing on a thought. "How was your relationship with Steve Bruker?"

"Mr Bruker was like a father figure to be honest, or even a grandfather figure," said Jarrod, still referring to his ex-manager by his surname. "I owe him a lot. Even when he farmed me out to Carlisle a few days after I arrived, there was a method to his madness. He had done it all, so I was in the best hands."

"And when he left," continued Mark. "What were your thoughts?"

"Yes, I was disgusted," said Jarrod. "He didn't deserve to get the sack, he worked miracles with us to keep us up the season before and he almost did it again. I guess that's just the way it works though. Nigel has done very well to establish us back in the Championship."

"Great," said Mark, clicking on his mobile again. "I'd better get back to work now. I should only really have an hour and it's been that already."

"I appreciate your efforts, Mark," said Jarrod. "It can't be easy juggling the website, a full time job, and supporting your team home and away."

"You're right there," said Mark. "Let alone the two kids, a wife, and a mortgage." With that, he stood up and made for the desk to pay. Jarrod slowly got to his feet and signalled to the waiter that he would be the one who would pay. That gesture would surely guarantee him a good write up. With the whole bill coming in under thirty quid, he was happy to leave a tip.

Mark was surprised.

"Hey, I'm the one who should be paying," he said. "Good on you, Jarrod." He turned and bounced down the steps and before he got around the corner at the bottom he yelled, "Look on the website tomorrow."

With that they exchanged a wave and Jarrod made his way to the car park, deep in thought.

# Chapter Twenty: Rumour

It was Friday morning and Marianne had been gone for an hour already before Jarrod was awoken by Aneka leaping on the bed. It was getting close to the end of the school year, but Aneka hadn't lost her zest for it. Sebastian came in with a face like thunder, asking Aneka to be quiet, but the opportunity for a rumble with Dad was seized and all three of them embarked on an epic wrestling match on the bed, Jarrod on the bottom.

There was just enough time for a bit of larking around before they had to click into gear and clock on to the morning routine. Jarrod's alarm on his phone heralded that moment.

"Breakfast. Clothes. Hair. Teeth. Lunch box. Shoes. Go, go, go!" he cried, confident his son would achieve all of this in about ten minutes before his daughter had even started the first task.

Time was going to be tight this morning, so he made straight for the kitchen to sort out the lunch boxes, quickly buttering rolls and unwrapping the ham from its paper wrapping. Jarrod was focusing firmly on getting the kids ready before he even thought about himself, and it wasn't until he had finished in the kitchen that he decided to hunt for some more unbranded football gear, eventually finding the same top from the last trial all crumpled at the bottom of a basket of clean clothes.

Time for Jarrod to pack his gear and make sure he had everything for the day, not that it was anything different from any other day at training, but he just had to be ready and relaxed, so nerves wouldn't affect him.

Jarrod decided to speed things up by finding Aneka's shoes and packing her school bag, finding a permission note in her bag for an excursion, which he hastily filled out, finally calling for her to get a move on.

"What's the rush, Dad?" asked Sebastian.

"I've got to be somewhere this morning and I've left it a little late," said Jarrod.

Sebastian obliged and turned off the TV and leapt upstairs to the bathroom and popped his head inside, politely urging his sister to hurry up as 'Dad is late!'

They made it to school right at the opening of the gates, and the small crowd of kids dispersed into the playground.

Today seemed eerily quiet. He gave Seb and Aneka a kiss before they burst out and closed their doors almost in unison and walked through the school gates banging shoulders.

Jarrod was relieved the morning had so far gone without drama, but he knew he was at the behest of the traffic gods to make it to Darlington in good time.

He tuned in to Radio Newcastle as he reached the end of the road, and they were talking sport as usual. They quoted a bit of headline news, referring to the Heed Army website who had run a piece suggesting club captain Jarrod Black had missed his opportunity to play Premier League with Gateshead.

Jarrod sat in silence. The radio pundit came to the conclusion that perhaps it was make or break time - either step up to the plate and deliver promotion or make the move to the Premier League at another club.

Jarrod was stunned. He recalled to himself how awkward his reply had sounded yesterday in that damned interview and how he thought he had papered over it sufficiently. The traffic lights had gone green and he found himself very close to the car in front, realising he had to get his mind back on today, but he was furious. Furious at Mark White.

Jarrod hadn't seen the article on the Heed Army website and couldn't exactly read it now that he was in the car, but he immediately dialled Mark's number and waited for him to answer.

"Jarrod," came the one word answer.

"Mark," replied Jarrod, almost leaving it at that before continuing. "Why am I not hearing very good things from yesterday?"

"Good question," said Mark. "I presume you've seen the article?"

"No, I haven't," said Jarrod. "But, Radio Newcastle have seen it and they're drawing conclusions."

"I'll admit, Jarrod, that the wording is a little ambiguous," said Mark. "You should read it first maybe." His tone was a lot less friendly than it had been the day before.

"Not happy, Mark," Jarrod stated. "Not happy at all." And he hung up, very unlike the model professional that was Jarrod Black.

That exchange was enough to fire him up even more, and some aggressive driving saw him reach Darlington's New Feethams stadium just after 9:30am, another five minutes to find a car spot, and then five minutes to walk from the car to the office.

Still seething, he caught a reflection of his angry self in the office window, which took his mind off it for a moment, made him collect his thoughts and also made him laugh at himself. Jeez, get a grip lad!

When he entered the office there were a few players in there already 'checking in', and Jarrod recognised most of them from the last session.

The friendly receptionist beckoned him over and gave him a warm greeting, already knowing who he was, and invited him to check over the details he had filled out last time and to sign some waiver form or other, probably to remove any liability if he got injured.

Des Davis was straight out to greet him, followed a few seconds later by a small but jolly businessman, whose suit jacket was a little too long for his arms. He introduced himself as Gerry, the owner of the club.

Jarrod could tell that Gerry had a presence, with Des having moved aside in a hurry to allow his boss the space to greet him.

"Jarrod Black," said Gerry. "I've been hearing good things about you, son, very good things."

"You're not talking to the right people then." said Jarrod, by way of a joke, not that he was really in a jokey kind of mood.

"Come," said Gerry, placing his hand behind Jarrod's back but not touching him. "Come into the office here and we'll have a word."

Sitting in the office was a familiar face, if a few years older than he was the last time he had run into him.

"Gary!" exclaimed Jarrod. "What are you doing here?"

It was Gary Hollister, ex-manager of Carlisle, and memories of his time there came flooding back. Jarrod was beaming.

"Jarrod, my good man," said Gary, standing up and walking around the desk to give him a handshake, although Jarrod would have hugged him in an instant. Gary's height made Gerry look even smaller, but Gerry was the one to lead the discussion.

"You two obviously know each other," said Gerry in an almost inquisitive manner. "I understand you were together over at Brunton Park for a while."

"Yes," said Jarrod. "Gary gave me my first start in English football. What a game it was too - I had a 100% scoring record for ages after that."

Jarrod was alluding that he didn't play any first team games for quite some time after that magical League Cup night in Carlisle until well into the season with Gateshead. "Played one, scored one."

"We could have done with some of your luck in the next round, mind," said Gary. "We got off lightly at Everton with only a five goal thumping."

Gerry moved in a step and took charge.

"Jarrod," said Gerry. "Gary is helping us out in the short term while we look for a long-term managerial team. We're hoping he can help attract the right candidates and who knows he could end up being our first manager back in the football league next month."

Gary smiled at Jarrod, while Des stared off into the distance. There was perhaps a bit of a power game at play here, but it could be that Des was simply tuning out as he had heard this same line used on more than one person in this situation.

"And..." continued Gerry, "Gary, in fact all of us here, we would like you to be part of this journey with us. We know more about you than you probably think we do. We've done our homework and talked to the right people. We are confident we can offer something enticing for you here at Feethams."

Jarrod's eyebrow had raised, and he was conscious of it, so he relaxed his face.

"We need to make things happen fast," continued Gerry. "And you are by no means the only 'big name' we are talking to, but let's say you are the one we really want."

Des clapped his hands together and said to no-one in particular, "But first, we need to get out onto the park and get this session up and running." He turned to Jarrod. "Are you ready?"

"Won't be five minutes," said Jarrod, who was clearly not fully dressed. "I know where everything is I think."

They filed out of the office, Jarrod and Des together, while Gerry and Gary chatted and slowly followed them out.

The session was quickly assembled and after a quick headcount, Des explained what was happening. First, they would have a warm-up and would split into three groups of eight to run through some drills, then they would choose two teams. The two teams would have a tactics session and would then play against each other for two halves of thirty minutes.

It was quite a schedule and would be a good test of the pre-season fitness. Jarrod hadn't quite taken note of everyone who was there as he had hurriedly pulled his shin pads, socks, and boots on and was quite late to join the group.

After the warm-up routine, he found himself with Piotr Jankowski, again a blast from the past. He strode up to his old teammate when he realised it was him and clasped him in an embrace. They had not been that close during their time together at Gateshead, but he was in a hugging mood after seeing Gary, so it felt like the right thing to do and Piotr was smiling.

They were about to launch into conversation when the allotted coach, an older guy with a grey beard and mad staring eyes, asked everyone to come in and listen to the instructions for the first drill; a running exercise around a large square of cones, where four of the players would chase the other four until two of one team overtook two of the other team.

Two more exercises and they were well and truly warmed up and ready to play.

The coach finally introduced himself, in his American twang, as Dion, and he was in fact a football scientist introducing new ideas to the club over the coming season.

Des grabbed his clipboard and read out the names of the players for Team A, Jarrod being the second off the alphabetical list. Team A were given bright orange bibs and led up to the far end of the field by another coach, who introduced himself as Tim.

He looked familiar, but Jarrod couldn't place him. Jarrod shook hands with a couple of the faces he hadn't yet met, and they huddled together in the light drizzle as Tim handed out a red cone to each player. He had already marked out a very small field with yellow cones and explained that the yellow cones represented their half and asked each player in turn to take their position and drop the red cone.

The players were then asked to step outside the square and pay attention while Tim explained some basics. Again, the fact that Jarrod had never had such a session made him feel excited, and Tim went through a sort of buddy system, where he expected players to be able to swap intermittently with their buddy frequently during certain phases of the game. The left back in this 4-3-3 formation, for example, was expected to buddy with the left sided midfielder when defending, but when attacking, the left back would buddy with the left sided attacker, compressing the game and allowing overlaps and very wide wing play.

This all seemed a little too good to be true, and so simple that it couldn't be a tactic that had not been tried and failed already. Team B were already lined up and ready to go, and they had obviously not had the same talk. The game soon got underway, with Des, Tim, and Dion joined by Gerry and Gary and a few others at the sideline on half way.

There was a little bit of confusion at the start of the game from Team A as they tried to implement the new buddy system, and they found that they had players out of position all over the place - Tim yelled at them to stop thinking too much and just let it happen, and sure enough, after about ten minutes, the first transition took place.

Being totally absorbed in the game it was a surprise to hear the half time whistle, and the teams went off to their coaches for some feedback.

Tim told Jarrod to watch the second half with the coaches on the sideline, which Jarrod wasn't too thrilled about after such a good run in the first half, but he explained that he wanted Jarrod to see it from their perspective and help identify the players that they needed.

After a five minute run-through of the first half highs and lows with the players, Tim left the second half preparation to Dion and started to explain a few things to Jarrod.

"Team B is mainly made up of players that we have already signed," said Tim. "But you might have already worked that one out." Jarrod certainly hadn't.

"They've never played together before though," said Jarrod. "There's not much conversation."

"True," admitted Tim. "Team A is made up of players we would like to sign, and a couple we don't expect to sign if everyone else signs up. I'd like you to have some input into this process."

"I can try," said Jarrod, feeling a little unnerved by the fact he was being assumed as someone who was already involved in the club, and also trying to downplay his knowledge.

"Good," said Tim. "We'll get this second half underway."

The second half began at a fast pace, Jarrod's place being filled admirably by the substitute, who was clearly eager to make an impression.

Tim asked Jarrod his thoughts on one or two players and asked if there was anyone who stood out from the rest of the team. Jarrod was beginning to feel less at ease - he was a player after all - all he wanted to do was get out there and get involved.

He got the sentiment of a big fish in a small pond and he wasn't used to it. With Team A toiling to maintain parity after an equalizing goal midway through the second half, and with energy levels dipping, Tim asked Jarrod whether he would like to go back on, and Jarrod jumped at the chance, if only to escape the coaching role he seemed to have found himself in.

After the game, Tim and Dion ran through the good and the bad, a lot more thoroughly than Jarrod was used to, and Des and Gary were in deep discussion over a clipboard. Gerry detached himself from the group and walked around to Jarrod, who was taking a long drink from a drink bottle.

"What do we have to do Jarrod?" he asked.

Jarrod kept drinking while he contemplated his question. He

took the bottle out of his mouth and breathed deeply.

"Gerry," said Jarrod. "You've got some convincing to do."

"Okay, let's have a chat in the office afterwards before you head off," said Gerry. "You don't need to be anywhere do you?"

"I can hang around," said Jarrod. "No problem."

Dion wrapped up the session by taking the players on a very slow lap of the field, running through some muscles the players may be feeling, the names of the muscle groups, and the possible injuries they could get.

It was again very informative stuff, and Jarrod was enjoying the detail. The players gave the coaches handshakes and started to head off, Jarrod enjoying a few words with Piotr, catching up after a number of years with all the major news items.

Jarrod chose not to take a shower - he hadn't brought any change of clothes so deemed it pointless - and made his way to the office where he was asked again to sign off by the receptionist and ushered into the back room where Gerry was waiting, reading the back page of the local paper.

"Can I invite you back tomorrow, Jarrod?" asked Gerry in a tone that was almost apologetic. "I would like to run you through our plans and give you the chance to meet a few more people who aren't here today. We can do lunch too."

Jarrod gave a face as if to say, 'Sounds okay,' bottom lip upturned and a small nod, à la Robert De Niro.

"Let's say 11am tomorrow," continued Gerry. "I know it's a Saturday and you might have plans, but I'm aware that you start back at Gateshead on Sunday and this might be the only time we get to do this."

"I'll be here. I might have the kids with me, but I'll be here," said Jarrod.

"Even better" said Gerry. "They can have a look around. We would be delighted to welcome your family."

They shook on it and Jarrod left the office. Piotr was waiting in the reception and stood up when he saw Jarrod and bounded over.

"Let's do lunch," said Piotr. "Let's talk."

Jarrod had always known Piotr as a straight talker, and he liked the idea. It sounded as though Piotr had things to tell him and the timing was good, nothing much on until school pick up and no engagements with supporters' websites or journalists.

They agreed to meet at the Hall Garth hotel, not far out of Darlington on the way back to Newcastle, Piotr on the way up to see family in the area, and parted ways to find their cars with an acknowledging nod.

A glance out of his back window when he first got into his car, and Jarrod was pretty sure he saw the car of one of the photographers from the local press pulling into the car park ahead. He wasted no time in pulling away and past the entrance to see if it was him. The car had moved on inside, so he would never know, but paranoia was starting to creep in and Jarrod sensed it.

Radio Newcastle was still tuned in, and it was coming up to the half hour mark, so no doubt there would be a recap of the news and sports. He flicked the radio to his staple of BBC Radio 5, and they were talking through the cricket, a welcome distraction from footballing matters.

He was at the hotel in no time at all, and first there. Piotr had obviously got stuck at the lights Jarrod had zoomed through on amber. Jarrod made his way into the restaurant and secured a table for two with a leafy outlook and ordered a large bottle of sparkling water from the bar.

He was sitting back down when Piotr walked through the door and, after the host had made sure he had a table waiting, made his way over to Jarrod and took the seat opposite.

"Are you signing for Darlington, Jarrod?" he said quietly. Jarrod had expected this line of questioning, no bull from Piotr, ever.

"Why do you ask?" came the shady reply, and it was a reply that didn't quite make sense, not even to Jarrod himself. "Are you signing?"

"I asked you first," retorted Piotr. "You're captain of Gateshead, why would you be here?"

"Timing," said Jarrod. "The timing is right. I don't think I'm ready for another play-off defeat and all that disappointment." Jarrod found himself giving up more than he really wanted, but as it was Piotr, with his abrupt manner of forthright questioning, he felt compelled to give forthright answers.

"You left Gateshead in a hurry yourself," continued Jarrod. "We never got the real reason."

"Yes, and thanks for your calls since," said Piotr, alluding to the lack of communication with him since he left three years ago. "It was Nigel who said I should go. We didn't see eye to eye. You know how he was with me. Leaving me on the bench while he tried his little experiments. Arsehole."

"Still," said Jarrod. "You were earning some good reviews and you seemed to be heading for a good season."

"I know when I'm not wanted," replied Piotr. "The move to Brentford seemed like the only option. I've had three good years in London, but I'm now ready for something else. These guys are offering good money and long contracts. It's what I need at this stage of my life, for my security and the security of my family."

Jarrod could sense that Piotr was trying to persuade him to join also, in not so many words.

"They are offering good terms," agreed Jarrod. "That's for sure. But, is a move to the fourth tier of English football the right move for any of us? Are they expecting to buy another promotion and then another and another?"

"That's what it looks like," said Piotr in a matter-of-fact sort of way. "I think I'm ready to make the move. It would be great if you were there as well. Wow," he said, reclining in his chair and looking at the ceiling for a moment. "Imagine being back alongside Jarrod Black..."

Jarrod was enjoying Piotr's company. They had gone out for a dinner together soon after Piotr had joined Gateshead, and Jarrod had seen it as appropriate to get to know the new player on a personal basis and show him what a good family-oriented team they were.

Piotr hadn't been a bundle of laughs that time, but after a couple of years playing with him and being around him on a daily basis, he got to understand and enjoy his sense of humour and his quirky abruptness. He never got the chance to repeat that dinner, and he had thought about it, when Nigel Shackleton announced one morning training session that Piotr had moved to Brentford.

No goodbyes, no leaving party, no farewells. He simply wasn't there anymore. That was one of a few things that had irked Jarrod about his time working under Nigel. There was no room for sentiment. The sense of business seemed to override every other facet of daily life and human interaction. Jarrod and Piotr discussed this.

They enjoyed a hearty meal. The hotel filled up fast with the business crowd as lunch time wore on, and they decided to forego the dessert to get moving and get out of the way of potential prying eyes. They swapped phone numbers before hitting the road.

Jarrod had the realisation that his mood had mellowed from the morning, and he was feeling relaxed. Not even a tractor causing a massive tailback on the main road could dampen his mood.

He arrived at the school with almost half an hour to spare, opting to get out and make his way to the locked gate. He parked himself on the wall and flicked through old photos on his phone.

The pick-up done, the kids were invited over for an impromptu play date at their friends' house. The Jones family had a boy in the same year as Sebastian and a girl in the same class as Aneka, and their mum Catherine was hairdresser to all the mums and girls from school.

Jarrod was happy to agree to the kids pleas and dropped them over, staying for a beer when he realised their dad Chris was also at home. Chris was a big Newcastle fan, and like most of them, he had a soft spot for Gateshead. He also had a lot of football knowledge, and always seemed to be able to turn the discussion to the absolute latest topic involving Newcastle United.

He asked Jarrod straight away whether he had heard the news about Jan Waagenar, the holding midfielder from St James, who had been involved in a car crash on holiday in Italy and was expected to be out for some time with broken vertebrae. Jarrod hadn't heard - in fact the news was so breaking that it wasn't even on the BBC sport web feed - and Chris was straight to the point, asking if Jarrod had ever considered moving to the Toon.

Jarrod played his usual professional card, taking advantage of the hours and hours of media training he had been through over the years to give Chris a reply that neither confirmed nor denied anything. It was an interesting thought, though - imagine if instead of switching down two divisions to join Darlington, he could surprise everyone and end up making a shock move over the Tyne to join his Dad's team. How happy that phone call would be back to Sydney...

The kids were having such a good time, larking around in the sunshine, running through sprinklers and spraying each other with water pistols, that they inevitably lost track of time, and Marianne turned up. Catherine had obviously tipped her off as to the whereabouts of the kids, which made Jarrod feel a little inadequate as he hadn't contacted his own wife.

Marianne walked back to the car to fetch four large pizza boxes and the kids all realized the evening would in fact be turning into a night. Good times.

The kids were having a ball. Catherine and Marianne were assessing Catherine's dress choice for her upcoming school reunion, and Chris was powering through the beers. Jarrod had already made his familiar choice of stopping at the first but enjoyed the banter with his increasingly jolly friend.

By nine o'clock, Jarrod decided he had to make tracks - Marianne was going nowhere though, and she was loving the company.

Jarrod had been invited to Darlington again tomorrow and he couldn't jeopardise it by having tired and ratty kids. There was no sport on in the morning as all the winter seasons had come to a close and Sebastian's cricket team had a bye. The kids were surprisingly co-operative when they were given their five-minute warning.

Marianne made the snap decision, now that she was going to find herself alone, and realising she had already shared almost two bottles of pinot grigio, to join her family and head home.

There were hugs and kisses all round as the kids said their goodbye, and the mums and dads said their goodbyes. It had been a great night, but Jarrod still had his smelly clothes on from the morning session, and still had all his smelly gear on the back seat of the car.

Jarrod decided, perhaps against his good judgement, given that Marianne was pumped up on wine and the kids were a little tired, to inform the family on the five minute car ride home that they would be joining him tomorrow at Darlington. Sebastian wasn't impressed - he just wanted to have down time and make the most of the free Saturday morning, but Aneka showed some interest at least.

Marianne checked her diary, knowing that Saturday mornings were traditionally a little unpredictable, and then said that it was okay. After the session, they would all venture down to Darlington to have a look around. They had never been to Darlington as a family, so at least it would be something different. Jarrod felt as though he had gotten away with murder, leaving the announcement so late in the day.

# Chapter Twenty-One:
# Family

Jarrod had deliberately tuned the radio to something totally sports-free before the rest of the family hopped in the car; he was aware there could be some media coverage of yesterday's escalating situation regarding his comment in the Heed Army interview.

He'd had a couple of texts on his phone that he ignored, and they set off on the journey to Darlington. Jarrod was keen to make sure it wasn't a long one, so he could at least have that as a positive when the inevitable crunch talks came with Marianne.

They took the now familiar route, which was pretty quiet, and were in Darlington well ahead of the meeting time of 11am, Jarrod making an effort to comment on how little time it had taken.

They were greeted as VIPs when they arrived. Gerry was there with Des and Gary and they immediately stopped their poring over a computer when they saw the new arrivals. Gerry bounded over to shake hands with Jarrod and start the introductions. Gerry had his grandkids with him in another office and he took Sebastian and Aneka through to meet them. They were a little younger and were playing Super Mario Karts on a projector on the wall. There were controllers for all, and they slipped seamlessly into the game.

Gerry sat Marianne and Jarrod down at his desk and they were offered coffee and water, which they both took gladly, and once Des was out of the room, Gerry began the sales pitch. It turned out Gerry was a businessman whose last business, specialising in mining equipment, had been purchased by a company from the United States, and that company was looking for a cut-price road to the Premier League.

Gerry had been retained as an advisor, which allowed him to effectively semi-retire, but this project had catapulted him straight back into a heavyweight role. He was a meat and potatoes man, but he was articulate and concise, which Marianne seemed to enjoy, and he talked with a confidence about the project that prompted much questioning from both Jarrod and Marianne.

The project even had a name, Project Delta, probably due to the amount of change that was going to happen in such a short time, and Gerry referred to that title numerous times, forgetting he was pitching to a football man and not a corporate decision-maker.

It turned out the club had made approaches to several high-profile players, some from overseas, offering the chance to finish off their careers in an exciting atmosphere instead of winding down with their millions of pounds in China or the UAE, and the names mentioned were certainly eyebrow-raising to Jarrod.

The club had even gone to the point of offering to purchase the infamous Darlington Arena, the white elephant that had effectively sapped the original club's resources and eventually forced the club to close. Project Delta had to expand quickly to make this a success, and the rugby club that part-owned the stadium, a poisoned chalice if there ever was one, was in a negotiating mood.

The New Feethams stadium recently built on land adjacent to where the old stadium once stood was definitely a stop-gap measure designed to see them through to the National League, but lack of available land to expand meant they would have to relocate sooner rather than later.

"If we can secure a ground share at the Arena, and I have a

meeting about it this afternoon," declared Gerry, "then we will move in straight away. There is not much that needs to be done to get us playing games there. It is more a question of what we do with it once we've bought in."

"The club will move into the stadium and ground share with the rugby club?" asked Jarrod, before pausing. "Doesn't that make for a poor playing surface?"

"You'd have thought so," said Gerry. "I'll take you there for lunch. You'll see. We should be able to walk on the field and see just how good the surface is."

He was already sold on the idea in his heart. It sounded so exciting and different, and his mission now appeared to be to convince Marianne this would be a good move. He was acutely aware he could pull the pin any moment and get cold feet. The scenarios rolled around in his head. It was a choice between the easy option of staying at Gateshead or the ridiculous and thrilling option of joining Darlington. There might even be multiple options if, and when, news gets out that Jarrod Black is leaving Gateshead.

"Tell me about Darlington as a town," asked Jarrod finally, totally changing the subject to something that would appeal to Marianne. "What does it have to offer?"

"Now, you're asking!" said Gerry in a tone suggesting he didn't have a whole lot of positive to say about the town, but he continued in his cheery tone. "Darlington's only 45 minutes from Newcastle. We're bordering North Yorkshire. We've got big towns nearby. We've got everything you could possibly need here, and the people are as honest and true as they come."

"Are you a local?" asked Jarrod, just fishing for a clearer picture.

"I'm from close by, aye," said Gerry, finally breaking into his non-businessman accent. "Sedgefield born and bred."

"Do you still live there now?" continued Jarrod.

"I still have a house there," said Gerry in a matter-of-fact way. "But I live right here in Darlington, over in the West End. Lovely spot. I'll invite you over for tea once you've signed." Gerry had a cheeky smile on his face, and Jarrod stopped probing.

"Gerry," interjected Marianne. "You will be having us round for more than tea if Jarrod signs." They all laughed, Jarrod a little awkwardly, not sure what to make of her statement.

Gerry arranged to meet them at the Arena in fifteen minutes, and Gerry gave Marianne a printed map from a pile on the reception desk of how to get there. Des and Gary were already over at the Arena with a couple of players. Gerry declared he was not very good at leading the way and he would probably lose them due to his 'lead foot.' The map was a good idea.

In reality they wouldn't need it as the lovely lady in the Sat Nav would lead them there anyway. Gerry did, in fact, lead them there, at least part way there until he took an amber light at full speed leaving Jarrod stranded at the lights. Marianne commented that 'he did say he would.'

They arrived in eight minutes, barely long enough for the lady in the Sat Nav to get into her flow. They saw Gerry's car, parked with a number of other cars next to what looked like the main entrance, and Jarrod slowly pulled up next to it.

The kids bounded out and Marianne followed. Jarrod caught himself looking at her and glanced at himself in the rear-view mirror, giving himself a raise of the eyebrow. This day was going well, at least so far. They found Gerry just inside the sliding door, in conversation with a very tall and broad man. Jarrod immediately assumed he was connected to the rugby club in some way. Gerry excused himself and greeted Jarrod and the family, ushering them into the next set of sliding doors and to the foyer, which was totally spotless and gleaming.

Gerry led them out through the next set of doors and down a long corridor, which led out on to the main stand. They were higher up than Jarrod had anticipated, and they had to negotiate some steps to get down to pitch level.

The playing surface was indeed impeccable, absolutely flat, and softer than some of the pitches he played on in the Championship. The stadium looked new, despite it being far from it, and there was no sign of wear and tear, no rust, no peeling paint, no stickers that had peeled off at the edges, someone was going to a lot of trouble to keep this place looking good.

Jarrod again got the impression Marianne was taking this all on board and even she was believing in Project Delta. Gerry led Jarrod and Marianne up to the corporate area, past where reporters would sit, and TV commentators do their thing.

A fine selection of canapés, sandwiches, rolls, were on a side table, along with a fresh pot of filter coffee, filling the air with a rich aroma. The mini-bar fridge was full of water and soft drinks. Jarrod made for the coffee and poured one out for Marianne, before going back for one himself. This was promising. More good impressions.

Gerry explained they were meeting in half an hour with the directors of the rugby club and with the mayor, and that Jarrod and Marianne were welcome to stay, although they might find the subject matter a little tedious.

Jarrod took the opportunity to thank Gerry, but declined the offer, knowing the kids wouldn't be angels for the whole day. In fact, just as he had finished there was squealing from the field - Aneka had taken a tumble and it had knocked the wind out of her, and Sebastian was showing no remorse or concern whatsoever.

Marianne took the opportunity to leave Jarrod with Gerry, grabbing a sandwich, and headed down to knock some heads together. Just as she got close, Gerry's grandkids raced across the field and got there first, Aneka recovering miraculously as a result.

"Jarrod," started Gerry, now that he had him to himself. "Please tell me there's a spark of interest."

"I'll tell you what," continued Jarrod, aware that Gerry was getting to the crunch. "I'll get my agent to contact you this afternoon and let's work out the details. I'm not going to make a decision right at this minute, but you've given us a lot to think about."

"Your wife is lovely," said Gerry. "I bet you weren't expecting her to be so accommodating."

"Yes, my wife is lovely," repeated Jarrod, saying it loud as if to run it past himself one more time and see if it sounded weird. "But she's not the one you've got to convince."

Jarrod could feel the self-doubt. Jarrod knew he needed no convincing. Marianne could present the obstacle, but he wanted Gerry to know he was still sitting firmly on the fence.

"Here," said Gerry, handing Jarrod a business card with the contract manager's details. "Get your agent to contact this lady. I'll let her know she might get a call this afternoon."

Jarrod put his hand out to offer a handshake, which Gerry accepted.

"Thanks for coming at short notice," said Gerry. "I'm sure you are aware of the time constraints. Enjoy your day tomorrow, I'll let you find your own way out."

"Thanks," said Jarrod, before remembering that tomorrow he was in at 7am for the first pre-season day. "Oh, yes, tomorrow. Thanks. I'm sure it'll be entertaining."

With that, Gerry turned to walk through doors back to the corridor. Jarrod jogged down the steps to the tunnel, where he could see Marianne chatting to someone. It was Jason Rhodes.

"Jason," said Jarrod, with an element of surprise.

"Hey Jarrod," said Jason. "I didn't know you two came as a package - bloody good golfer your wife. Taught my wife to play. She's got a lot of patience."

Jarrod smiled.

"Are you signing up to join us?" continued Jason. "It would be amazing to have you here."

"We'll see," said Marianne in her mysterious and somewhat flippant manner.

"Yes, we will see," said Jarrod. "There's a long way to go just yet, but stranger things have happened."

"Time to go?" asked Marianne.

"You picked it," confirmed Jarrod. The kids were just teetering on the edge of the abyss, ready to plunge into an afternoon of ill behaviour. "I reckon we've got five minutes before they go feral."

"Jason," said Jarrod, offering a handshake. "I'll see you soon my friend."

"Good to see you, Jarrod," replied Jason. "Hope to see you here soon."

Jarrod gave a whistle to the kids, who recognised it as a signal they were going, and raced across the field, followed by Gerry's grandkids who were keen to continue playing. Once they had reached Jarrod and Marianne, the kids said their goodbyes and Marianne thanked them for playing with Sebastian and Aneka.

They made their way out, following the way they had come in, stopping to thank the receptionists on the way, and climbed into the car. Jarrod felt pretty pleased with himself and had one question for Marianne before turning the key in the ignition.

"So, what are your thoughts?"

"I like it," replied Marianne honestly, more honestly than Jarrod had imagined. "I think you're crazy, don't get me wrong, but this looks like fun."

The kids were buzzing and asking all sorts of questions about the stadium, the town, and whether they could play with the other kids again, and when they were coming back. By the time they were back on a main road, the conversation had stopped. Aneka was slumped against the window and Sebastian was dozing with his head bowed down, which Marianne reached over to prop back up as it didn't look too comfortable.

Jarrod took the opportunity to make a call, picking up his phone with the Bluetooth in the car, something that he rarely did. He felt a level of comfort though with Marianne. She appeared to be on the same page and in a good mood. He decided this was the time to give Dad a call. A quick glance at the time said that it would be evening in Sydney, not too dramatically late.

"Dad," said Jarrod, when the phone was picked up with the customary 'hello.' "It's Jarrod." Before Dad had time to talk, he added, "You're on speaker with Marianne and the kids. Well, the kids are asleep in the car."

"Hi there," said Marianne, always cheery but unsure whether or not to call her father-in-law Dad or Mr Black.

"Hello, Jarrod. Hello, my darling, Marianne," said Dad calmly. "Going somewhere nice?"

"Just heading back home," said Jarrod, shifting in his seat like he had something to share but wasn't allowed to say it. "We've been in Darlington for the morning."

"Oh, yeah?" said Dad. "Have you signed for them?"

"No, no," said Jarrod, trying to make out that his Dad was getting ahead of himself, purely for Marianne's benefit. "We're not at that stage yet. We've had a look around, met the owner, we had a quick tour of the stadium. Didn't see much of the town mind you, but it looks okay."

"Right," said Dad, in his very practiced matter-of-fact manner. "So, what happens next?"

"Ah, I need to get Manny, er Mr Leonard, to give them a call to talk through options. Can you ask him to make a call tonight? I'll text through the number. It's the contract manager and they're looking to finalise an offer."

"Jarrod," said Dad. "You know you should be contacting Mr Leonard yourself."

"I know, I know" said Jarrod, having been told this many times previously. "But you do it so well..."

"I'll give him a call after this one," said Dad. "Send that number through now."

Marianne picked up the phone out of the middle console of the car and, with the business card in one hand, began transcribing the number into a message, not an easy thing to do in the car. The very fact that Marianne had taken it upon herself to do that demonstrated she was keen, so keen that Jarrod made a note of it to question why she was indeed so keen.

"So, how is everyone?" asked Jarrod as a time-filler as the message travelled around the world.

"Mum's been a bit crook the last couple days," said Dad. "She's in bed already, bit of the flu, I think. Anna is good. She had a cracking game tonight. She's out with her team in Sydney."

"Did they get a win?" asked Jarrod, suddenly embarrassed he had forgotten all about his little sister's success.

"They drew," said Dad. "Anna scored the third equalizer in the last minute, then her goalkeeper saved a penalty in injury time. So exciting!"

It was great to hear Dad excited about his sister and it gave him a twinge of homesickness.

"Ah," continued Dad. "There's the message through now. I'll give Mr Leonard a call and get back to you. I'll send you the bill for the telephone calls."

"Speak soon," said Jarrod, and Dad hung up abruptly.

Jarrod put on a surprised face and looked at Marianne who was smiling. The kids were fast asleep, and the road was pretty clear ahead. Marianne put her head back and exhaled heavily, she was obviously still struggling after last night. They were by now half way back to Gateshead, at least, and Dad was soon back on the phone.

"Dad," said Jarrod. "All good?"

Dad didn't answer straight away but sounded to be fumbling a little, and all of a sudden came back.

"Jarrod," he said, shouting. "I've got Mr Leonard on a conference call. Manny can you hear us?"

Jarrod was bewildered. His Dad was holding a conference call on a mobile phone. Jarrod couldn't remember the last time he'd done that himself and would have been pretty sure his Dad would have had no idea how to do it. Wonders never cease.

"Wow, Jarrod, sounds like you're just in the next room," said Mr Leonard. "I understand you're driving, so keep your eyes on the road."

"Hello Mr Leonard," said Jarrod. "Has Dad filled you in about what's happening?"

"Yes, he has," said Mr Leonard, the delay making it necessary to speak in sentences and not interject like a normal conversation. "I've got your Gateshead contract sitting in front of me, as well as the proposal they put together the other day. I've been out of the loop for a couple years now, so I'm probably not the best man to do this, but I'm happy to negotiate on your behalf."

"I'd love that," said Jarrod, although he knew straight away his contract was just about to be discussed in front of his wife and he was ready to feel a little violated. "What do you think needs negotiating?"

"Let's start with basic wage," started Mr Leonard. "That's a drop of 40%. That's a lot of money, but it's still a very good deal, considering the length of the contract."

"Okay. So, should we go for more?" offered Jarrod, unsure as to where Mr Leonard was heading.

"Well," continued Mr Leonard. "Promotion bonus is generous, but still under the figure in your Gateshead contract. Win bonus is again well under, but you'd effectively be playing more games, appearance rate is about half, there's no goal bonus, but that's not what brings in much for you."

"Hey," said Jarrod. "No need for that."

"I'd say we go for a small increase in basic wage," said Mr Leonard, pausing to swallow. "Then get you another small increase in appearance money. We'll insert a buy-out trigger amount, just in case some club wants you and offers loads of money, and we'll make it high to demonstrate good faith. You'll need a clause allowing you to attend all international commitments, just in case you want to go back. That's probably all."

"Great," said Jarrod, conscious and grateful Mr Leonard had been careful not to talk in monetary terms.

"Now," said Mr Leonard. "How are they going to afford to buy you from Gateshead?"

"I was thinking the same thing," said Dad. "Darlington must have a lot of ready cash."

Jarrod hadn't contemplated that - he still had two more seasons on his current contract, and that was enough to keep his transfer value high. Marianne looked at him and raised an eyebrow.

"Not sure what's going to happen there, to be honest," replied Jarrod. "Guess I should have asked that question."

"That's not really your problem, is it?" replied Dad. "As long as the contract is right, the two clubs can do whatever deal is necessary."

"Jarrod," said Mr Leonard. "Maybe your age and the length of time left on your contract gives Darlington some room for manoeuvre. I would have to do a bit of research. See if you can find out how they're proposing to buy you."

"Will do," said Jarrod, as if it was a simple request. "When are you going to make the call? Can you call me when you're done?"

"Give me half an hour to run through the figures and I'll give this lady a call," said Mr Leonard. "You do realise the time here? I might be a little sleepy."

"Really appreciate it Mr Leonard," said Jarrod, feeling like a schoolboy once again. "And thanks Dad. Speak soon."

"Now, if I can just work out how to hang everyone up, here..." said Dad, before the phone call was cut. Marianne had a chuckle - she could just picture Jarrod's dad holding his mobile phone at arms' length with his reading glasses perched on his nose, swearing under his breath.

# Chapter Twenty-Two: Digs

It had been over five months since Jarrod had signed for Gateshead, and after succumbing to the hamstring injury on his loan spell with Carlisle, he was back to full training and appearing regularly for the youth and reserve teams. It was exhilarating and exciting, and the onset of cold, wintry conditions hadn't dampened his desire at all.

The club had continued to house Jarrod and Reggie with Doris. Reggie led the search for more permanent digs, and was also leading the way with the excuses for not finding any. They were very settled at the guest house and were putting in a lot of extra training in order to maintain the level of fitness that was now expected.

"I reckon I've got this one..." said Reggie, bursting into the changing room after taking a call on his mobile. "You've got to come and see it with me."

"Excuse me for not showing too much delight," said Jarrod. "But I reckon we've been in this situation at least a dozen times."

"No, no," said Reggie. "This is mint. It's a rock star pad, and it's just a tiny bit over the budget. Come on, we can have a look in twenty minutes. Let's get our skates on!"

With a roll of his eyes, Jarrod hurriedly got ready, while Reggie didn't bother getting showered and simply took out his shin pads and changed his boots for his trainers.

"Come on..." pleaded Reggie, dancing on the spot nervously.

With Reggie leading the way, they burst through the office, Senthil barking something at Reggie, which he simply waved away, and they broke into a jog to get to the trusty old car parked askew in a visitors car spot.

Reggie slammed the car into reverse, just missing the other cars and Jarrod jumped in, the car speeding off even before he had started to close the door. Reggie was quite a character and loved making the everyday mundane stuff as exciting as he could. Reggie found the place without using his phone, to which Jarrod stated, "You've been here before, haven't you?"

"I scoped it out last night when I spoke to the real estate agent," he said, talking like a private detective might. "You know, a reccy to suss out the area."

"It looks pretty new," said Jarrod.

"Yep, it's only a year old," continued Reggie. "Just enough time to iron out any problems while still being really fresh and modern."

"Who are you?" asked Jarrod. "Has the agent brainwashed you?"

"Nah, nah," said Reggie. "Come and see. You'll love it."

They parked and walked over to the entrance of the building, which had an intercom. Reggie pressed the button and a voice told them to come on up, top floor, and a buzzer sounded to signal that the door was open. Jarrod leaned on the door and it opened. They walked past the lift and raced up the three floors to the top, where there was a landing and only one door with 301 printed on it in a large industrial font.

The door was slightly open, so Jarrod knocked and pushed open the door slowly and walked in, Reggie following very closely behind. The estate agent, a well-groomed man in his thirties in suit and tie was there. He abandoned his brochures and files and the table, gliding over to greet them. Reggie took over the talking role, as he had already discussed the apartment with the agent, and they had a look around the property. Reggie pointed out things as he went, eagerly showing Jarrod the second bathroom, commenting on the size of the kitchen, raving about the third bedroom, and basically doing all the sales work for the agent.

They came to the end of the mini-tour and the agent and Reggie stood between Jarrod and the door as if to subconsciously block his exit, Reggie standing there with his arms open and head to one side, waiting for his reaction.

Jarrod had never lived out of home until he had come to England. His time with Doris, and in the guest house in Carlisle had given him a small insight into living away from home. He revelled in the independence. The fact of sharing with someone so they could get a much bigger and better place was appealing, but the actual sharing part he felt would be a challenge.

The apartment was, it had to be said, an absolute marvel - a penthouse overlooking the River Tyne, walking distance to night life, two car spots in an underground secure car park. It was massive. Possibly even bigger than the house he had grown up in back in Sydney. There was, of course, the small matter of price. They had both been given their budget, and combining it, the weekly rent would surely be achievable.

"How much?" asked Jarrod as they walked down the stairs afterwards.

Reggie finally gave him the figure. "That's way over the limit!"

Jarrod was immediately plunged into disappointment, but Reggie was his cheery self and retorted, "I've got this sorted, my son."

Jarrod smiled, knowing that Reggie would indeed have something up his sleeve, and he pictured him almost crying, in front of the managing director, pleading, making out that it was the only place they could find.

There was no rush anyway. The club had almost resigned themselves to housing the pair with Doris indefinitely, and they had become somewhat of a meet and greet team at the guest house when new players arrived at the club, or when loanees and triallists rocked up for short stints.

"If you can pull this off Reggie, you're a legend."

They raced over to the car, and hurried off, even though they had nowhere in particular to be and no need to hurry. Life was good.

Two days later, Jarrod and Reggie were called in to see Mr Pederson before training and they made their way there half an hour early. They were sitting in his office waiting when Mr Bruker walked past, and they caught his eye.

"Okay boys?" asked Mr Bruker, quizzically.

"Hello Mr Bruker," said Jarrod, before Reggie had the chance to say anything.

"Waiting for something?" asked Mr Bruker.

"Mr Pederson asked to see us," said Reggie. "Don't know what it's about."

Mr Bruker shook his head.

"Doesn't sound too promising," he said, with a smile and a wink. "Mr Pederson is running about five minutes late. Jarrod, can I borrow you for that five minutes? Come with me."

Jarrod glanced at Reggie, who gave a little shrug with no explanation. Jarrod slowly got to his feet, then bounded after Mr Bruker, who had already walked off in the direction of his corner office. Mr Bruker put his bag down on the desk, beckoned Jarrod in, then walked over to the door and closed it. Jarrod didn't know what to do or say or what to expect.

"Jarrod," said Mr Bruker. "We have a situation at the moment, in our first team games. We are losing too much ball in midfield. We win the ball in defence, then the midfield play just lets us down. Too many passes going astray. Too many aimless balls. Have you seen?"

"We're losing games," said Jarrod. "But I couldn't quite put my finger on why."

"So, you think we're playing well?" asked Mr Bruker.

Jarrod paused, unsure as to where this was leading. Then he got the courage to continue.

"The endeavour is there," said Jarrod, immediately becoming conscious of using the word 'endeavour.' "But the belief is not."

Jarrod winced as he thought about what he had just said and how clichéd and pompous it sounded. Mr Bruker paused and contemplated.

"Wise words from such a young man," admitted Mr Bruker, before changing direction and clarifying the reason for the chat. "Will Daykin tells me you're a star in the making."

Jarrod wasn't sure what this meant, and how would first team coach Dayks know? Perhaps he had been talking to Senthil.

"So, I want you to be part of the first team squad this weekend."

Those words sat there for a moment before being grasped.

"Wow," said Jarrod. "Wow...I wasn't expecting that."

He broke into a smile. The thought of telling Dad was in the front of his mind, mixed with the thought of telling Reggie, who was sitting on his own waiting for Mr Pederson. He knew Reggie would want to experience the first team squad at the same time.

"You'll be joining the first team in training today," said Mr Bruker. "Just get ready as usual and do your warm-ups with your squad, and we'll come and get you when we're ready."

Mr Bruker beckoned him to the door.

"Fantastic," said Jarrod, jumping to his feet. "Thanks for the chance."

"See you soon," concluded Mr Bruker.

Jarrod raced down the wide corridor, checking back when he realised he had run past Mr Pederson's door, and could hear Mr Pederson had arrived and was around the corner talking to the receptionist. Jarrod took his seat where he had been sitting when they saw Mr Bruker earlier.

"What was that?" asked Reggie.

Before Reggie could finish his sentence, Mr Pederson entered the room and commanded their attention, walking over to the desk and placing his brown leather case on the floor next to it.

"Thanks for coming boys," said Mr Pederson, with almost a resigned tone of voice, that tone when you are bowing to the inevitable and feel as though there's no choice.

"What can we do for you?" came the slightly quirky question from Reggie.

"Your accommodation situation," stated Mr Pederson. "Tell me the latest."

Reggie shifted uneasily in his seat, while Jarrod remained deep in thought about his call up to the first team squad and the chance that had suddenly fallen into his lap.

"Yes," said Reggie. "We are still at the Guest House."

"With Doris," said Mr Pederson, letting Reggie know he knew that and knew the situation.

"Yes," said Reggie. "And I...we've been looking for flats and houses for quite a few weeks now with no success."

"You're maybe not looking in the right places," said Mr Pederson. "There's a lot of stock in Newcastle, and out Shields way. You should be able to pick up something relatively easily and cheaply."

Reggie paused, knowing he was being led into a tricky situation.

"Yes," said Reggie. "You'd think that. Truth is, I...we've looked at a number of options over the last two months and we are still at the guest house. Not through choice, I might add. And not that Doris isn't great or anything."

Jarrod clicked back into the conversation after allowing his mind to wander for what seemed like an hour.

"Mr Pederson," said Jarrod. "We looked at a place to share the other day and it was fantastic. It was a bit more than we were given as a budget, but it was ready to move in to and it was just what we're looking for."

"Yes," said Mr Pederson, having patiently waited for the boys to talk themselves into the real reason they were there. "That is quite a sum of money to fork out as a deposit. Tell me. Why should we house you in such a 'fancy' place like that?"

"The deposit is the problem," admitted Reggie. "Any difference between the budget and the rent we can cover ourselves."

Jarrod turned to look at Reggie, eyebrows raised.

"We can't stay with Doris forever, surely?"

This might have been the clinching factor. Mr Pederson changed direction.

"So, boys," he said, looking at both of them in turn. "We will put up your deposit and be your guarantor. We will pay the rent, as agreed in your contracts, for the first six weeks."

He stared at them, making them feel nervous.

"Please remember we have a code of conduct. This covers footballing and non-footballing matters. To make it easy for you, let's just say if there is any nonsense that comes across my desk with regards to you two and your fancy new pad, you will be in breach of the code of conduct, and you will be punished accordingly. Understand?" stated Mr Pederson.

Jarrod could feel himself blushing. Reggie was smiling.

"Yes!" shouted Reggie, before giving a fist-pump. "We won't let you down!"

"No," said Mr Pederson. "No, you won't. Our contracts manager Jean-Claude will take care of the details. Make an appointment at reception to see him and bring a copy of the rental contract with you."

"Right," said Reggie, in slight shock. "We'll do that."

Mr Pederson got up from his seat and opened the door and with some grovelling thank-yous and nods of the head, the boys filed out and back into the corridor, before walking through to the reception area strutting like John Travolta, beaming from ear to ear.

What a result. Jarrod could see Reggie was sweating, as well as nervously laughing when he made the appointment with Jean-Claude for later that afternoon.

They were now in a mad rush to get the rest of their gear on for training. Reggie sprinted off through the door as soon as he had his boots laced up to join the group on the field.

Jarrod was always a bit slower getting ready, as he always had to don a brace on his left ankle, the product of turning his ankle over too many times as a youngster. The brace had a really long lace that seemed to get out of alignment every time he took it off and needed correcting every time he put it back on. On occasion he would forget to put it on or realise after he had put his socks and boots on, and he felt uneven without it, but the freedom of motion of his foot was welcome. Jarrod was finally ready and trotted through the door and off towards the group, knowing he was already late.

The group turned to Jarrod as Senthil looked up at the new arrival.

"Good afternoon," came the good-humoured sarcasm from the Gateshead coach. "Jarrod, Dayks has been over, and would like you to join him over on the other field." Senthil showed the way with the palm of his hand.

Jarrod saw Reggie with hands on his hips and an eyebrow raised and gave him a cheeky wink as he jogged off in the direction of the first team training.

"Jarrod," said Dayks as he arrived at a slow jog. "Welcome to the fold."

Dayks had his arms folded.

"Lads," he said, addressing the group, who were on their knees at various stages of a warm-up routine. "I trust everyone knows Jarrod Black."

Some nods of the head came and a few calls of, "Alright?" along with an acknowledging wave or two. Jarrod knew every one of these players - they had been to a few team bonding sessions, a few runs on the beach up at Tynemouth, and they all had lunch together after training on Fridays.

Micah Oli trotted over. He had just arrived on loan from Ipswich Town and Jarrod had never been formally introduced. They shook hands with a smile, which Dayks saw and seemed to be impressed with. Dayks told Jarrod to join in the stretching session, and they began the warm-up routine: a set of drills that was now second nature. Jarrod joined the end of one of the lines and did the exercises with precision and was consciously a little bit more flambuoyant than usual.

The training session went longer than the reserves or youth team training sessions; after the usual fitness, drills and game routine, they started to set up some set piece training and went through, probably for Jarrod and Micah's benefit, a series of defensive and attacking corners, analysing the positioning at each one.

Jarrod was loving this. It was right up his alley. Getting right to the bottom of the reasons why a player should stand in a certain position and when to move away from it. Some of the information was like a revelation to him. Thoughts that he thought he owned were, in fact, in the training manual.

This was a level of professionalism he had never seen before, and whilst there were some jokes and a bit of laughter, the general mood was one of determination to get the job done properly. Jarrod could feel his muscles getting sore from the running, his thighs felt like rock, but his eagerness kept him going. The session ended with a free kick session, and to Jarrod's surprise they didn't use dummy walls, they did it properly.

Dayks called the end of the session and pulled in his players to collect the equipment and bring it to a central spot. Jarrod liked that - they might be first team players but needed to be grounded - and Mario Franz, the tall central defender, set off on a lap of the field at a decent pace. The rest of the team clicked into gear and following him for what was a warm-down jog.

Dayks had a few words to say at the end, but nothing of much substance, just that they would be working on attacking play in the morning and for everyone to rest tonight and see the physio team if there were any issues from today.

Jarrod walked off, steam coming from the top of his head and making a swirling pattern in the light. He made his way back through the back door and into the changing rooms. When he got there, the warmth of the showers and the bright lights changed the feeling, and tiredness started to take over. A huge yawn came across his face and he sat looking rather ragged.

Senthil came through the changing rooms, showing a young player around, maybe a new youth player or a triallist. When he saw Jarrod, he introduced him.

"Jarrod Black," said Senthil. "This is Brett Jamieson, joining us for a month from Clydebank in Scotland."

The boys shook hands. Jarrod snapped out of his semi-comatose state and smiled at the new arrival. Memories of his first day at Gateshead coming back. It had been an eventful few months that's for sure, and that day felt like a few years ago.

"Jarrod joined us as a youth player back in the summer," continued Senthil. "He's in line for a first team debut this weekend."

Senthil smiled. Brett looked on with admiration. The words didn't sink in for Jarrod.

"Welcome to Gateshead, Brett," said Jarrod. "Senthil's a hard task master. Stay on his good side..."

Senthil was already moving on but checked back with a raise of an eyebrow. Brett followed obediently.

Jarrod's demeanour suddenly changed from a tired and slightly spaced-out youngster into a determined young footballer, and his focus was immediately back. He showered, even remembering to take his shower gel with him, then got himself in comfortable post-training clothes: a thin, loose fitting grey tracksuit bottom, and v-neck sweater. The outfit looked the part despite being an unlikely combination.

Back at the guest house, after being kindly offered a lift by one of the other late departing players, Jarrod breezed in to Reggie's room. Their doors were always open, partly because they didn't really have anything worth stealing, but mainly because they enjoyed it that way.

Reggie was reading a book, something Jarrod wished he had the stamina for, but which often ended in a two minute read before waking up an hour later when the book finally thumped on the floor. He gave the air of someone being a little stand-offish but that was clearly a ruse as he went in for the big hug, congratulating his mate for making it to the big time.

"You kept that quiet," said Reggie, once he had uncoupled himself from the headlock he had ended in. "Straight to the first team!"

"Hey," said Jarrod. "I didn't have a clue until this morning in the office. I didn't even know what he was talking about to begin with."

"It's about time they got some proper new talent in the team," said Reggie. "It's not looking good at the moment."

"That's what the boss said," admitted Jarrod. "But enough about me. What about the apartment? We're meeting the agent there in half an hour. Did you get the paperwork from Jean-Claude?"

"He was out," said Reggie. "But he sent through something to the agent and they called me this afternoon."

"So we're good?" asked Jarrod hopefully.

"We're good!" said Reggie, diving back in for a second rumble. This time he sent Jarrod to the floor, but still ending up on the bottom in a tight embrace. Jarrod seemed unbeatable in a tussle today.

"Hey," said Jarrod. "Don't injure the star player!"

Reggie gave him a swift punch to the mid-riff, catching Jarrod off guard and taking the wind right out of him.

"Let's go then..." said Reggie.

The night was getting dark. Traffic was pretty dense for a few hundred metres, then filtered out and they made it to the apartment building well in advance of the meeting time.

The agent was there, or at least his car was there and they went up with a mixture of excitement and expectation. The feeling of relief and exhilaration was obvious for Jarrod, and he could see that Reggie was loving the scene - all the paperwork having been finalised by the club beforehand, and it was only a token gesture to sign the contract, which they both did with genuine haste, eager to wrap up the deal before it was whipped away from them.

The agent handed over the keys and walked them through

the basics, the locks, the electricity box, the stop valve for the water, and the water heater instructions.

Reggie was especially concerned with the parking situation, and the agent took them down the lift to the basement where the car park was full of high end luxury cars and personalised number plates.

The final item to cover was the door code, and this made it feel real. They had secured their first ever rental and scored an absolutely amazing place. After wishing the agent a good evening, they tried out the door code, which took them into the foyer. They tried the lift which cranked into action, making the short journey from the basement.

They decided to go up one last time to check it out and decide who would go in which bedroom. Jarrod eventually made the call by getting the one nearest to the living area with the two-door bathroom, with the logic he would always be closest to the action.

They went through the kitchen, checking out the appliances and the massive pantry. This was living! About half an hour later, after making a quick list on Reggie's phone of the basics they would need to move in, they left, making sure the lights were off and the windows were closed, and made their way to the car.

"Party this weekend?" asked Reggie as he put the key in the ignition.

"Shouldn't we get some furniture first?" answered Jarrod with a question, "Not much of a party without."

"Good point," admitted Reggie. "Let's get that sorted first and then we can have a house warming on the weekend."

"Done," said Jarrod and they clasped hands in their rapper style and went in for the hug.

# Chapter Twenty-Three: Clean

The next day at training, Jarrod was again in the first team set up, and as a result was there for three hours longer than usual.

Reggie used his time to get to Ikea and Homebase to check out some basics, like a microwave, a bed, and kitchen table.

Jarrod caught up with him at the Metrocentre, where it had late night opening, and found him looking at sofas.

"Ha ha," said Jarrod. "Never thought I'd see this day."

"I know," said Reggie. "I didn't realise how much money we'd have to outlay. There'll not be much left after rent when we start paying it. We should get it all now while the club covers that."

That's exactly what they did; a massive shop on Reggie's credit card, buying two beds, both available for delivery in the next 48 hours. They picked out sheets, towels, a kitchen table, and a microwave, as well as ordering crockery, cutlery, pans and utensils.

They moved on to the cheap shop around the corner from the Metrocentre where they bought even more basic items like toilet paper, cleaning products, and salt and pepper shakers. This was intense. They had bought almost everything except a sofa and a coffee table by the time the shops shut.

"We have to get Sky connected," said Jarrod. "I'll organise that. What about the water, the electric, the gas, and all that stuff?"

"Do we have to pay for all that?" asked a shocked Reggie.

"I'd expect so," said Jarrod. "It's not free."

It was clear that Reggie had no idea about real life in general, but Jarrod loved the fact, and felt it was an opportunity to make life just that little bit more exciting for the two of them.

If Jarrod was doing this solo, he would have ended up with a dingy one bedroom flat in a dodgy part of town, for a fraction of the rent, and would be saving money from the word go.

This way though, he could live like a king but save no money. If they played their cards right, they could have the best time of their lives. Jarrod was in line for a first team debut. So, who knew what the future would hold.

It was Friday morning not long after breakfast, and the boys walked in to the kitchen at the guest house and Reggie greeted Doris with a great big hug, as she was folding some tea towels.

"Eeeh, what are yee deein?" she screeched in her best Geordie.

"Doris," started Reggie. "The time has come."

"Time for what, man?" came the reply from a slightly flustered Doris.

"We've found a place, Doris," said Jarrod. "How much notice do we need to give you?"

"You got that apartment?" exclaimed Doris. "How the devil did you get that?"

"Contacts," said Reggie. "And lots of smiling."

Doris picked up the next tea towel to fold and flicked it at Reggie, catching him on the arm.

"Right," said Doris with a determined look on her face. "Upstairs with me."

Jarrod and Reggie looked at each other with a puzzled look.

"What..." said Jarrod as Doris breezed past them both.

"Upstairs," repeated Doris, and they didn't need any further invitation - crossing this lady was not an option. Doris made her way calmly up the stairs, holding the bannister as she went, with the boys slowly loping up behind her. She reached Reggie's room, door open as usual.

"Right," she said, hands firmly on hips. "See this bed? See that it's made."

Reggie nodded compliantly, his words failing him.

"Clean up your floor. Put things away in your cupboard. Take the cups downstairs. Oh. That's where my good glass went."

Reggie rushed into action, realising he was now being the subject of a test. Jarrod looked at Doris, Doris smiled and flicked her head as a sign to follow her out the door. They walked to Jarrod's room and Doris pushed fully open the thin brown wood-panelled door, a t-shirt getting caught underneath it as she pushed, causing her to push harder, the t-shirt riding up right underneath the door in a right state.

She glanced at Jarrod, whose eyes were wide. After a moment of wonder, Jarrod also kicked into gear and didn't need any instruction. He started off by picking up his clothes from the floor piled in the corner and placing them on his bed to sort out. The bed was made, albeit in a haphazard fashion. Jarrod was conscious of Doris standing at the door with her arms folded.

"You boys need to get a grip!" she yelled, her voice raised to make sure Reggie also heard. "How the devil are yees two ganna live in your own flat?"

With that, she walked off, probably to have a look at Reggie's room, and there was a clink as she picked up some of the mugs and cups Reggie had placed outside the door. She was clearly going downstairs now, so Jarrod nipped to the door and crept to Reggie's room.

"What was that about?" asked Jarrod in a low whisper. "What brought that on?"

"I think she's happy for us getting our flat," said Reggie. "She's probably just concerned that we're going to live in a mess. Gotta love Doris. She's only thinking about our welfare."

Once the boys had endured half an hour of tidying and almost military room inspections, it was time to get moving to get to the stadium for training. Jarrod rolled his eyes with a chuckle as he had to dig out his tracksuit from underneath all his neatly folded clothes in the drawer.

Jarrod suddenly remembered he was due on the first team bus that afternoon for the Saturday away game at Watford. He searched for his club jacket and got a few things together in his small day bag, grabbing toothbrush, toothpaste, and shower gel.

They got to training just in time. Reggie chose to get changed with Jarrod and the rest of the first team squad, simply because he could, and he also wanted to give the impression he was part of the first team. The mood was very good, and all the players were having a bit of banter, everyone laughing as defender Ferenc Kalic walked in with a large four-wheeled suitcase.

"What? I meet my family at the game tomorrow," he said by way of defence. "I take them Newcastle United stuff, they bring me food from home."

Training was light, which Jarrod wasn't used to. The intense warm-up was the same though, but this was a tactical session. Jarrod was the centre-piece of the majority of the discussions.

It was clear that most of this was being done to accommodate him in the first team and bring him up to speed. After the final warm down, which involved twenty minutes of stretching with an incredibly fit-looking gym instructor from the local gym, a few of the boys stayed behind to do some set piece practice.

Harry Lowndes, the first team goalkeeper, offered a challenge to everyone that they would fail to score half of their penalties; everyone taking one each, twenty quid riding on the result.

Jarrod watched as six of his new teammates took a penalty one at a time against him, two of them hitting the post, one being expertly saved, and the other three being placed beautifully in the net.

Jarrod knew his penalty would be the deciding penalty in the bet. As with all scenarios that involved blokes betting against each other, the stakes were high, and the nerves were jangling - this was more intense than the World Cup final.

Jarrod placed the ball on the spot, Harry cajoling him with some mind-games, saying that the ball wasn't on the spot. Jarrod simply smiled and got ready to take his run up and raced in at speed before dinking the ball. Harry had already made his mind up to dive, leaving the middle of the net unguarded. The ball sailed on to the underside of the bar and dropped down. The flailing leg of the prone goalkeeper kicked out at it and simply turned the ball into the net.

"It's got to be clean..." said Harry, immediately to his feet.

"Ha ha," said Jarrod. "No chance. Gooooaaaaal." He embarked on the slowest celebration, arms out wide and head bowed like the Brazilians of old. The luckiest of goals. Jarrod walked up to Harry and gave him a mock cuddle, to signal no bad feelings, and then with a finger tapping his own chest he signalled the winner.

It was a fun moment, and there was genuine camaraderie and a good feeling. The stragglers all got showered and changed into their club attire. Jarrod had been presented with a business shirt that formed part of the first team look, and all the players then congregated in the cafeteria.

The receptionist walked calmly into the cafeteria with a clipboard and announced the coach had arrived. Anyone requiring luggage to be loaded was to make their way out first, Ferenc first on the scene before she had finished her sentence.

They filed onto the coach. The front window had the club crest and in the front side window by the front door, a sign marked, 'Gateshead FC, Watford (Away).'

# Chapter Twenty-Four: Journey

Travelling by coach to a game was not new for Jarrod. He had been on some decent trips already. This one was a bit special though, as he was on the coach with the rest of the first team.

He got out his mobile phone and started recording, commentating a little bit as he panned around for an imaginary audience, familiar faces coming into view, some of them giving a little smile or a wave of acknowledgement.

The journey South was quite a hike, but once they hit the motorway, there was no traffic to hold them up and the players settled in for the journey. Jarrod had a couple of travel pillows to lean on and a few players were getting some sleep.

The novelty of the lengthy journey was definitely beginning to wear off as the coach pulled in to the hotel just outside Hertford, and the quiet that had descended over the squad about two hours beforehand was broken as the players started to rouse from their seats.

Jarrod was starving, but there was still a wait. After the pretty admin lady Jenny had gone ahead to check in the team at reception, the driver began the process of unloading the bags. The hotel porter then took the bags to reception where the players would walk by after getting off.

They filed in and picked up their belongings and were given a room key and told to be down in no later than thirty minutes for a late evening meal. Jarrod was sharing a room with Neil Cottee, a player he had never previously had anything to do with.

Jarrod wasn't going to wait for his roommate and after quickly washing his face and running his fingers through his hair, he bounded out the door and down to the dining room. The room was already buzzing, players free from the confines of the coach and ready to let loose. Jarrod, if he was honest, was ready to go out and explore, but Mr Bruker was there, and he seemed to want everyone to stay within earshot. When the majority of the players had arrived, Neil having been the last, the manager clapped his hands and the players fell silent.

"Lads," he stated, setting the relaxed tone of the speech. "Welcome to Hertford. We don't normally stay over like this but with the early kick off tomorrow, the 'powers that be' decided we should do what we need to do to be fresh for the game. While I'm not your Dad, I'm urging you to enjoy a hearty dinner, and a glass of wine perhaps. I would like you to get to your rooms by 11 and be back down here for breakfast at 7:30. Jenny?" He glanced over to the admin lady, who continued for him.

"Thank you," she said, "Kick off is at 1pm. We will be leaving here at 10:30am sharp on the coach. Make sure you have all your belongings and leave your room key with reception."

Jarrod had never known this level of care. He could now enjoy his dinner and get some rest safe in the knowledge that everything was taken care of. Just as he sat down at the long table, squeezed in between Jenny and Richie Bernard, he felt his phone buzz in his pocket and stood back up and backed away from the table. It was a message from Reggie: 'Call me. NOW!'

This was followed in the list of messages by three missed calls that he had not noticed. Jarrod was just about to flick the mobile phone off and re-take his seat when the phone rang. It was Reggie. Jarrod couldn't resist.

"Gotcha!" said Reggie. "How's Watford?"

"You rang me up four times to ask me how Watford is?" said Jarrod. "What's up really?"

"Party is ON tomorrow!" Reggie exclaimed. "I've got a DJ coming. Don't worry, he'll keep it down, but he's got lights. Russ in the reserves used to work in a cocktail bar and he's bringing his gear. I picked up a table from the Oxfam shop and I'm borrowing some chairs tonight."

Reggie was stuck in gear and continued at full pace.

"Here's the plan," said Reggie, pausing for dramatic effect. "My cousin Marianne is coming up tomorrow, driving from London. She can stop in at Watford on the way and pick you up. You'll get back earlier, you'll be back by eight, and we can party on!"

Jarrod's first thought was, 'Oh, no.' But conscious of how little he wanted this distraction right now, he knew he would be up for it the next day. And spending the evening in a car with his fit cousin, well, that could be a game changer.

"Hey," shouted Jarrod, his mind starting to click. "I'll ask Jenny. She'll know what to do. I'll text you."

Jarrod walked the few steps back to the table and was relieved his seat hadn't been taken by anyone else, and wedged himself back in. Jarrod tapped Jenny on the arm.

"Sorry, Jenny," he started, apologetic for interrupting. "Can I ask you something?"

Jenny sat upright and turned in her seat to face him.

"Anything, Jarrod," she said. "That's what I'm here for."

"I've got a friend coming to the game tomorrow..."

Before he could continue, Jenny finished his sentence, "...and you'd like a couple tickets to give them? Sure! We'll have a few spare tickets."

"No, no," said Jarrod, then after having the thought of giving free tickets to a hot girl. "Well, yes, that would be great. But, what I really need to know is if I can go back in the car with them after the game as we're going out tomorrow night."

Jenny was a little puzzled. Jarrod was careful not to mention the gender of the friend.

"Mr Bruker does like everyone to travel together," she said in a voice that suggested doubt. "But I think Fez is off to London afterwards, so it shouldn't be an issue. I'll find out for you."

Jarrod was looking at her with pleading eyes, and Jenny leaned back in her chair to tap Mr Bruker on the shoulder who was sitting two up from her. She was in conversation for about a minute, and Mr Bruker afforded himself a glance over at Jarrod which suggested she was indeed discussing him. Jarrod's brain was, by now, frothing with anticipation. Jenny finished her conversation and pulled her chair back in, taking her time to turn to Jarrod.

"There is one condition, Jarrod," said Jenny.

"Go on," said Jarrod, lowering his head but raising an eyebrow.

"Mr Bruker says you have to score a goal tomorrow." And she broke into a smile.

"Great," exclaimed Jarrod, the jovial response going over his head. "And those tickets?"

"I've actually got them in my bag now," said Jenny. "I'll give you two. Is that enough?"

"Thanks," said Jarrod, not knowing how many tickets he would need. "Two will be fine."

He felt very pleased with himself and somewhat excited, more about seeing Marianne again than making his debut for

Gateshead. The rest of the evening was a really happy affair.

Players started to head away upstairs to call it a day, and Jarrod made sure that he wasn't one of the first but wasn't far behind. He stood up and waved both hands above his head to signal 'goodnight' to the remainder of his teammates, parting with, 'I've got a goal in me, lads.'

Just as Jarrod contemplated what to do first, whether to have a quick wash, jump in the shower, or dive into bed, a jangle of keys signalled Neil's arrival. Clearly he was a little tired and irritable by the way he forced the door when it didn't open after the first wave of the magic key card. He didn't say much, just a quick 'how's it going?' and headed for the bathroom, where he closed the door and started his night time routine.

Jarrod decided to follow up his phone call from earlier, as it was getting late, and decided a text would have to do: 'Got two tickets for the game for ur cuz.'

He had sent it and put his mobile phone on the bedside table when it rang. It was Reggie.

"Ha, that's great," said Reggie, "Marianne's coming up with a mate. I'll let her know."

"Should I leave the tickets at reception?" asked Jarrod. "Is that how it works?"

"Makes sense," affirmed Reggie. "I'll tell her to pick em up there, should be after midday. You nervous?"

"Haven't had time to think about it to be honest," replied Jarrod. "I'm more nervous about meeting your cousin again."

Reggie paused. He clicked on to what he was saying.

"Aaaaah." He sighed. "Have you got the hots for Marianne?"

Jarrod was silent. Of course he did.

"You're going to have to wait in line my friend. She's hot property!" blurted Reggie.

"She'll not be able to resist when she shares a car with a match-winning hero tomorrow," said Jarrod, to which they both roared down the phone, Reggie in disbelief and Jarrod in jest.

"Catch you tomorrow, mate," stated Jarrod.

The phone was down now for the night. Jarrod changed into some loose silky boxer shorts and a t-shirt and went through his bag to check if he had everything he needed for the morning.

He picked the tickets out of the pocket of his trousers, making sure he folded the trousers over a chair so they wouldn't get crushed, and put the tickets in the end pocket of his sports bag.

Jarrod headed to the bathroom. Without even closing the door behind him, he did his last pee of the day and as he flushed, he noticed a syringe in the bin, and a couple of used vials with a black label and a red stripe with writing he couldn't quite make out.

Jarrod took a step back, a moment to pause and contemplate what he had seen, and then took out his toothbrush and squeezed a bit of Neil's toothpaste on to it, careful not to make a mess on the tube. He looked at himself in the mirror. 'So what do I do now?' He brushed his teeth, then reached down to the bin and carefully picked up one of the vials, making sure the syringe wasn't anywhere near his hand. He then opened the bathroom door slowly and peered out.

"What's this?" he asked, making sure Neil had turned over to face him before producing the empty vial from behind the door jamb. Neil sat upright in an instant and stared at Jarrod, then at the vial, and back at Jarrod.

"You've got to keep this quiet," said Neil, blind panic written all over his face. "It's just something to help calm my nerves."

Jarrod held the vial in his open hand for a moment, the start of the name Erythro making him think of times when he had tonsillitis and the doctor had given him something like that, but as a tablet. He slowly closed his hand, walked back to the bin, opened it and made a point of the vial hitting the edge so the noise would let Neil know it was back in the bin.

He walked out and Neil was still staring, at a loss for words. Jarrod walked past him and around to his own bed, wishing his roommate goodnight and climbed into bed, turning the light off before slipping lower in the bed and kicking out the sheet that was tucked in tightly.

He had too much going on in his head now, thoughts of making his debut for the first team the next day, thoughts of driving home with Marianne, a party being planned in his home he hadn't even slept in yet, all this tempered by the expectation that Narco Neil would do something weird in the middle of the night like go missing or strangle Jarrod.

He was fast asleep within seconds.

# Chapter Twenty-Five:
# Dreaming

Opening his blurry eyes, Jarrod glanced over to his mobile phone, clicking it on to see the time before clicking it off immediately.

Neil's bed was empty. He then heard him in the bathroom. Neil returned and rolled into bed again, he was off deep breathing within seconds.

This was it. Today was the day.

Jarrod left Neil stretching in his bed to make the 7:30am breakfast, having thrown on the same clothes from the night before. He raced down the stairs. There were only a handful of players there, along with the coaching staff and support crew. Jarrod said his hellos as he headed over to check out the buffet. He sat on the end of a table with the rest of the players.

Talk was of the game ahead. There was no training today, they were going to relax after breakfast and check out straight onto the bus, and once all the players had arrived, around the 8am mark, Jenny stood up and addressed the squad.

"Morning everyone," she started. "Once you've had your breakfast, can you go and check out of your room and bring all your baggage down to reception where you can hand in your room key and assemble in the foyer."

Jarrod appreciated the clear and concise instructions, and complied, finishing his breakfast with a hearty bowl of grain clusters and yoghurt, and left with three of his new teammates to go up and get packed up.

He flicked on the TV and remembered he had left his phone

on the bedside table, so picked it up, flicking channels with the remote in the other hand until he got to the news.

A text message on his phone: 'Looking forward to seeing you! Thanks for the tickets. See you after the game. M x'

The number wasn't in his phone – it was Marianne though, and he smiled, conscious that his heart rate had just gone up and he could feel himself blushing slightly.

Neil was in soon enough as Jarrod settled back to watch the news. He was especially chatty and friendly, totally unlike what he had been the day before. Jarrod didn't really know how to take this, but they ended up having a good old catch up until it was time to get moving.

They walked down to reception together, still chatting about Neil's experience of his trip to Australia two years previously, but as they boarded the bus, Jarrod was quick to find his centre seat at the back and Neil was keen to take a solo position at the front of the bus.

The team were all in their white 'business' shirts, Grant Burgess had his unbuttoned almost to the waste, and it took some intervention from Jenny to get him spruced up and looking smart.

The bus was moving. Jarrod had enjoyed the hotel and felt quite at home there, but this was the adventure of a lifetime, and he was ready to grasp it with both hands.

The journey to Watford was shorter than he had imagined, and the bus came to a stop just around the corner from the main entrance before reversing skilfully in through the gates. It was only just coming up to eleven thirty, and the sun was starting to break through the heavy cloud cover making Jarrod squint as he got off the bus. There was a smattering of interested bystanders watching the players file off the bus, and a couple of the players went across to a barricade right by the entrance where they started to sign autographs.

Jarrod walked over to have a look, and was immediately accosted by two girls, and it took him a moment to realise that it was Marianne, and a very pretty blonde girl, both of them laughing their heads off and making such a fuss, hands all over Jarrod, pretending to be massive fans and making the remaining players stop in their tracks and wonder what was going on. Jarrod simply stood and waited for them to finish their charade, which they eventually did, and they all burst into laughter, Jarrod grabbing them both for a group hug.

"Salut les filles," said Jarrod in his pidgin French. "Thanks for the welcome!"

"Ha ha," said Marianne. "Got you! Now your teammates think you are a superstar. Jarrod, this is Nadine." Making sure the 'i' in Nadine was excessively long.

"Bonjour Nadine," said Jarrod, conscious that his French accent was ropey and he had effectively exhausted all his foreign language knowledge already in this conversation. Nadine reached in for a kiss on each cheek. Jarrod flinched, but then realised that it was perfectly normal.

"Where do we meet you after the game?" she asked. "Should we wait here? You'll be out quickly?"

"Yep, seems like a good spot to meet. See you right here," said Jarrod, as he put up his hand and remembered he had to get the tickets from the sports bag being wheeled past him on a trolley. He found his bag and turned back to the girls.

"Thank you," said Nadine, giving him a really cute look. "Hope you have a good game. Hope you can hear us shouting."

"I'll look for you," said Jarrod, as he walked to the entrance. "I'll be able to spot the jacket."

He pointed to Marianne's bright orange jacket and the girls waved as he left. When he was inside, he found Jenny directing traffic, and she showed Jarrod the way to the dressing room. Harry Lowndes spied him first and pointed with his hand outstretched as if to present to the crowd.

"Here he is, the gigolo!" he said in his booming voice.

A massive roar went up and Jarrod didn't really know what to do or say, so he let the roar die down and then smiled before finding a free spot between players of various state of undress. He was floating on air.

The players went out in threes and fours onto the field once they were fully ready, Jarrod having been handed a first team training top by Jenny when he was about to leave the tunnel.

The stadium was virtually empty, but there was a lot of activity around the perimeter and a lot of set up still being done. The early kick off was obviously not welcomed by everyone.

The Gateshead team were almost all out on the field, and there was not a single Watford player. Coach Will Daykin was calling all the players in for a chat. He waited until everyone was there, the first of the Watford players appearing to a smattering of applause. Coach Will gave the players a moment then snapped them into focus with a big clap of his hands. The players shuffled closer in a semi-circle to hear his voice.

"We know what we're up against here," he stated, in no mood to be interrupted. "We've done our homework. We have the players to do the marking jobs. We have our central defence ready for the aerial threat. We know we're going to fight for possession, and when we get it, we're going to keep it as long as we can, even if it means going backwards and using Harry."

A few Watford players were trotting out, the applause growing louder as the trickle of fans continued into the stadium.

"Standard warm-up," said Will. "Go."

Tibor Calinz, the quiet spoken captain, clapped his hands to signify his troops needed to fall into line, and they formed their two lines, completely second-nature and very smoothly done.

The warm-up was exactly as they had done at training the previous day, and Jarrod felt some stiffness in his leg, probably due to the coach trip. The longer sprints at the end were welcome to get the blood circulating and get some of the burning sensation out of his lungs.

The players looked very professional in their identical kit, and that continued as they split into three groups for a running and turning drill that they executed with total precision.

Jarrod was letting the professionalism rub off on him, and he could feel his concentration and technical skills being enhanced as his mind was set firmly on the job.

Some screeching from the sidelines caught the attention of a few players and they stopped what they were doing. It was Marianne and Nadine going crazy again having made their way down to the front.

The girls upped the volume again when Jarrod got his first touch. He turned with his foot on the ball and his arms crossed; basically telling them it was enough while secretly hoping they continued.

The stadium was starting to change colour, the bright seats starting to fill with fans. The noise level was at a murmur and the stadium was slowly coming to life.

Will called the players in one last time and told them to collect any equipment and head back to the changing room and to assemble there in five minutes, to which some of the players raced to get some cones before disappearing down the tunnel. Jarrod simply walked off, taking whatever he found in his path. The screams from the sideline went up again as he reached the tunnel and as he put his hand over the side of his face, feigning embarrassment, the screams got even louder.

Jarrod took a seat when he got in the busy changing room, and the door closing meant Mr Bruker had just entered the room and was ready to address his troops.

He held a clipboard to his chest and surveyed the room looking at certain individuals, holding their gaze before going back to his clipboard. Coach Will seemed edgy. Mr Bruker then burst into action, moving to the mobile whiteboard in the centre of the wall.

He talked fast, writing his team up in semi-scribble onto the whiteboard using a blue pen, starting at the back with the goalkeeper Harry, a back four of initials in a flat formation, then a three man midfield, again straight across the middle. JB was scrawled in the left midfield spot and Mr Bruker pointed with his marker pen at Jarrod who could scarcely believe what he was hearing.

He hadn't really been concentrating as he was expecting only a spot on the bench, if anything, but now his senses heightened and the adrenaline kicked in. His concentration switched on like a light.

He caught Neil's eye and raised an eyebrow - Neil had been dropped and was staring straight through Jarrod. He had the look of a beaten man. Jarrod had a flash of guilt. What if Neil thought he had talked to Mr Bruker, or Will, or even Jenny about what he had seen the night before? Jarrod could feel his face reddening and looked away.

Mr Bruker gave the final instructions - they were playing to win today. The formation was attacking, Watford would not be expecting it. This was almost make or break for the season even at this early stage and he urged his players to make the most of the attacking set up and to get forward as often as possible.

The players seemed totally transfixed, as if this was a revelation. Perhaps it was, and Jarrod was stumbling in to something new and exciting. On the other hand it could be a throw of the dice that could end up with a six goal drubbing, but that wasn't the feeling he got.

The door opened and the players confidently stepped out in the corridor that took them to the tunnel area. The Watford team were entering the tunnel at the same time and could sense the confidence from their visitors.

The stadium announcer was at the end of the tunnel. There was a line-up of cameras and there was a lot of activity coming from the field.

The referee turned to the captains to signal their entrance onto the playing field and they strode out. Jarrod took his spot fourth in line, dwarfed by teammate Jerome Blondeau. He gave his legs a few sprints on the spot as he crossed the white line.

The stadium looked and sounded totally different. The wall of sound as they came out was now replaced by a loud buzz of over 20,000 people chanting. The stadium was more or less full. The miniature Watford mascot was the first to come through for the official handshake, along with the Watford captain.

The Gateshead team ran towards their fans, and Jarrod made a point of saluting the black and white area of the stadium with applause, his hands high above his head. Every fan in the section was doing the same in return. Quite the welcome.

This was real. This was why he was in England. This is what he craved. He would just now have to produce a performance to suit the occasion.

The players got together in a huddle. Tibor roared at the top of his voice to make himself heard and give the impression they were entering into a war. Jarrod could feel his chest swelling with every word.

The blood pumped through his body with an intensity he had not felt for some time. Tibor peeled away to do the coin toss and handshakes with the referee and his opposite number. Harry took the mantle. Standing in the centre of the tight circle and giving Jarrod a thump in the chest.

"This man," he said. "This man is going to win us the game today."

Jarrod could not have felt any prouder at that moment. The referee blew the whistle to signify the change of ends - Tibor had obviously won the toss.

The two teams trotted past each other, some players feeling the urge to wish their opponents a good game, others offering a final handshake, some just walking past without word or gesture.

The players lined up in their formation. Jarrod made a point of not standing in his position until the whistle blew, and the crowd roared their approval as the first move of the game saw a long ball down the Gateshead left headed behind for an instant corner.

The resulting corner was fielded by Harry, who took Mr Bruker's instructions on board by bowling the ball long down the right, setting Gateshead immediately on the attack. The home side were definitely up for the match, but they were a little taken aback by the running game Gateshead had brought to the occasion.

There were instructions being barked from the Watford bench and arms stretched out with puzzled looks as Gateshead started to run at the defenders down each wing, Jarrod doing his best to keep up with his left winger Nate Carisbrook whenever he tried to beat his fullback.

Jarrod found himself drifting to the centre to pick up the ball from the defence and was quickly confirmed as the focal point for everything going forward; spraying the ball out wide or making the telling through balls over the top. It was the wingers though who were doing the damage, and when Nate skipped past a lunging tackle to keep his feet, the referee stretching his arms to wave play on, he galloped to the edge of the box, drew the last defender wide before accelerating past, smashing a ball across the six yard box where an onrushing defender reached for the ball and sliced it up over the keeper and into the corner of the net for a freakish own goal.

The Gateshead fans behind the goal were jumping around like total lunatics. What a way to round off a fabulous period of dominance, and the cheers turned to chants, '1-0 to the Geordie boys' being the song that morphed out of the din.

The players were quick to celebrate, although there was no goal scorer, and they made a point of taking their time with their bonding in front of the away fans.

Kick off saw the Gateshead team reset and refocus on the job at hand. It was only a matter of time before Watford were caught out throwing too many players forward as they searched for more options upfield. Gateshead won the ball and embarked on a remarkable counter attack. Jerome found himself providing the overlap for the through ball in behind. He raced into the box and after taking a heavy touch, slid to the keep the ball in, hooking the ball over to the far post where his towering central defensive partner Fulvio Marceda met the ball at full speed with a simple header and bundled the ball into the net along with the goalkeeper.

What a goal! Jarrod raced up to the goal after the players had started to untangle themselves from the net. The unfortunate Watford player caught in the celebration stayed down with a bloody nose. The fans were still jumping. They couldn't believe what was happening.

The scoreboard clicked over to 0-2. The stadium announcer gave the news the goal scorer was number 2; totally mispronouncing the name but receiving a huge cheer from the Gateshead end. Gateshead were two goals up away from home against a team much higher in the table than themselves.

Jarrod was struggling to understand how on earth his teammates could have gotten themselves in to such a predicament in the league. The half time break was still five minutes away, and the home team could sense that, despite the disquiet they could feel from the watching masses, a single goal before half time could and probably would change the game.

Jarrod picked up a loose ball, skipping a challenge that got a slight nick on the ball taking it away from his control. The ball bounced in the centre circle and a Watford midfielder reacted first and made a play for the ball. Jarrod was committed to the challenge and launched himself at the ball making sure he started sliding before the impact, tackling with studs raised or feet off the ground being so inflammatory in this day and age.

Jarrod got there first and squeezed the ball to his left but braced himself for impact and when it came it was big. The Watford man, a big black guy with massive legs, crashed into him feet first followed by his whole weight.

Jarrod was sent flying in the air and braced himself for the landing, finding himself cushioned by his assailant with a crack as he hit the ground. Jarrod was dazed, and two of his teammates rushed over to see if he was okay, another rushing in to make sure the Watford man knew what he had done was not okay. Jarrod was fine and was concerned for his opponent.

Jarrod stood with arms spread over the Watford player, shielding him from any potential abuse from his irate teammates. The referee called on the home team's physio with a shrill blow of the whistle, and the stadium fell almost silent as the realisation of the seriousness of the situation took hold.

The Watford player, Ricardo Owasu, was not moving, and the Gateshead physio also ran on. The temper of the players dissipated and the majority of the players went over to the sideline to take on water and to talk with the coaching staff.

Owasu finally gave an indication he was alive, before the Watford physio called for the stretcher. He was slowly removed from the field and taken straight down the tunnel. The stadium and players from both teams broke out in huge applause.

Jarrod didn't realise that his quick feet, ability to take a hit, and concern for his fellow player were to catapult him very quickly to stardom. The fans roared as Jarrod walked down the tunnel after the six minutes of injury time had finally elapsed. The Gateshead dressing room was as buoyant as he had ever known a dressing room to be at half time. Mr Bruker walked in beaming.

"That," he stated, "was the best half of football I have ever seen."

This was coming from a player who had seen it all. His players were not in a position to doubt that statement, after all they were two goals up away from home against a team nine places higher than themselves. The mood was simply electric.

"Will here says we should defend our lead," said Mr Bruker. "But today, I'm going against the wishes of my good friend and we are going out there and going for more."

The dressing room was rocking. Mr Bruker could have said anything and the result would have been the same. It was like a US presidential roadshow. Mr Bruker was able to get a reaction out of his flock regardless of what he said.

"All right, all right," barked Will, his arms stretched out in front of him to calm the crowd. "Nate, we need more. We're going to give the ball to you every time and you are going to beat your man."

Jarrod was surprised that Nate was targeted as someone who needed to up his game but given the amount of ball he had and the space he was creating, he could see why Will was geeing him up. This was, after all, an amazing performance, and the whole team knew it. No point in resting on their laurels. It was time to go out and do it all again.

"And Jarrod," said Mr Bruker. "Keep holding the centre. Tibor can drift upfield, but you make sure you are there in the middle always."

Will opening the door was like opening a cage of hungry lions, exiting the change room with purpose and resolve. The Watford players had already headed back out on to the field.

Jarrod heard Marianne and Nadine squealing as he came out of the tunnel and turned to give them a fist-pump. They were cheering, fists in the air, before collapsing in hoots of laughter.

The players took their positions, Gateshead ready to kick off. Jarrod turned to his teammates in defence and urged them to push ten yards further up to give the impression they were going to swamp their opponents. That is exactly what happened.

Options were everywhere, and Jarrod took the right one, slipping in a low ball behind the attackers for Tibor to run on to and bury the ball comprehensively past the keeper for a third goal, barely thirty seconds on the clock in the second half.

The whole team, Harry included, raced to congratulate their captain, and they managed to kill about two minutes from the game time before the referee blew to restart.

The fans behind them were in full voice, the home supporters stunned. The game descended into a procession of substitutions and time-wasting from Gateshead from then on. Jarrod was finally replaced with five minutes on the clock, making sure he was as far away from the bench as possible when his number came up, and even then pretending that he didn't know, before slightly irking Mr Bruker by running off instead of slowly ambling, letting supporters know this was tactical and not because he was injured.

The game was still going on, but it was almost at walking pace now. The Gateshead fans were belting out tune after tune, and the players were applauding their fans from the field even as the game was going on. The final whistle sounded after an uneventful minute of stoppage time in the fast-emptying stadium, and the noise was immense from the Gateshead end.

The players shook hands with the Watford team before walking across to their fervent fans, giving them fists in the air and applause which was whole-heartedly reciprocated. Jarrod found himself in Jerome's arms at one point, hoisted in that infamous Pele pose, beating his fist at the away fans.

Will and Mr Bruker came over and joined the celebrations, urging their players to continue giving thanks to the considerable support that had made its way down from Tyneside early that morning. Jarrod didn't want to leave, but as soon as he could see some of the away fans heading for the exits, he knew the moment was over, and turned to walk back to the tunnel, a feeling of utter exhilaration coming over him.

Nadine had jumped the fence and was in his face before he knew it and she jumped into his arms before Marianne joined her. Clearly there was no worrying about getting a stadium ban - this was a one off visit after all! Jarrod lapped it up, and eventually managed to get himself down the tunnel and into the sanctuary of the changing room.

He pushed open the door to find the room booming with conversation, an excited chatter filling the space and was instantly caught up in it. It felt like a Grand Final win, and FA Cup triumph, qualifying for the World Cup against all odds, all rolled into one. Jarrod wanted to relive some of the moments of the game with his teammates, and he couldn't stop talking. Neil came up to him and gave him a handshake, not a word spoken. He had played the last ten minutes and was looking a lot healthier as a result.

Jarrod grabbed his towel and took off all his clothes with total abandon before walking into the shower area, strutting like a peacock.

By the time Jarrod got out of the shower, a number of players had left the change room. Right-back Ferenc Kalic was wheeling his great big suitcase out the door, whistling. The mood was calming down. He grabbed his phone to see that the time was after three and was conscious he had now moved into the next part of the day. He quickly dried himself off before making a meal of getting dressed, struggling to get his pants past his damp backside and then pulling his t-shirt on backwards before realising and turning it back round.

The crisp white club shirt was stuffed unceremoniously into his bag, and with a quick survey of the area to check for stray socks or a misplaced mobile phone, he was straight out the door and headed towards the foyer area. The media conference was taking place in a room off the main entrance and Jarrod poked his head around the corner. Mr Bruker caught his eye and immediately beckoned him inside, making reference to his 'new breed' of Gateshead player and singing his praises.

Jarrod backed away much to the merriment of the media crowd and made for the doorway where he saw Jenny chatting with a couple players.

"Jarrod," she said, opening her arms to wrap him in a warm embrace. "There's two girls waiting for you outside. Am I ticking your name off the list to say you have left the building?"

"Yes, you are," said Jarrod. "Thanks for everything, but I will have to love you and leave you. See you on Monday." He planted a kiss on Jenny's cheek before pushing open the heavy door and walking out into the cool breeze. He was expecting some more hysteria from the girls, but slowly walked down the stairs and it was a moment before the girls saw he was there, Marianne spying him first, pulling herself away from the conversation they were both having with a male-heavy group of Watford fans.

"Wow, Jarrod," she stated, her voice singing as she talked in her exotic accent. "That was ah-ma-zing."

"Glad you liked it," said Jarrod, and Nadine walked over, abandoning the group to greet her new idol.

"Jarrod," said Nadine. "You were great. We loved it. Can we come again?"

Jarrod was beaming. The feeling of contentment from giving pleasure to people was something he could get used to.

"Of course you can," he said, and with that they all joined arms, one girl on either side, and they led him off to their car, which was parked a good ten minute walk from the stadium.

# Chapter Twenty-Six: Soiree

Jarrod sat in the back as Nadine drove and Marianne directed her using her mobile phone. He was loving being the question master and wasn't fazed when they broke into French on the odd occasion. Jarrod had no idea what they were talking about.

They had made it off the M1 with only a couple of wrong turns, after going three times around one of the large roundabouts as they contemplated which exit to take. Nadine was proving to be an excellent driver, making some deft lane changes and showing no mercy to fellow road-users.

The traffic was light, and they made good time, Jarrod flicking off a text to Neil to ask if they had left the stadium yet, to which he got the reply, 'Are you kidding? Mr Bruker will be talking to every newspaper after this one.'

Jarrod was enjoying the company of the two girls. Their French accents were music to his ears. Nadine was a good-looking girl, but he was fixated with Marianne. He remembered meeting her way back at the trials and remarked how pretty she was then. Of course, he hadn't mentioned it to anyone at the time.

They stopped for a bite to eat at a motorway service stop near where the M62 meets the A1. Jarrod watched the sports wrap up on the news while the girls were in the bathroom. Spurs had beaten Newcastle to his dismay but the league table for the Championship showed that Gateshead had moved up two places in the table and further away from danger at the bottom. He stood there taking in the results until the girls came out and they found a seat.

He could feel himself trying to send Marianne signals to see if sparks would ignite, but if he was honest with himself he was a total novice at this game. It was purely experimental. Jarrod would hold her gaze for that split second longer, he would then make sure Nadine was the focus of the conversation just to see how Marianne reacted. And he would, subconsciously or not, move closer to and then further away from Marianne and see if she would move with him.

Knowing there was still two hours before they got to their destination, and the party would be in full swing by then, they made the call to get moving again. Marianne drove this time, Nadine insisting Jarrod rode in the passenger seat.

By the time they were heading past the Angel of the North and into familiar territory, to Jarrod at least, the conversation had died down somewhat and Nadine had tuned out. It was after all quite a long journey. Jarrod made sure he kept things going along with Marianne to keep her alert behind the wheel and to get to know her better.

He got the basics out of her - where she was from, where she was living, even who she was seeing; the answer was what he was hoping for. As they drove into Gateshead and off the A1, Marianne asked where he lived and it dawned on him he didn't actually know the address or how to get there from where they were, much to the amusement of the girls.

A quick phone call on speaker to Reggie sorted that out, and it ended up being remarkably easy and after following instructions to pick up some ice and two bottles of vodka from the off-licence around the corner, they were parked and unloaded.

Jarrod could hear the hum of the music from the basement, and although it wasn't excessively loud, he was sure it would be loud for the immediate neighbours and hoped Reggie had prewarned them. He thanked the girls for coming and they got their bags from the boot of the car and summoned the lift to take them up to where the tunes were coming from.

He really had no idea what to expect. Nadine and Marianne seemed to be 'au fait' with the situation and walked into the open door and headed straight for the bathroom, presumably to get changed and made up. Jarrod walked in and looked around. It was dark with some flashing lights from the main living area.

As soon as Jarrod saw Reggie he raced over and grabbed him around the shoulder as he talked to a very pretty girl.

"Yes!" shouted Reggie. "You f-ing champion!"

Jarrod wasn't used to hearing Reggie use that sort of language, but felt it was justified.

"No, you f-ing champion," retorted Jarrod. "How good is this?"

"Enjoy, mate," said Reggie. "Stick the ice in the sink and we'll put some beers in there. Russ was running low for the cocktails."

Reggie and Jarrod pulled off the most amazing party. It was all Reggie's work. He had the connections, he knew the girls, it was all him, but it was also Jarrod's apartment, so he could lay claim to it, and it would be known as Reggie and Jarrod's party from then on.

Some of the party-goers were heading out to a nearby nightclub to finish off, but Jarrod and Reggie were happy to wind down in their new home, Reggie helping the DJ pack up while Jarrod got his mobile phone connected to his portable speakers to continue the tunes.

The apartment looked great - there wasn't much furniture, but Reggie had done a great job in making it look as if it was fully furnished, and he was gushing in his praise of his new flatmate.

The four or five guys that remained were sitting around a low table, which turned out to be a sheet of plywood on two milk crates with a white sheet over it, and they had what looked like crystal glasses in their hands, with a bottle of Jack Daniels on the go in the middle. A cigar would not have been out of place.

It was getting late, but Reggie made the decision to move and they collected what rubbish they could see, turned off all the lights and headed down the stairs and into the night to make the short walk to the nightclub.

Jarrod had worked up the courage to ask Reggie about Marianne.

"Marianne's gorgeous, eh?" said Jarrod.

"Yes, she is," said Reggie. "My Auntie married a French guy. We've been there on holiday a few times and even though she is my cousin, I can safely say that she is indeed gorgeous."

"So, is she off-limits?" asked Jarrod. He knew he would have a tough time if someone asked him about Anna, so he was prepared for any answer.

"Off limits?" came the surprised reaction from Reggie. "Nothing would make me happier! I might be able to crack Nadine then!"

They were both loving life at the moment. They had pulled off a great party. They had girls staying overnight, and Jarrod had even made a winning debut today. So much to take in!

The music was intoxicating. Jarrod had taken on more JD than he ever had, which wasn't that much, and he just hit the dance floor, grinding with whoever was near and pulling out all the cheesiest of moves. It didn't take long for Nadine and Marianne to find them. They danced together for a good hour, each familiar tune being met with cheers and outrageous moves.

# Chapter Twenty-Seven: Result

Jarrod opened his eyes to find himself in bed with Marianne, and they were naked.

A quick 'freshness' check indicated they had not gotten up to anything, but he could not believe his luck. He remembered unwrapping the sheets from their packaging the night before and making the bed and stuffing a couple of cushions from the sofa into a pillow case to make a pillow after they had used all the new pillows for their guests.

He was absolutely bursting to see if he could make this situation even better and ran his hand over Marianne's hip and up between her breasts, turning to press himself into her. He was taking a massive chance here, but the feeling was obviously mutual, as she squirmed and pressed herself even closer to Jarrod and then turned to face him.

Despite her mascara being a little less perfect than it had been previously and her hair being a little wild, she could definitely pull it off, and Jarrod was instantly smitten. They didn't say a word as they enjoyed some quality time together for a good half hour, keeping the noise to a minimum, but it was highly likely the same thing was happening in Reggie's room.

Marianne's body was athletic and toned, Jarrod's muscled legs wrapping around her slender frame. When Marianne's phone sounded to break the silence, they snapped out of their embrace, and it wasn't long before Nadine waltzed in, dressed only in her bra and pants, to sit on the end of the bed and start a conversation with Marianne in French as if Jarrod wasn't there.

Reggie slinked in and sat next to her clicking his fingers and winking at Jarrod as he walked in. This had been a truly epic night. Jarrod was a total novice with girls and relationships, but he felt some pretty strong emotions towards all of the people in the room at that point and he was sure he was in love.

Perhaps he was simply in love with his life at the moment, or maybe he really had fallen for this beautiful girl who was naked in his bed right now chatting with her really hot mate and Jarrod's best friend. Wow!

It wasn't long before Jarrod and Marianne were seeing each other regularly, or as regularly as their chaotic lives would permit. A reserve team trip to Queens Park Rangers gave Jarrod the chance to head to London the day before the game, and then Marianne's course took her to Liverpool, which coincided with a youth team game in nearby Manchester.

Jarrod was flirting with the first team while still making appearances for the youth and reserve teams, but it took a cancelled game just before Christmas for Marianne and Jarrod to spend a longer period of time together. Marianne invited him to join her in Paris for the weekend when she went to a family engagement out in the western suburbs.

They were totally wrapped in each other, Jarrod still having the comical yet wise words of his teammate Harry in his head: 'you shag a French girl, she'll be expecting you to marry her next.' Jarrod was in love, or at least lust, and he enjoyed meeting all the relatives and hearing all the stories, at least from the English speakers amongst them.

He also enjoyed the sex, and found he was well matched in that department. Marianne didn't hold back and was always keen to take advantage of any moment alone to get together.

Reggie and Nadine were also still together, Nadine taking advantage of Jarrod being away and making herself at home at the apartment in Gateshead.

Life was good and Jarrod was quite aware of it.

# Chapter Twenty-Eight: Season

Jarrod hadn't slept that well and found himself on his back staring at the ceiling and at Marianne.

He eventually kicked off the duvet from his feet and spun onto the side of the bed, sitting with his elbows on his thighs, looking down at his feet ready to make the first move of the day.

It was six. It was light but the blackout blinds he had installed recently were doing their job and Marianne was still asleep.

It was the first day of the new season at Gateshead and Nigel had called the team to the stadium for a day of testing, admin, and light training, before the real work began on Monday.

Jarrod could sense his own apathy, but after getting to his feet and taking the first few steps, his mind clicked into gear and he was straight in the shower, lost in thought about the day ahead.

Sebastian walked in, headphones on, already engrossed in whatever computer game or video he was obsessing over at that moment and walked straight back out without going to the toilet when he realised his Dad was in there. Sebastian walked back in just as Jarrod had turned off the shower and asked, "Dad, are we moving to Darlington?"

"I...I'm not sure Seb," came the reply. "Would you like that?"

"I don't know. I'm just interested," said Sebastian.

"We'll know more this week coming up I suppose," said Jarrod. "These things tend to happen quite quickly when they do."

That was enough for Sebastian and he backed out while

Jarrod got himself changed and headed out after him. He found his son on the couch, with the TV on but his tablet computer taking his concentration. Jarrod put his hand on his shoulder and sat down next to him, flicking his headphone off his ear.

"So, if we did move," asked Jarrod, "would your life be over?"

There was jest in the tone of his voice, but he was genuinely concerned.

"No," replied Sebastian. "But I'd like to know sooner rather than later."

That was a very mature response and Jarrod felt as though his son was growing up and thinking more like an adult.

"I'll keep you informed every step of the way," said Jarrod honestly, and he got up and walked over to make himself a coffee from the pod machine. He glanced at the clock, which made him judder, and he rushed into the laundry to get his football gear ready. Aneka and Marianne would be in bed for another two hours at least, and by now Aneka would have sneaked into their room and taken Jarrod's warm spot.

Jarrod made himself presentable and packed up everything he needed, which wasn't much, before jumping in the car and roaring off out of the driveway. The journey to work was a well-worn path. The roads were clear, no surprises given the time of day, and the trip seemed even shorter when compared to the drive to Darlington that was fresh in his mind.

He arrived at the stadium to find quite a change. The car park had a new gate that was relocated about a hundred metres further along the road, and the car park itself had been expanded and resealed with freshly painted lines. The stadium entrance had also undergone a makeover, fresh paint and new livery, and Jarrod wasn't sure whether to embrace it or take it as a sign that sands were definitely shifting at his club.

A warm greeting though from the reception staff inside made him feel right at home, then seeing his teammates brought a smile to his face. There was a flurry of activity going on through the door into the entrance to the bowels of the stadium. The players were lining up to undergo physical tests in a makeshift sports lab. The scenario was akin to clearing customs at an airport as players removed shoes and placed bags in an area on the floor before filing in for a weight check, then a height measurement, a body fat test, and finally a saliva test, that last step taking the most time and causing a bit of a delay.

He spied Ferrazzo and the diminutive Italian looked every bit the superstar, immaculately turned out despite the ungodly hour and like a well-groomed stallion in a pack of shabby work-horses. His crisp white shirt was unbuttoned two buttons from the top, and he gave the Alessandro Del Piero vibe, a player Jarrod had seen play in Sydney a few years back as a kid.

"Welcome back lads," started Nigel rather quietly, everyone consciously taking a step closer to hear. "Today we are going to get to know the football again. It's been a few weeks and we need more than ever to get to know this thing very intimately." He held up a gleaming match ball, yellow and blue, with many small panels, unlike the ball that had been in use in the previous two or three seasons. This was the match ball for the new season, and it was a very nice touch to be able to make its acquaintance at this early stage.

"Get changed," continued Nigel in as big a voice as he could muster. "And we will meet out on the field at ten past seven—it is now 7.03, so please move quickly."

Nigel strode out with his entourage of three coaches, one an unfamiliar face, and the players quickly changed into their gear, or in Jarrod's case, simply changed from trainers to boots, and made their way over to where they were standing.

The new face was introduced as a Nike technician, and he was to run through the features of the new match ball. He grabbed a volunteer and they started describing the new features, how the ball could be struck to cause movement in the air, how tight a curl they could expect.

Jarrod was struggling to stay focused. A ball was, after all, a ball, and the differences would be picked up as soon as they played with it. The demonstration went on for almost half an hour, and the technician received a round of applause at the end of the session for his in-depth input.

The club photographer had since arrived and was taking snaps. Jarrod became conscious that he was struggling to show much enthusiasm and tried to stir a little life into his body with some bouncing and jogging on the spot.

Jarrod was called over for a chat with Nigel. They shook hands and Jarrod sat down at the desk that had been set up near the field, which was littered with folders, one for each player it seemed.

"Good to see you, Jarrod," said Nigel. "I trust you have had a relaxing pre-season and your head is in the right place."

Jarrod nodded. "What happened in May is in the past now," he said. "We have to make it happen this year, we really do."

"We've brought in Emilio. I see you've met." Again Jarrod nodded in Ferrazzo's direction. Nigel continued, "We're bringing in Walter Besa in a couple days from the Spanish second division to help us in midfield this season."

"I hadn't heard that one," said Jarrod.

"I hope you can make the two of them feel welcome and help them integrate to our style of play," stated Nigel. "These two guys could make the difference this season. This could be our year."

"Sure," said Jarrod. "Let's see what you've got for pre-season."

Jarrod smiled and Nigel held out his hand which Jarrod shook firmly, piercing his eyes with his stare. He remembered previous pre-season sessions, not quite in the same format, where they had openly discussed the captain's role, who should be vice-captain, and who should make up the team leadership committee. There was none of that today.

Either it was assumed the status quo from last season remained, or there were others in line for those positions. Jarrod liked the ambiguity and stored that one up as a reason to leave, in case he had to justify himself at a later stage if it came to it.

He jogged over and re-joined the game, which had upped in intensity since he had left it, and the team that scored the most goals in five minutes would avoid a lung-busting two minute fitness drill. There was only a minute left of the first game, and Jarrod's team was behind by a goal.

He put his foot on the ball and drew a challenge, flicking the ball to his teammate who advanced and laid the ball back to Jarrod who launched a low shot straight through the cones for an equaliser. The five minute session was up and the coach decided that both teams would do the two minute drill - four seconds in a squat position followed by four seconds rest for two minutes.

The players found it easy to begin with, but as the two minutes reached their end, the talking stopped and the grimaces started, and when they finished there was an audible groan. No time to rest though, it was round two, and they were into the small sided game again, the stakes raised and the intensity even higher.

The session was a lot of fun. Jarrod began to get his rhythm back and was clearly enjoying himself, giving out some strong tackles and keeping the banter flowing. The players were covered in sweat as the sun beat down and the session came to an end, all four teams moving over to the doorway where the lab was set up where they were to go in for round two of testing.

This involved a blood sample. There was quite a wait while this was done, and then a urine sample which meant taking on a lot of water to induce the feeling in order to deliver the required amount and there was a great deal of laughing, some players taking on litres of water in what became a pub-like atmosphere.

This was good. He felt at home and felt at ease, and that helpless feeling of defeat that had shrouded the club in May had gone. By the time the players were changed and sat down for a brief chat in the media room, it was gone 11am.

The club managing director Sjonni Pedersen gave them a welcome and a brief outline of what the goals were for the club this season, and what changes in personnel behind the scenes had taken place since the last season had finished. There was thanks to those players who had moved on - there were only two - and welcomes to the three players who had been signed, and some introductions of two new coaches, Victor Rundle and Mitch Argeles, Mitch having been the coach who took Jarrod through the session outside.

There was a new head of media relations, a fan liaison officer and there was a physician who would be in charge of nutrition and well-being. There really did seem to be a genuine change to become a more professional and forward-thinking club. The media team finished the briefing with a five minute video about social media. This was a short version of something the players had seen before, with updates of the latest crazes and traps for online participants. Jarrod had struggled to maintain his social media presence, having only a twitter feed that he sometimes let Sebastian update, under his supervision, with comments about signings and match results. The final point reinforced the club code of conduct that abuse of social media was not tolerated at any level.

Nikolai asked Jarrod to join him for lunch. It was early enough to find somewhere before the Sunday roast crowd. Nikolai would drive, dropping him back to the stadium afterwards.

The next session was in the morning, so they had the rest of the day to themselves. Marianne was taking the kids to the beach for a day out up North somewhere. The two elder statesmen, as they clearly were, said their goodbyes and Nikolai led Jarrod to his car, a brand new white BMW with tinted windows. This was ostentatious, but at least with the tinted windows and non-personalised plates, they could be incognito. Nikolai drove fast and very efficiently to a car park along from Central station, and they walked up the steps to the first floor where the beautiful smell of lamb and garlic wafted in their faces.

The restaurant was a no-booking restaurant, but they were early and they were seated right away by the front window overlooking the street below. They had not talked deeply in the car, but as the waitress was bringing them water, arranging their menus and taking their drinks order, they both looked at each other and knew there was a lot to discuss.

"Walter Besa," Nikolai started. "Emilio Ferrazzo. What is happening?"

"I'm not being paranoid, you see," said Jarrod. "There was no talk of captaincy. There was nothing about forming a committee. Nothing."

"You're convinced that you're on the way out, aren't you?" said Nikolai.

"I am," Jarrod paused. "I am, but I thoroughly enjoyed today's session."

"Yes, me too. A little different, short and sharp fitness, not ridiculous long runs, pre-season has evolved." They both smiled.

Jarrod changed direction. "I have an offer on the table."

"It's Darlington, isn't it?" asked Nikolai, resigned to the fact that his earlier intervention had fallen on deaf ears.

"Who else?" said Jarrod. "They've started making moves early before anyone has started pre-season, and I'm going through the process of negotiating the best I can get."

"Sol Campbell is back," said Nikolai.

They continued their conversation over lunch. Nikolai grilling Jarrod, playing the perfect devil's advocate before stopping Jarrod in his tracks and turning it around, inviting Jarrod to give him his own reservations about what he was contemplating. Jarrod took the invitation and poured out his concerns, Nikolai agreeing to some and waving away others, and finally, as their amazing main courses came out, and the starter plates that had brought them olives and haloumi with extra ripe tomatoes were taken away, Nikolai asked, "So can I sign up too?"

They both laughed. Jarrod had a glass of red wine, Nikolai was drinking sparkling water, but they clinked glasses and Jarrod felt as if he had the justification he needed. As they continued their conversation, it turned out that Nikolai had been subject of an offer from Holland, and he himself was being tempted.

They started to go through the same process – this one seemed a little more straightforward as it was to a club in the top flight and was a big money move for both club and player. Jarrod was genuinely excited for his teammate. They talked for a good hour, enjoying each other's company, and revelling in getting everything off their chests.

Dessert and strong black coffees were next, and Jarrod made sure he paid at the counter before Nikolai could claim it was his turn, returning with the bill and commenting how good value the place was considering the quality and quantity of food they had eaten. They ducked out of the restaurant, acknowledging that a few eyes had been on them inside, and back down to the car. Nikolai drove them back to the stadium where there were still a hundred or so cars in the car park. His parting words to Jarrod were :

"Jarrod, you know when this gets out, you will all of a sudden become both a traitor and hot property. Don't be surprised if Darlington is not where you end up."

Jarrod took that thought with him and waved off his mate, unsure as to whether or not they would be able to have a long lunch together in the future. That had been perhaps the last supper.

A text message popped up on his mobile phone as he hopped in his car, it was from Sebastian - he wasn't sure how he could send text messages without a mobile phone, but knew he had a device capable of pretty much everything else. It read: 'Dad, check out the heed website.'

And there was a link attached. It took him straight to the top story which showed a disinterested looking Jarrod staring into space while his teammates appeared to be listening intently. It was captioned ambiguously but suggested that his mind was elsewhere, following up on that story earlier in the week suggesting he could be thinking of leaving.

Jarrod cursed, but knew it was time to do something.

# Chapter Twenty-Nine: Fast

It was after one in the afternoon when Jarrod walked into the empty house. He checked the phone for messages.

There was only one. It was a brief voicemail from Dad, asking Jarrod to call him, no matter what time. It was actually quite a civil time, just before bed in Sydney. Jarrod picked up the phone and dialled home. The phone rang for one ring, and Dad picked it up.

"Jarrod," he said, knowing it could only be him, or a fifty percent chance of it being him or Mr Leonard.

"Dad, what's happening?" asked Jarrod.

"Mr Leonard has done some negotiating and got exactly what he asked for." Dad paused. "Which begs the question, should he have gone for more. But that's a different story."

"No, no," said Jarrod. "If he's got everything, I think we have a green light."

"Are you sure about this?" asked Dad.

"I'm sure. It's time," said Jarrod.

"No going back. Once this breaks, it's all over at Gateshead."

"Yes, I know. I understand. Thanks for supporting me, Dad."

"No question of that, son. Now tell your family and then get in touch with Darlington and let's see what happens."

"Onto it. I'll keep you updated. Love to the family."

Jarrod hung up the phone, dialling Marianne on his mobile

who answered straight away.

"Darling," she said. "How are you?"

"Good, Marianne." Jarrod had his business hat on. "I'm going to ask you one final time - are you okay with me signing for Darlington?"

"Yes, of course," replied Marianne almost immediately. "You have to look after our best interests and I trust you to do that."

"Thanks, hon," said Jarrod. "Let the kids know."

"We're here!" came the shouting down the phone. "You're on speaker!"

"Go, Daddy!" shouted Aneka, and that was enough to seal the deal.

Jarrod wasn't entirely sure how this was going to pan out. It was Sunday after all, and surely not everyone worked all day every day, but he picked up the phone and made the next phone call to the Darlington contracts manager.

The receptionist answered and there was a long pause while they located the required person, June, and she came on the phone with a bright and cheery 'hello.'

Jarrod explained that he was willing to accept the terms as set out in discussions with his representative Mr Leonard. He could hear movement at the other end of the line, and envisaged the contracts manager waving over her colleagues to listen in. He then asked what the process would be from here, and June explained there was still a great deal to do from this point. It was a slightly unusual situation in that Jarrod had come to them, therefore, there was nothing technically illegal or immoral about it, but it would still be an unusual scenario.

She would make first contact with Gateshead and urged Jarrod to be contactable all day as there could be decisions that needed to be made quickly.

June promised to ring him to update him, before asking if she could transfer him to Gerry.

"Jarrod," came the cheery voice on the phone. "Thanks for getting in touch with us, and I'm hearing all the right things. If there is anything we can help you with, anyone we can put you in touch with to help you, just ring us."

"Thank you, Gerry," said Jarrod. "It sounds as though we will be in contact a lot today."

"It's not as complicated as June is making out. Don't you worry. But we might need you to come in this afternoon. Speak to you later." And he hung up.

The five seconds of silence after the call had ended left Jarrod a little stunned, but the mobile pinged with a message, and it was from Anna, wishing her brother congratulations.

Jarrod jumped into the shower and took his time, lost in thought and trying to wash away the dirty feeling he had.

He could hear his phone ringing when he turned off the shower and rang back the missed number without checking who it was. The voice message he received when it wasn't answered said that this was Sjonni Pederson's mobile phone, the Gateshead managing director. He was probably on another call or still leaving a message for Jarrod. The phone then gave the beeps to suggest another call was coming through, and this time it was from the Darlington number he had in his phone. It was June.

"We have made contact with Gateshead to explain the

situation," she stated. "They will be contacting you to discuss."

"Yes," said Jarrod. "I've just missed a call there."

"Okay, ring them back," June said. "Hear what they have to say. Don't agree to anything, just give me a call back after you've spoken with them. As soon as they understand you have made the decision by yourself, you can leave it with us."

"What if they come back with a counter offer?" Jarrod asked.

"You will have to make that decision on your own. I'll wait to hear from you," she replied.

"Thanks, June," said Jarrod.

"Thanks." June hung up, giving Jarrod another five seconds of silence before continuing the ring-around.

"Jarrod," said Mr Pederson upon answering. "I've just left you a message, but I'm glad you called back straight away. Talk to me."

It was an incredibly open way of starting a conversation. Mr Pederson obviously knew what was happening after being a party to the conversation June had had with him or his contemporaries at Gateshead.

Jarrod felt that it was a way of trapping him into saying something he didn't really want to, even though he had always maintained a professional relationship with his managing director, and he had to think of a way to turn the conversation around.

"I'm assuming that June from Darlington has been in touch," he replied, almost tempted to put his tongue in his cheek.

"Yes," said Mr Pederson. "That is why I'm calling you back. You do understand what you are embarking on here could be deemed as a little underhanded. I wish you had talked with me first. I only saw you this morning."

"I appreciate that, Mr Pederson," said Jarrod. "This has been a sensitive situation from the start."

There was a moment of silence, Mr Pederson clearly expecting more.

"Have you ever had the feeling that the time is right?" asked Jarrod, unsure which way he was going to take this. "An exciting opportunity has arisen, and I've decided to take it."

Jarrod winced. That sounded like the sort of talk Mr Pederson would use when trying to convince a player to leave when an offer had come in, and the player wasn't keen on taking it.

"Jarrod," said Mr Pederson. "You have been our club captain for five seasons now, and we have enjoyed some great success with you. We have brought in some quality players to play alongside you. We have signed players to complement the way you play, and now you want to leave us. And leave us for a team in League Two. I must say I am shocked and a little upset."

"Mr Pederson," said Jarrod. "How can we make this as smooth as possible?"

That was a good move, Jarrod figured. Playing it as though there was no going back, no way of changing his mind.

"What will make this smooth is if you sign a one-year extension to your contract," countered Mr Pederson. "We can discuss terms right now."

This was not about money, so Jarrod responded to that effect:

"There is no need to sign contract extensions, Mr Pederson," said Jarrod. "What I need at this stage of my career is a challenge.

Whilst the challenge of getting Gateshead up into the Premier League is there, it is one that is getting a little long in the tooth."

"I'd like to think that we're making statements of intent this pre-season already," said Mr Pederson. "We've signed quality players. I'm offering you a new contract. We can work together and get that spot in the Premier League. We almost did it last year."

Mr Pederson was sounding excited, but it was failing to stir any enthusiasm in Jarrod.

"I wish you the best of luck with the season ahead, Mr Pederson," said Jarrod, trying not to sound condescending. "I have made the decision to join Darlington, and I would appreciate your help and guidance in making this move a positive for Gateshead Football Club and for Jarrod Black. Can I count on you?"

"Jarrod," said Mr Pederson, almost resigned. "We have to put a positive spin on a lot of things we don't like. This one is going to be a little tricky though. How can we justify letting our captain go with two years left on his contract? You realise we could keep you for those two years?"

Jarrod felt himself blushing. He knew what he was doing was not entirely ethical.

"Yes, I do," said Jarrod. "But we are all grown-ups here. We need to come to an arrangement and do this with minimal loss of face on both sides. Can I trust that we can work on this together amicably?"

There was a long pause, and some rustling of papers in the background from Mr Pederson's end. The phone then went muffled for a moment, Jarrod sure that a hand was being put over the receiver at the other end.

"Jarrod," said Mr Pederson after a while. "Is there nothing I can do?"

This was the last roll of the dice, and the fact he had repeated his name yet again made it quite definite.

"Mr Pederson," said Jarrod, with a soft sigh. "There is nothing you can do. My intention is to join Darlington."

"Okay," said Mr Pederson. "We've worked together very well over the years, I'm sure we can work together one last time to make this a positive move. Let me get our PR team onto it to get the fans on board."

"Thanks," said Jarrod, relieved and feeling his rosy cheeks calming down as the blood rushed from his face. "I will talk to June, and I thank you for your understanding."

"Darlington though," said Mr Pederson. "Darlington. Have you been to Darlington?"

"Yes I have," said Jarrod, matter-of-factly. "It's only down the road and it's actually quite a friendly place."

"I'm only pulling your leg," said Mr Pederson. "I know it is. Look, I'll be in touch later today, or someone will be. I'm going to give my friend Gerry a call. Hope your day goes well."

Mr Pederson hung up, managing to have had the last word and giving Jarrod something to ponder. The bugger! So he knows Gerry. And why wouldn't he?

Jarrod put his phone down on the bench and stood looking at his blurred reflection in the fridge door. His heart rate was well and truly up, and his body language was tense. He gave himself time to stand on his toes, give a deep breath, before his moment of meditation was punctuated by the phone ringing, yet again.

"Jarrod speaking."

"Hi Jarrod," came the cheery voice of June. "June here. Just a quick update."

"Yes," said Jarrod. "I've just got off the phone with Mr Pederson at Gateshead."

"Oh," said June, caught off guard as she was the one phoning to give the update. "Go on."

"I think we're good to go," said Jarrod. "He did offer a contract extension but I managed to steer him away from it and I'd say that he now knows this is happening."

"Good," said June. "Although I think Gerry might be on the phone with him right now. I'll keep you updated."

"Now," said Jarrod. "You had an update."

"Yes," said June. "I have a contract for you to sign, and we need to go through a medical procedure to make it official."

"I did a medical this morning," said Jarrod. "Can we use that?"

"Unfortunately not," said June. "We need to do this independently."

"Okay," said Jarrod. "Where and when?"

"We have our doctor available at short notice today," continued June. "So, it might be a good idea to come over to Feethams this afternoon. That way we can do the medical, walk you through the contract, and if we've got time, organise a media conference. Are you available to come over in an hour and a half?"

"Yes," said Jarrod, glancing at his watch. "I can be there at 3pm"

"Perfect," said June. "See you then. Usual entrance."

"See you soon," replied Jarrod, and ended the call, placing the phone on the benchtop.

He stood and opened the fridge, looked at it for a moment, before closing it again. He didn't know what to do with himself for a couple minutes, and sat down at the bench and leaned back, putting his hands on the back of his head and staring up at the ceiling.

That was enough to snap him into gear and he climbed the stairs to his bedroom and started to work out what to wear. He opted for a dark blue sports jacket, a crisp white shirt, and black jeans. A winning combo he had used several times in the past at official night-time functions. It wasn't too dressy and the jeans had some 'designer holes' as Aneka called them.

He left a scribbled message on the white board: 'At Darlington, might be back quite late.' That was to alert Marianne that he might not be around for the kids bedtime. He checked for his keys, wallet, phone, and skipped out the door with purpose.

He slid into the car, confidently negotiating the driveway in reverse before speeding off towards Darlington.

# Chapter Thirty:
## False

Jarrod strode into reception at Feethams and was immediately welcomed by June.

She called Gerry and a couple of other official-looking members of staff. They went through the next set of doors together and into a small room which had a partition, clearly another player on the other side of it getting a once over.

"Jarrod," said Gerry. "Thanks for making a brave choice."

"Thanks for giving me the opportunity," replied Jarrod.

"Dr Bhanu here will go through a swift medical process with you," said Gerry. "If you need anything just holler."

"Thanks." Jarrod nodded.

June walked out with Gerry, leaving the doctor to introduce himself and explain the procedure. Jarrod was asked to strip down to his underwear and sit on the side of a bed which the doctor pumped up to a height where he could easily manipulate Jarrod's legs.

He went through a series of tests on his knees and ankles and tested reflexes and asked Jarrod to tell him when his manipulations made a stretching sensation. This was followed by some heart monitoring on an ECG machine, before a five minute run on a treadmill and being hooked back up to the machine for some post-exercise monitoring.

Dr Bhanu didn't give any indication as to whether there were any issues, simply making notes on his clipboard. There was obviously someone going through exactly the same procedure on the other side of the partition, but Jarrod didn't catch a name. It might be Piotr.

Jarrod was all done before the patient on the other side, which made Jarrod come to the conclusion there was a medical being failed. The final requirement was a urine test, which Jarrod took some time to produce, having neglected to take on any extra fluids since the morning's activity. He was quick to point out he had taken a glass of red wine with lunch.

Time was ticking away, and it was four by now. Dr Bhanu thanked Jarrod for his time and let him get changed. Jarrod then walked out in to the corridor where June met him and took him back through the doors. They went around a corner to an office where Gerry sat with his two colleagues, reading through a document.

"Sit down, Jarrod," said Gerry. "June, you too."

"Everything okay?" asked Jarrod, sensing some edginess.

"Yes, yes," said Gerry. "We've got your contract as agreed with your agent Mr Leonard."

"Okay. I trust I will have time to speak with him to make sure it is all present and correct," said Jarrod.

"Yes," said Gerry. "Feel free to use the phone here. Dial zero to get a line. Truth is, Gateshead are dragging their feet at the moment. They haven't formally given us permission to talk to you yet, so we can't get the contract signed. You might have a few more hours."

"I see," said Jarrod. "Do I need to ring someone at Gateshead?"

"Nothing we can do to be honest," said Gerry. "June is in touch with the right people and they are taking their time. We'll leave you to make that call." They got up and walked out, closing the door behind them.

Jarrod chose to use his mobile phone instead of the phone that had been offered, as he had the number in memory. Mr Leonard answered after a few rings, Jarrod apologising for the time, and they walked through every page of the contract together, which made Jarrod feel at ease, knowing they were reading through the same document.

It took only five minutes. Mr Leonard left Jarrod with the instruction to use his own name where the 'Player's agent' name and signature were required as Mr Leonard was no longer officially a registered player agent. They ended the call cheerily and Jarrod was confident the contract was sound.

He got up and opened the door slightly to let those outside know he had finished his call, which prompted June to walk over and open it fully, beckoning Jarrod out in to the corridor.

"We've not heard anything from Gateshead," she said. "That might be it for tonight. Not much we can do until we get word from your current employers."

"That's a shame," said Jarrod. "I'll get myself home then. Call me if you need me to come in tomorrow."

"Yes," said June. "We will definitely be in touch as soon as we hear. Sorry we couldn't wrap this up tonight, and thanks for coming at short notice."

"It is what it is," said Jarrod. "Look forward to hearing from you tomorrow."

Jarrod walked past reception and courteously said goodbye to the receptionist before heading out to the warm early-evening air. He was home by five, and only just beat the rest of the family who were coming in after their day out and were full of chatter.

Aneka raced up to give her Dad a big cuddle. Jarrod picked her up and held her like a baby, enjoying the moment.

"Is everything done?" Marianne asked as she walked in, carrying an oversized handbag.

"Not quite yet," replied Jarrod. "Should be done tomorrow morning. Paperwork issues."

Marianne clapped her hands as Sebastian shaped to pick up his handheld computer, shooing him up the stairs and shouting, 'Shower, now!' while lunging at him to smack him playfully on the back of the legs.

The evening was like any other. Marianne prepared the evening meal for a change, stirring away at a Mornay for a good ten minutes, while Jarrod cast his eye over Sebastian's final homework for the year with him. Dinner done and books packed away, it was time to relax in front of the TV together while David Attenborough described the migration habits of the Monarch butterfly.

This was a time of week the whole family enjoyed, and once the show had finished, Marianne walked up the stairs with Sebastian to go through the tooth-brushing routine and Aneka was carried up by Jarrod, the whole family finding themselves in the bathroom all at once.

"Dad," said Aneka in that melodic way that tells you that a question is coming next.

"Yes, Aneka," said Jarrod.

"Which team do you play for now?" asked Aneka. That was a good question.

"I play for Gateshead," replied Jarrod. "But tomorrow I might be playing for a new team. Remember that place we went to for the day and you played on the field with the younger kids?"

"They were fun," said Aneka.

"That's where I might work tomorrow. I'll tell you when it's done."

Aneka was happy with the simplistic answers. She was asking the question knowing the answer anyway because she had been listening to Mum and Dad talk about it. Jarrod was at peace with himself. They put the kids to bed.

The evening had been idyllic, everyone was happy, everyone was content.

# Chapter Thirty-One: Intense

Jarrod had left his phone downstairs on charge when he and Marianne finally went to bed that night after watching three episodes of the latest Netflix series they were into at the time. He had also forgotten to switch on the dishwasher too, so that was running in the hope it would be ready in time to load up again with the breakfast dishes.

His phone beeped and there were messages, even at this early hour. The sun was beaming through the window and giving an almost religious feel to the kitchen. He picked up the phone, half knowing what to expect, but as it turned out there were even more messages than he had imagined.

One that stood out was Mark White, with a request to call him. There was also a message from Gateshead detailing the agenda for today's training session which was due to start in about five minutes. Jarrod was staying away. Mr Pederson had asked him late last night to steer clear until the matter was resolved. The excuse being used was that he was down with a cold.

He grabbed a two litre milk bottle from the fridge and poured half a glass, quite symbolic he thought to himself, as he wasn't sure what sort of mood he was going to be in today.

Sebastian was up next, and raring to go, always keen to get through the morning rush as fast as he could so he could have some relaxation time before the usual panic to get out the door. After getting a rough hug, perhaps a hangover of the previous night's rumblings, he poured himself some of the home brand cereal Marianne had insisted on buying, and sloshed the milk in with total abandon, leaving a puddle underneath his bowl.

Jarrod decided to tackle his messages sooner rather than later, picking up the phone and dialling Mark from the fanzine. He hadn't left on the best of terms that last time they spoke, and Jarrod felt up for a confrontation.

"Jarrod Black," said Mark, in a manner that suggested Jarrod was about to be accused of something, quite a confrontational way of starting the conversation.

"Yes, Mark," replied Jarrod. "What can I do for you?"

"I'm hearing some noise coming out of the club," said Mark. "Mixed messages if you will."

"Oh, yes?" said Jarrod, feeling the need to cough lightly to give the impression he was, indeed, sick. "You seemed to make your own mind up about me yesterday with that photo, so why do you need my viewpoint on anything?"

"Jarrod," he stuttered, obviously a little embarrassed. "We write about things we hear, and I want your input so that we don't end up publishing anything that is factually wrong."

"Right...?" replied Jarrod, waiting for a question.

"You are not at training this morning," stated Mark.

"That is correct," stated Jarrod.

"You are 'under the weather,'" Mark stated.

"Yes," said Jarrod.

"So will you be in tomorrow for training?" probed Mark.

"We'll have to see how I am tomorrow morning, Mark," said Jarrod. "Now, can I just take another call that's coming through? Nothing to see here."

"Okay, Jarrod." Mark sighed. "I'll not keep you any longer. Get well soon."

That last sentence was clearly designed to be sarcastic. Jarrod scowled as he ended the call.

Sebastian had run upstairs and was replaced by Aneka, peppering him with orders thinly veiled as polite questions. Jarrod got her cereal, a dish, and retrieved a spoon from the whirring dishwasher. He was just about to pour the cereal when the phone rang.

It was Mr Pederson, not really the person Jarrod was hoping to be ringing.

"Hello, Jarrod," he said cheerily. "We're nearly there."

"Is there some kind of hold up?" asked Jarrod.

"Actually, there is. I am duty bound to provide you with some information," he said.

Jarrod feeling puzzled at this stage. "Go on..." Jarrod offered.

"Upon contacting the FA to discuss your situation, the grapevine went into overdrive," he said. "We have had six enquiries this morning as to your availability for transfer. We already have two transfer bids for your services: one from the Premier League and one from China."

"How has this happened?" asked Jarrod.

"It's happened because you are a sought-after commodity, Jarrod," said Mr Pederson. "If it is now known you are set to leave Gateshead, you will now be the subject of offers and counter-offers from all manner of clubs."

"A sought-after commodity," repeated Jarrod. "But after this news breaks, damaged stock."

"Yes, that is an unfortunate by-product of this stupid process that the FA insist we go through in order to make transfer dealings transparent," said Mr Pederson. "Now, put your shoe on the other foot. Gateshead are being offered money for this transaction by a number of clubs, and you are asking us to let you go for nothing. How can this work?"

Jarrod's heart sank. He had been concerned that this scenario could play out, and it appeared to be coming to fruition.

"Mr Pederson," pleaded Jarrod. "How can we make this situation work?"

"Jarrod," retorted Mr Pederson. "If you want to play for Darlington that much, and Darlington want you to play for them that much, then you are going to need to instruct them to pay us a transfer fee comparable to what we have been offered."

"How am I going to know that those offers exist?" asked Jarrod, concerned at this predicament.

"I have no interest in ripping you or your new club off, Jarrod," said Mr Pederson. "I can assure you we are receiving enquiries this morning and you will most likely start to see this develop into something big very quickly."

Jarrod stood staring into space in the kitchen.

"I suggest you talk to your people, and be prepared," stated the almost smug Mr Pederson.

"Thanks for the heads up, Mr Pederson," said Jarrod, his heart beginning to beat slightly faster. He ended the call. This was the kind of situation, outside actual football, where Jarrod felt the least at ease - all eyes on him, difficult decisions having to be made and justification required for those decisions. He put his hands to his face and rubbed up and down, a way of waking himself up and re-booting to start the day in the right mind. This was going to be a rollercoaster.

"Daaaad," came the shout from upstairs. That was the starter's pistol, and he leapt up the stairs, clicking back into parent mode, his mind getting back on focus and back into the game.

Jarrod had ignored his mobile phone while getting the kids ready for school, and they had ended up leaving the house and getting to school in good time. Aneka wanted her Dad to come into the school gates, as he often did when they were early enough, but Jarrod waved them off instead at the drop-off near the gate, making sure they were in.

He walked back in the house to find Marianne down in the kitchen slowly getting into gear for her late start, taking the opportunity to give her a warm cuddle then made his way to the small office they had set up out the back. This was a space they rarely used and it was in fact quite a dumping ground for paperwork, but within a couple minutes he had cleared the desk and sat down to an iPad, a pad of paper, a pen, and began to survey the carnage on his phone.

08:15 MARK WHITE: 'Call me when you get a chance.'

08:17 DAD: missed call (3)

08:25 MANNY LEONARD : missed call

08:27 DFC : missed call

08:33 NIKOLAI TOPF: 'Something happening?'

08:45 JASON RHODES : missed call

08:47 Unknown number : missed call

08:55 Unknown number : 'Please call me ASAP. June.'

There were options where to start, and he started at the least appealing, but probably the one that would give him the most information about where he stood, and he surprised himself by calling Mark White.

"Jarrod Black," said Mark, quite shocked to be receiving the call. "I'm glad you called."

"What can I do for you, Mark?" asked Jarrod, unsure as to where this was going.

"How's your Chinese language skills?" he asked. "Guangzhou sound appealing?"

"What are you talking about?" asked Jarrod, becoming slightly impatient. "Is there something I don't know?"

There was a bit of shuffling from the other end of the phone, and then Mark continued, a little distant as if reading from his phone while he talked into it.

"Guangzhou Evergrande in for Black," said Mark. "Big play by big club to lure Jarrod Black to China to push for Champions League glory."

"Sounds interesting," said Jarrod truthfully, writing the name on his pad and getting the spelling totally wrong. "I've never been to China. Anything else I can help you with?"

"Are you leaving, Jarrod?" asked Mark outright.

"You just keep reading, Mark." With that, Jarrod ended the call and got back to his messages, another two having popped up while they had talked for that thirty seconds.

He rang Dad next. Marianne came in with a tiny coffee cup, the fresh aroma of strong black espresso wafting in with her. She placed it down and offered a wink, as Jarrod already had the phone pressed to his ear waiting for the answer.

"Hello?" came an excited Dad on the other end of the line.

"Dad!" said Jarrod, sensing the excitement.

"This is more like it, Jarrod," continued Dad. "Chinese Super League or Leicester in the Premier League. Two big opportunities! Which one sounds best?"

"Dad, I've just dropped the kids at school," said Jarrod." I'm just catching up on all this. I've got no idea what's the latest rumours doing the rounds, but I'm aware there are offers and enquiries."

"Mr Leonard called me half an hour ago," said Dad. "He's been getting calls this afternoon."

"I see," said Jarrod. "I'd better give him a call."

"He's playing football at the moment," said Dad. "Kick off was at six. I'd give him an hour, by the time he's all done."

"Right," said Jarrod, doing the maths with the time difference. "I'll speak with him later."

"So, what are you thinking?" asked Dad.

"I'm thinking how I'm going to get through today," said Jarrod dramatically.

"You'll be right," said Dad. "Go and make some good decisions. Call me if you need me, but I'll be thoroughly biased to where the big money is!"

"Righto," said Jarrod, chuckling. "Speak soon." He ended the call and wrote Leicester City on his pad.

Next he flicked a text reply to Nikolai: 'Not sure. What do you know?'

The next call was to Darlington. The receptionist replied and he recognised her voice as the pretty brunette but couldn't remember her name. She announced her name, Keira, as part of her practiced welcome. He asked to speak with June, and Keira put him through in her cheery melodic voice which gave him a bit of cheer in his tone when June answered.

"June," said Jarrod, when he heard the hold music abruptly halt.

"No, it's Gerry. June's just out for five minutes. Jarrod, how are you today?" asked the Darlington owner in his commanding voice.

"Good, good," said Jarrod, and then after a slight pause. "Well, to be honest, I don't know!"

"We've never talked about a transfer fee have we?" said Gerry.

"No," admitted Jarrod. "That was not something I had even considered."

"Well," said Gerry excitedly. "We have funds. We're not going to offer any silly money, but we're going to offer something that would effectively buy out your contract."

"Right," said Jarrod slowly. "Keep going..."

"We'll need you to offer your resignation to Gateshead," said Gerry.

"They'll not take it," said Jarrod.

"That's right," said Gerry. "When they don't, you will ask them if you can buy out the final two years of your contract."

"That would be crazy," said Jarrod.

"That would force them to give us a figure to work with," said

Gerry. "Besides, they would get nothing for you in the final year of your contract anyway. So, it's more like buying out a one year contract."

"Is this normal?" asked Jarrod.

"Not really," said Gerry. "But if you want to come here, and I think you do despite all the talk that's starting to happen, then that's your option."

"Okay. Let me make some calls. Thanks, Gerry."

Jarrod had made some scribbles on his pad as he had talked with Gerry, and decided he needed a little official assistance. The number for the PFA was in his phone, and he made the call, eventually speaking with a liaison officer, Victor, who he had communicated with the previous season over a matter of bullying at Gateshead. Victor was amazing.

They went through the scenario together, even getting other members of the PFA involved in the discussion, and they quickly came to the conclusion that this was in fact a viable method to force the hand of Jarrod's current employer to negotiate fairly with Jarrod's potential new employer.

The half hour discussion gave him enough tools to be able to steer himself through the situation, and he had made three pages of notes, underlining the key action points where decisions had to be made. He thanked Victor for his time and was asked to keep the PFA informed along the way. Jarrod was feeling confident.

Without delay, he was straight on the phone with Gateshead, eventually talking directly to Mr Pederson who, as expected, turned down his resignation and, as if reading from the same rule book as the PFA, agreed to work with his contracts team to get a figure for buying out the final two years of his contract.

The time frame was one hour. Nothing would happen until then.

Marianne sensed Jarrod was off the phone and popped her head around the door. She blew him a kiss and Jarrod smiled as she made her way out and off to the golf club for her 11am start.

His phone pinged with a message from Nikolai: 'Lots of talk. Deflects away from me. Talking to Twente this afternoon. Exciting!'

This made Jarrod smile - he wasn't going through this alone. It was perhaps now time to have a look at what was brewing online, and the internet page that opened when he turned on the iPad was the Evening Chronicle website. The headline thankfully showed Newcastle United news at the top, pushing his breaking story into second place.

That damned photo of Jarrod looking disinterested was used, and there was mention of China, Leicester, Ipswich Town, and even Osasuna in Spain, as being candidates for his signature, and not one mention of Darlington.

This was going to be some coup for them if they could pull it off, and Jarrod already had a sense of excitement at the prospect. Jarrod had a flick through some other websites, the Heed not updated since yesterday, the Shields Gazette having pretty much the same story as the Chronicle, and the BBC simply having a two-liner about Guangzhou's interest.

Jarrod's phone rang. It was Mr Leonard.

"Jarrod, how are you?" asked Mr Leonard in a business-like manner.

"Good," said Jarrod. "I missed your call earlier."

"Yes," said Mr Leonard. "I just need to know where things

are at. I've had some calls this evening from agents asking about you, and I want to set them straight."

"What have you been telling them?" asked Jarrod.

"Nothing as yet," said Mr Leonard. "But if you want me to stoke the fire and start a feeding frenzy, say the word."

"No. I've offered my resignation to Gateshead," said Jarrod.

"And they declined your offer," said Mr Leonard. "Now you're getting a figure to settle the remainder of your contract. Risky."

"In what sense," asked Jarrod.

"Well..." Mr Leonard stated. "If they still say no, then you'll become a piece of meat being tossed around on a very hot barbeque until someone you don't like gobbles you up."

Jarrod winced at the very crude analogy but appreciated the picture it painted.

"I'm confident of a resolution," said Jarrod. "They're not bad people at Gateshead."

"Sure," said Mr Leonard. "But business is business."

"Understood," said Jarrod. "I'll keep you in the loop. Oh. How did you go tonight?"

"Tonight?" asked Mr Leonard, unsure of his questioning but then realising he knew he had been playing. "Ah, yes. A come from behind victory in the Over 45s comp against the top team. We'll sign you up in a few years. Take care Jarrod."

He was just about to launch into another internet search when the phone sounded again. This time it was Mr Pederson.

"Hello, Jarrod," he stated, by way of confirming it was Jarrod he was talking with.

Jarrod responded with a curt, 'yes.'

"We've got a figure for you as you asked. Two years at your current salary, rounded down to 2.8 million pounds."

"2.8 million. Right," said Jarrod, hardly able to contain his shock at the size of the figure. "Let me get on to Darlington and see what transpires."

"Before you go," said Mr Pederson. "Can I make a final plea?"

"I'll give you the opportunity," said Jarrod, almost cringing at his own words as he was in no place to hold the high ground.

"Stay at Gateshead and we'll make you part of our coaching team at the end of the two years. We can get that in writing now in a contract and get you on the courses straight away."

"Interesting," said Jarrod. "But, I'm already part way through my licence - I've been doing it independently for the past year with one of the local clubs."

"Oh," said Mr Pederson. "Been moonlighting?"

"Gateshead has even given me time away from duties to do it. Hasn't anyone filled you in?" Jarrod exclaimed.

"Clearly not." Mr Pederson sounded annoyed, before changing his tactic. "Have you had any contact with the supporters?"

"Minimal," said Jarrod. "I'm getting a sense there's going to be more changes besides me."

"Jarrod," said Mr Pederson. "We were hoping to build a team to get us into the Premier League. Doesn't that excite you?"

"I am excited for you, Mr Pederson," said Jarrod. "I just don't think I'm really part of the grand plan." Before Mr Pederson could interject, Jarrod finished off, "I'll take your figure to Darlington and they will be in touch. Thanks for your time."

Jarrod felt he had burnt that bridge now, and any olive branch had been well and truly snapped. He now had an eagerness and phoned June straight away and quoted the figure to which she gave a whistling sound. It was obviously higher than anticipated. June thanked Jarrod for helping out in the matter and said she would be in touch by midday.

Jarrod called Nikolai after his name came up on the Heed website. He answered immediately.

"Wow. Were you sitting by the phone?" asked Jarrod.

"Waiting for a call from the club to give me permission to talk with FC Twente," said Nikolai. "I bet you've been on the phone all morning."

"How did you guess?" asked Jarrod, smiling. "I have never known it ring so hot. The phone is actually physically hot in my hand. Any concrete offer on the table?"

"My agent tells me there's a three year deal," said Nikolai. "That's all hearsay at the moment. Gateshead needs to give the green light. Next thing I'll put in a transfer request, I guess. What about you?"

"Bubbling away," said Jarrod. "It is not as easy as it should be."

"Hang in there, Jarrod," said Nikolai. "I've got a call. I'll catch you later."

"Go, go, go," said Jarrod as the call cut off.

There was a spare moment for Jarrod to head to the toilet, after realising he had been busting for the best part of an hour, and on the way back he grabbed a glass of water and gulped it down. It was a welcome break. With the clock ticking towards midday, he noticed he had been in the office for more time than he had ever spent in there.

June called. She was speaking almost breathlessly. She explained he had to get on to Gateshead as soon as he could as it was possible they had finally reached an agreement. She explained Gateshead had negotiated, or at least Gerry had negotiated with Mr Pederson, and that the figure agreed was within the realms of possibility, if not probability. This could be it.

Jarrod thanked June and immediately called Gateshead and got connected through straight away to Mr Pederson.

"Jarrod," started Mr Pederson. "We're going to miss you, my friend."

"Mr Pederson," replied Jarrod, feeling a wobble in his voice and a lump in his throat for the first time as he talked. "I can't express my thanks enough to you. I have been at the club for my whole career and I have only ever had a good working relationship with you."

"There is still plenty more to do, Jarrod," said Mr Pederson. "I'll put you back on to reception and they can organize a time for you to come in later this afternoon and we can sign the cancellation of your contract. You can also return anything that belongs to us, and you can collect anything from here that belongs to you, we'll leave that to you. I'll put you through."

"Thanks so much," said Jarrod, and the hold music took him by surprise.

The receptionist came on the line with a time slot and they agreed on a 3pm meeting. The contract termination document would also be sent via email to Mr Leonard in Sydney. The call was then hastily ended.

Jarrod immediately called June back and explained what had just happened and he could hear her slap the desk at the other end of the line before exclaiming, "Excellent!"

June agreed that Gerry and Gary would meet with Jarrod later in the day and they would arrange a press conference for 6pm, before which there would hopefully be time to complete any paperwork and make the move official before announcing the transfer.

He had to be there by 5.30pm at the latest and realised he had some work to do before then and also needed to get some food into him before too long.

Jarrod went straight upstairs and got his Gateshead branded hold-all and started to fill it with unused branded Gateshead gear. He then took most of them back out, thinking he could find a home for them with friends, family, and keep some as souvenirs.

There were a few things he would definitely give back - a set of scales from four or five years ago he never used, a Garmin watch lent to him by one of the coaches, and a laptop from a few years back used exclusively for Gateshead material, but pretty much rendered obsolete from the day he got it. He put playing gear, boots, and merchandise into the one bag.

Next he started looking through his paperwork in the office. There was a whole series of training manuals he had been given last year for Train the Trainer course, and the trophy from last season's Wearside Cup he had ended up with at the end of the night after the reserves had overcome Shildon in the final. He did sift through his contracts and pulled out the latest written copy then made a point of logging into his email to check that the contract termination notice had been sent through to Mr Leonard, and, like all paperwork from these transfer dealings to date, it was there as promised.

He had a quick read. It was quite a lengthy document, and Jarrod printed it out after losing his place halfway through the first page. Once the fifth and final page had appeared from the printer he picked it up and read it from start to finish. This all made sense, and the majority of the text dealt with confidentiality and confirmation of cessation of insurances. It was all very detailed and covered many more topics than he had thought it would.

Nothing sprung out as ambiguous or unreasonable, and Jarrod placed it in a clear folder and took it with him to the front door where he had started to pile up things to take. He took five minutes out to make himself a coffee, foregoing the real coffee machine in favour of an instant hit from the kettle, the smell filling the air with memories of mornings back in Sydney.

He dialled Marianne to say hello, and to check in after an emotionally draining morning, but her phone went straight to voice mail. She would be back in time to get the kids from school, so there was no drama, he just wanted some reassurance from someone who was on his side.

A message pinging on his iPad then tempted Jarrod into a browse of the day's football news, and straight up was a story linking Gateshead to 31-year-old England midfielder Jackson Porteous, and there was a strong chance he would be making the move. It quoted Nigel saying, 'he will do everything he can to persuade the quality player to the International Stadium,' and Gateshead were, 'ready for an assault on the automatic promotion spots.'

Jarrod found himself impressed by Gateshead's audacity in trying to sign Porteous, and likened it to Darlington trying to sign him, but the wheels could have been in motion ages ago and this was only just coming to fruition now. In fact, this could have been the signing that would lead to him being pushed out of the club anyway.

Jarrod's point of view was swaying along with his level of anxiety and seeing the pile of things he was taking took him closer to the realisation that this was the end. The phone rang and it was the Gateshead receptionist again, telling Jarrod they were sending a car over to pick him up, the stadium having become quite busy with press. Jarrod had a glance in the mirror and quickly dashing back upstairs to change his shirt that had a dribble of coffee down the front.

The car was out the front as he raced back down the stairs, almost slipping, which gave him a fright and slowed him down. He'd definitely be damaged stock if he took a tumble now. The driver knocked on the door and he recognised him as Jack, from times when he had been picked up to go to the airport for a few away games and gave him a friendly handshake, before asking him to help him load up the car with the items by the door.

When they were done Jarrod did a quick check around the house, making sure the doors and windows were closed and the heating was off - his mind had been elsewhere all day and he was conscious he needed to check the basics - before dashing to the car and climbing in the passenger seat beside Jack. He was accustomed to riding in the front as opposed to the back seat as Jarrod's house was the third or fourth stop before the airport and the passenger seat was usually not taken - over time it became habit to sit up front.

Jack was surprisingly quiet on the short trip to the International Stadium as if he had been briefed that this was something serious. Jarrod continued to scan his phone for news; nothing dramatically different appearing in the ten minute drive. As they turned into the car park, Jack made sure the lightly-tinted windows were up as he made his way slowly through the public car park to the staff car park, where he parked in such a way that Jarrod would get straight out of his side and into the stadium out of sight of any onlookers.

Jack instructed Jarrod he would bring all the items in for him. Jarrod thanking him before reaching back for the contract termination, taking a deep breath and bundling out of the car, through the open door into the area behind reception. He spied Jenny who gave him a smile, and beckoned him over to enter Mr Pederson's office, where he sat with Nigel and two other people in sharp suits who were reading through a document together.

Jarrod gave a cough to announce his arrival and Mr Pederson looked up and smiled before getting to his feet and offering his arms out, to pull Jarrod in for a fatherly hug.

"That's where the trophy got to," he said, lifting the Wearside Cup out of Jarrod's hand, checking it for dents. "The engraving place was asking what had happened to it."

"Ah, yes, sorry about that," said Jarrod. "It was quite a big night after the game and the boys asked me to hold on to it when I went home as it was getting a bit messy."

Nigel quickly walked out with papers in his hands without saying a word.

"Meet our new contracts management team, Jason and Dennis," he said. The two men stood up, shaking Jarrod's hand each with a curt, professional smile, Jarrod having no idea which was which. "We had better get on with this."

The taller of the two men sat back down and moved the majority of the paperwork to one side while the other brought out a folder from his case and opened it, revealing the same document Jarrod had in his hand.

Jarrod half expected Mr Pederson to try to convince him again, but there was none of that and Mr Pederson offered him a seat next to his own and the taller of the two men started to go through the document, Jarrod following on his own copy with Mr Pederson sharing.

The process took just over five minutes, there were initials to put on each page, a signature and date required on one of the pages regarding insurances and then at the end was a page for both parties to sign, Jarrod signing first and Mr Pederson smoothly gliding the document his way and signing underneath.

They caught each other's eyes after that and both smiled, Jarrod unsure as to what that meant, but he hoped it was a warm show of affection and respect for each other.

"Thank you, Mr Pederson," said Jarrod, after an awkward pause. "Thank you for helping make this happen."

"Jarrod," said Mr Pederson. "You are clearly a man of principle and I wish you every success in the future. Good luck at Darlington and say hello to Gerry for me."

They shook hands, Jarrod made a point of shaking the others' hands, before striding back into the open area behind reception which was buzzing with activity.

Jenny was there, talking with two young players, but Jarrod walked up to her anyway, Jenny ushering the two players off to their intended destination as she turned to face Jarrod. He put her arms on his shoulders, which was quite a reach for her, and smiled.

"Congratulations on the move, Jarrod," said Jenny. "We've had you here at the club so long it's going to be odd without you here."

"I'll definitely miss you," said Jarrod sincerely. After all Jenny had looked after him when he was a youth player, had been with him when he made his debut, had helped him when he was injured, and had been a confidante on many occasions. "I'll not be a stranger."

"Okay," said Jenny, nodding solemnly. "Jack will take you back home, unless you've got other business to take care of here. Nigel is out with the reserve team."

"Sure. Thanks," said Jarrod. He reached in and gave Jenny a kiss on the cheek. He turned and caught the eye of Jack who got to his feet.

"Jack! See you out the front," stated Jarrod.

He decided to head out the front door instead, stopping for small talk with the receptionists and having a quick read of the back page of the Journal before Jack turned up outside. He opened the front door and was immediately surrounded by flashing cameras and reporters with phones thrust in his face. He didn't say a thing and calmly edged his way to the car where Jack had opened the passenger side door. Jarrod climbed in, closed the door, making sure he didn't catch any reporters' hands, and Jack screeched off quickly.

"You're leaving aren't you?" said Jack, breaking his professional code.

"I just did," said Jarrod. "I just did."

Jack nodded and kept his eyes on the road. Jack was in a position where he saw a lot of goings on around town, and he may have even been ferrying players to and from the International Stadium all week for contract talks and medicals, Jarrod would never know.

"Well, you've timed it well," said Jack.

# Chapter Thirty-Two:
# Done

They continued in silence to Jarrod's house, where Jarrod jumped out and waved off his driver and raced back into the house to fetch his car keys.

He plugged his phone in to charge in the car before slowly reversing up the drive and into the street. The kids would be back any moment but he was keen to be on his way so he wouldn't be held up and could continue on his own timetable.

The fuel gauge was touching empty, so he decided the first stop would be the petrol station and took a slight detour in the opposite direction to the one where he could use his receipt from the supermarket to get 4p off a litre. After all, he was unemployed now. The pumps were quite slow, and the lady on the opposite side had just started filling up when she caught sight of Jarrod.

"Eeeh, hello Jarrod," she screeched.

"Hello there," he replied, smiling politely, unsure as to whether he should know her.

"Big Gateshead fan, I am," she said. "Just you wait there. I'll have to get an autograph."

They both continued filling up and she finished first, quickly striding around the car to get a pen and a programme and bound over to Jarrod who had just put the petrol cap back on.

"Can you sign my programme?" she asked. It was a programme from the Wembley final in May.

"Sure thing," he said. "I'll write something for you. What's your name?"

"I'm Kathy," she replied. "Oh, wait. Can you make it out to my son Calum? That's one 'l' in Calum."

They walked over to pay together, Jarrod thinking as he went, and just before they got there he started to write: 'Follow your dreams Calum. I have followed mine. All the best. Jarrod Black.'

After they had both paid, Jarrod asked her for her phone and they did a quick selfie, then Jarrod asked the attendant to take one for them, making sure the background was a flashy car outside, instead of the confectionary aisle. They walked over to their respective cars and said goodbye, Kathy absolutely beaming. She was still sitting in her car tapping furiously away at her phone as Jarrod drove off.

He had two missed calls since he had stepped out of the car, Mark White clearly keen to get hold of him, and Jarrod decided to ignore him, even when a text came through asking if he had met Jackson Porteous today.

The journey took him past the Angel of the North and down the A1, about a 55 minute drive in total with a little hold up with rush hour underway. Marianne had finally been in touch by text asking if he knew where Seb's basketball shoes were, which again he ignored guiltily, and resisted the urge to call Australia.

No. He was going to do this unaided. As he turned into the Darlington Arena car park, he noticed there was a flurry of reporters out front, some of which he had seen just before at Gateshead. He found a park easily, not too close to the throng, and coolly walked over to the main door. Once one of the reporters had spotted him, they all turned, some of them rushing over, some of them waiting patiently by the doorway. Jarrod pointed at one of them and gave them a puzzled face.

"Didn't I just see you an hour ago?" he asked, jokingly, before continuing smoothly through the pack and making his way through to the reception area.

He recognised one of the receptionists from the last time he had come, said hello and asked to see June. The receptionist offered him a seat in the waiting area away from the door so the press could not see him and made the necessary call for someone to come and greet Jarrod.

His heart was starting to beat quite fast and he definitely had nerves.

June walked around the corner and offered her hand to Jarrod, which he shook firmly with a smile and she led the way, thanking Jarrod for being so prompt and explaining what was about to happen in detail. They walked into the office that Gerry had made his own and Gerry got to his feet with a cheer and they shook hands.

"This is great news, Jarrod," said Gerry. "Let's get the business over and done with first. Can I get you a drink of anything? Tea, coffee, water?"

"I'll get a water, please," said Jarrod, and Gerry himself went out of the room and brought in a glass of water while June sat Jarrod down and started to go through the contract.

"You've already been through the contract I take it," said Gerry as he placed the glass down at an appropriate distance from the paperwork.

"Yes, I have," said Jarrod. "It's just a case of signing it. Let me just check it."

Jarrod took the time to compare the copy he was signing with the copy he had, and it appeared to match in every way, the pages and paragraphs lining up on each page. June and Gerry stood there watching him for a minute before Jarrod asked where he needed to sign. June instructed him to initial each page and then there was space for his signature in two places on the final page, and one space for June to fill in her details.

"All done," she said, and left the room, handing the contract to a colleague to be scanned and sent to the relevant authorities. She came back a moment later and continued, "We now have to register your signing with the Football League, and we should have an acknowledgement in five or ten minutes - they've fully automated their system this year. It's very efficient."

"No more fax machines then?" asked Jarrod, alluding to a famous story where the fax machine was out of paper at the FA on deadline day.

"No more fax machines..." said June.

"I'll take you to meet a couple of people," said Gerry and ushered Jarrod along with him.

"No," June interrupted. "We still need to prepare for the press conference. It's on at five-thirty and it's nearly five now." June left the room to pop her head around the corner and ask another colleague to come in.

"This is Mal," said June, introducing the smartly dressed man who had breezed into the room. "Mal is our media liaison officer and will give you a few pointers for today's press conference."

Jarrod and Mal shook hands and sat down at the desk side by side with a blank sheet of paper in front of them. Mal started to write and wrote out the sequence of events for the press conference. There was an introduction and thanks from Gerry, a description of the events leading up to the signing from interim manager Gary, who would be sitting alongside Jarrod, and then an opportunity for Jarrod to say a few words before the floor was opened up for questions.

Jarrod suggested what he might say, Mal instructing him to keep off the subject of Gateshead and focus on Darlington, as this was a Darlington news event. Jarrod practiced his speech twice. The first time Mal interjected and corrected Jarrod's flow, the second time Jarrod delivered it unhindered. Mal smiled and nodded as if to give it the green light.

Mal then went through a set of increasingly difficult questions that would come up from the press, giving a suggested answer where Jarrod was lost for an answer, and again steering the answers towards his new club. While this was going ahead, there was quite a lot of movement in the corridor outside and a murmur coming from around the corner.

It was almost time. Gary walked in and greeted them both.

"Jarrod," said Gary. "We're ready to go. Mal, thanks for coming in at short notice."

Gary turned to walk out, Jarrod moving alongside, and June looked them both up and down to see if there was anything out of place or not right with their clothing, pulling Gary's sleeves down on his suit jacket to make them even and brushing off a few hairs from Jarrod's shirt.

They both left the room and walked the few metres along the corridor to the media suite, where they appeared from behind a wall on to a slightly raised stage. Jarrod was surprised there were no photographs being taken, only a single video camera trained on the stage with the warm lights beaming almost in their faces. The press sat in individual seats with flip down tables, ones he had seen before in a school museum. The thirty or so reporters all seemed to sit up straight at the arrival of the official party and the murmur stopped.

As Gary and Jarrod were taking their seats, Gerry strode in to the main part of the room, past the waiting press and on to the stage and stood next to his manager and new signing. He thanked the press for being in attendance and asked them to have patience and only ask questions when invited. He even gave a practiced spiel about where the exits and toilets were located, before introducing his manager Gary and retreating behind the table to take his seat.

Gary explained that the club had exciting news. They had secured the signature of high profile player Jarrod Black and their new marquee signing would be a statement to the Football League that Darlington were not going take their sudden promotion lightly.

There were raised eyebrows from the press and fervent typing on phones to relay the news to their respective headquarters. A slight hum filled the room. Gary paused nicely for effect.

Jarrod gave a one minute statement of his delight in signing for the club, his desire to help Darlington establish themselves in League Two, and that his family was looking forward to the next chapter in their lives. Jarrod was talking with an excited tone and sounded genuinely happy.

Gerry then invited the press to ask questions, and they did so in classroom style; hands going up and Gerry inviting the first journalist to ask his question. The journalists introduced themselves with name and publication before asking a question. This was from the Northern Echo and directed at Gary.

"Is this the first of many major signings, Gary?" Gary quickly redirected the question to Gerry, who deftly answered diplomatically without really giving an answer. This gave birth to a few other questions along the same line, which Gerry answered impeccably, allowing Gary and Jarrod to relax and afford themselves a smile.

A question was then asked about transfer fee, which again

Gerry answered, letting the press know the two clubs came to an agreement over transfer fee and the fee would be officially 'undisclosed.' A question was then asked directly to Jarrod.

"Brian Toley, Chronicle Live. Jarrod, this comes as a surprise after you were linked with moves to the Premier League and overseas. Can you give us a reason why you chose to move down two divisions instead?"

Jarrod paused and Mal's instructions aligned in his head.

"This is an exciting time at Darlington," he said. "This is an opportunity to build something special and the two gentlemen to my right have made this possible. As you can appreciate, the ability to influence the future of this club on the pitch is the main reason for my decision."

This last sentence inferred he was not going to take the dollars and sit on the bench. Jarrod thought he had delivered it well.

"Mark Priest, Shields Gazette. Gateshead are building for another promotion push. Are you disappointed to be leaving that behind?"

Jarrod thought for a moment, trying to think of a way to start this off.

"The challenges at Darlington are now my primary focus. Next month's away match at Accrington is what I will now be concentrating on."

Jarrod winced at his less than ideal wording and would have liked to thank Gateshead but felt he had answered well enough. Plus, he had studied the fixture list over the last few days and was pleased to have added some knowledge to his answer.

Gerry fielded another three questions, Jarrod sitting back

listening to Gary and Gerry expertly answering them, before Gerry glanced at June who had appeared in the doorway behind the journalists and calmly thanked the press for being in attendance and invited them to remain in the media suite if they needed time.

Jarrod was first to stand up, Gary and Gerry taking their time and they left all together behind the wall and back in to the corridor where June had repositioned herself and guided them along and out on to the pitch.

A table was waiting with a selection of Darlington playing kit. Jarrod cast off his shirt and donned the home shirt. He was then handed a ball. He put the ball down and dribbled it over to the sideline and made a point of placing his hand on the pristine grass.

The club photographer then started to guide him into several different poses with and without the ball, with a scarf, and with another home shirt that already had his name on it and his cherished number eight.

Jarrod felt immensely proud at this moment and his chest was puffed right out, so much so that the photographer asked him to relax a little. Once the session was over, the press were invited to take photos, instructed only to take upper body shots. Jarrod repeated some of the poses for them before June wrapped it up and ushered the press back into the main stand.

Some squealing then came from the doorway. It was Aneka, followed closely by Sebastian who ran straight for their Dad. Aneka jumped into his arms and Sebastian went in for a hug, the club photographer taking a barrage of snaps of this golden moment. Marianne breezed in.

"Surprise!" she said and walked over for a kiss. "Bet you weren't expecting us here."

"I'm gobsmacked," said Jarrod. "How did you know this was all happening?"

"Your Dad," said Marianne. "He's been hounding me all day for news and I made a couple calls and found out you were here."

The photographer asked them to stand for a family portrait. The camera fired off a barrage of shots, all four of them standing with beaming faces. Jarrod Black had arrived.

# Chapter Thirty Three: Breathe

It was a warm Saturday morning. Jarrod and the family were just leaving Darlington after visiting a high school open day where they had met with the headmaster to discuss Sebastian starting year 7 in a couple years.

The accent on sport had really given Jarrod a good feeling, and Sebastian was giving off vibes he really wanted to go there after being 'buttered up' by the headmaster. Jarrod appeared to take a wrong turn and ended up in the countryside, passing under what was presumably the main route North and heading off through farmland on a road seeming to be heading in the wrong direction. Marianne finally caught on and asked where they were going.

"I've seen this house for sale," said Jarrod. "It's open for inspection this morning."

The kids gave a mysterious 'oooh,' while Marianne smiled. They came to a tiny village with several old stone houses, some whitewashed buildings, and tall hedges.

A sign pointed them off to the left and they took what looked like a driveway in past an opening to a grand old house built of stone with modern white windows that had a For Sale sign proudly in front. The front door was open and there were people in the back garden.

Sebastian and Aneka raced to the door, where the estate agent was standing ready to greet them. They waited impatiently for Marianne and Jarrod to catch up before they went in.

The modern twist on the interior and the wide open living

room that led to a covered outdoor area was simply breath-taking. The kids raced to head outside into the huge garden. Marianne took a peek in the kitchen, Jarrod choosing to stay by the door, observing his wife and kids to gauge their reactions before heading upstairs to see the bedroom layout. It was exciting.

Marianne joined him then the kids came upstairs and they all sat on the balcony of the main bedroom on a bench strategically placed to get the best view. This was magnificent.

They were due at Cath and Chris' place, their friends from school, for a late lunch, so they couldn't stick around for long, and Jarrod had to be back in Darlington by five for the first pre-season friendly of the new season, a good test against York City of the National League.

There was a bit of driving involved today, and Jarrod knew he would be heading back to Darlington alone as the kids would be loving spending school holiday time with their school pals and Marianne and Cath were lethal together, able to hold conversation for hours on end.

Dad called as Jarrod was driving back down the A1 after leaving the party and picking up his playing kit from home.

"Gidday, son," said Dad, sounding very relaxed.

"Dad, just heading down to Darlington for my debut," said Jarrod.

"That's great," said Dad. "I'm so pleased everything has worked out for you. Did I did tell you that Anna got the call up for the Matildas?"

"No way," said Jarrod. "She's back in after all these years?"

Jarrod was alluding to the fact that Anna had flirted with the national team in her early twenties but had been overlooked ever since she suffered an Achilles rupture some six or seven years ago. Jarrod was as proud as a big brother could possibly be and delighted with the news.

"When's the game? I'll see if I can find it on TV," asked Jarrod.

"Game's on Tuesday night, she flew out of Sydney on Thursday," said Dad. "They're playing an Asian Cup qualifier in Dubai."

"Fantastic," said Jarrod. "I've just arrived. Better get my game face on."

"Aye sure," said Dad. "Good luck tonight."

"Thanks, catch you soon, and big hug to Mum."

The Arena was looking resplendent in the late afternoon sunshine. The York City team bus was parked outside in the main carpark; the opposition already here.

Jarrod parked nearby and trotted with purpose to the entrance with his boot bag tucked under his arm, catching up to one of his new teammates who was chatting with a stadium worker.

Jarrod already felt at home here and gave his teammate, fellow midfielder Gavin Selley, a warm handshake and they walked in together sharing football small-talk. Jarrod couldn't help but compare this whole experience to his time at Gateshead and even at Carlisle. The professional edge to the whole place, with its pristine white walls adorned with spectacular shots of local landmarks, was giving him the sense of occasion that today merited.

Greeting the rest of his teammates as he walked into the dressing room, saying hi to Gary and exchanging some tactics, making sure he went out of his way to say hello to everyone he passed - it was all familiar, but it was also very new.

Pulling on the predominately white shirt was all too familiar too. Darlington's new shirts for the season were strikingly similar to a Gateshead shirt from two years ago and were made by the same company. Gary gave a team talk before they went on to the field to warm-up.

Once they were heading out there, it was clear that playing football here was going to be an amazing experience, with the closeness to the pitch making the likelihood of a great atmosphere if things were going well.

Just as he ran on to the field he looked to his left and checked his stride, almost tripping as his brain took over his body.

There was Dad!

He raced over and gave him a big hug over the fence, visibly shocked.

"Surprise!" said Dad.

"I thought you sounded a bit strange on the phone before," said Jarrod. "There was an extra delay. What are you doing here?"

Some of the fans around them cottoned on to what was happening.

"What do you think?" said Dad. "I flew over with Anna to Dubai and continued on to Newcastle. I've got to see my wee laddie play his first game."

"That's amazing," said Jarrod, before grappling him into a hug again.

"I'll be heading back to Dubai on Monday, so we've got tomorrow to catch up. Off you go and warm-up," said Dad, with misty eyes and a slight wobble to his voice.

Jarrod sprinted out on to the field. A cheer went up and fans gave him some warm applause. Joining his teammates for a warm-up, he was scarcely able to contain his excitement.

Although he wasn't to know it yet, Jarrod had just made the best move of his career.

# Acknowledgements

Thanks to Fair Play Publishing, Jarrod Black now has a home via Popcorn Press. This book began as a whimsical idea during the winter of 2012, and over a seven year journey it has finally emerged as the completed article and the start of a series. Hopefully the result is a few hours of enjoyment for the reader and an appetite for more.

I would like to give a shout out to everyone who has come along the footballing journey with me and given fuel for writing football fiction. Starting at right back in a successful Chantry Middle School team, the King Edward VI School team then played me as a wide midfielder, and this continued in junior football at Morpeth Villa and the battlers at Morpeth Rangers. A two year hiatus was ended when signing for Telemecanique in the Western suburbs of Paris as a striker, also enjoying a season at La Courneuve with the international Paris Gaels team in 1994. Moving to Stafford Uni for a double-winning season and trialling as centre back for the GB team for the World Student Games, another three year break was ended when signing for Gladesville Ravens in Sydney. After over ten years paroling the midfield with the black and whites, the temptation was too strong and local club West Ryde Rovers secured my signature on my 40th birthday.

From the goalscoring feats of Michael Whale, an unbelievable central defensive partnership with Si Bonham and the sublime skills of Sjonni Runarsson, you've all had a hand in shaping the footballing landscape of someone who absolutely loves the game.

# Want some more really good football books from Fair Play Publishing?

**Encyclopedia of Socceroos** - Every National Team Player
by Andrew Howe

**The World Cup Chronicles** - 31 Days that Rocked Brazil
by Jorge Knijnik

**Playing for Australia**  The First Socceroos, Asia and World Football
by Trevor Thompson

**Support Your Local League** - A South East Asian Football Odessy
by Antony Sutton

**Jarrod Black - Hospital Pass**
Part 2 of the Jarrod Black series by Texi Smith

**'If I started to cry, I wouldn't stop'**
by Matthew Hall

**Coming Soon:**

**Soccer in Australia to 1949**
by Peter Kunz

**Encyclopedia of Matildas** - Every National Team Player
by Andrew Howe and Greg Werner

**From US partners, Powderhouse Press:**

**Whatever It Takes** - the Inside Story of the FIFA Way
by Bonita Mersiades

Find them all at www.fairplaypublishing.com.au

END

Lightning Source UK Ltd.
Milton Keynes UK
UKHW020646180320
360541UK00012B/763